ADVANCE PRAISE FOR
WHAT A TIME TO BE ALIVE

'Playful and witty . . . with her sharp prose,
Mustard conveys a vivid sense of longing, and the
difficulties of finding your place in the world'
Cecile Pin, author of *Wandering Souls*

'Fierce and heady – this intensely stylish
novel captures the fever of youth'
Rowan Hisayo Buchanan, author of *The Sleep Watcher*

'I loved it . . . a novel I found to be beautifully
forthright, unexpected, and totally absorbing'
Amina Cain, author of *Indelicacy*

'Jenny Mustard is that rare thing, a timeless writer, in that she
writes intelligent, and elegant prose . . . reminiscent of the power
and grace of writers like Rachel Cusk and Raven Leilani'
Molly Aitken, author of *Bright I Burn*

'A beautifully plangent coming-of-age novel . . . written
with an openness and a melancholy that frequently catches
you off guard, and will go straight to your heart'
Lucy Caldwell, author of *These Days*

'With a crisp sense of humour, Jenny Mustard explores
the great themes of love, sex, friendship and freedom
in a campus novel that for all its cool Swedish restraint
is also suffused with a beguiling tenderness'
Niamh Mulvey, author of *The Amendments*

'A novel about innocence, curiosity, and discovery, full of
the big and small questions of stepping into oneself'
Ayşegül Savaş, author of *The Anthropologists*

'In *What a Time to Be Alive*, as in life, old questions are made new again. A fresh, tender, and resonant bildungsroman from the wonderfully large-hearted Jenny Mustard'
R. O. Kwon, author of *Exhibit*

'*What a Time to Be Alive* is a beautifully observed story about the chaos, fear, and passion of youth. Told with deliciously sharp wit and styled to perfection by Jenny Mustard. Not a single line is wasted'
Scott Preston, author of *The Borrowed Hills*

'Luminous and sharp, *What a Time to Be Alive* offers not only a dextrous recounting of a young woman's giddy, volatile journey in Stockholm but also an invitation for all of us to reconsider and rediscover our notions of self'
Yan Ge, author of *Elsewhere*

'Jenny Mustard has conveyed with subtlety, precision and wonderful follow-through a worldview and sensibility that is both original and recognizable. A coming-of-age without pretensions; *What a Time to Be Alive* offers a freshness, curiosity and authenticity that readers will want to emulate'
Caoilinn Hughes, author of *The Alternatives*

'A highly readable and unusually flinchless novel about the desperate and doomed desire to become a "normal person"'
Aidan Cottrell-Boyce, author of *The End of Nightwork*

'I loved *What a Time to Be Alive*. A young woman from southern Sweden searching for herself in love, in friendship and, most of all, in the micro-awareness of one's own endlessly dissectible nature. Heartfelt in all sorts of surprising ways. Romantic too'
Rónán Hession, author of *Ghost Mountain*

PRAISE FOR
OKAY DAYS

'A perfect Millennial love story to be filed alongside Sally
Rooney and Naoise Dolan'
Irish Times

'This debut is nothing short of brilliant, a love story that is
achingly contemporary'
Glamour

'A complex and joyous ode to being in love, messing up and
finding your way'
Stylist

'Mustard is a talented portraitist in whose hands these two
characters become real, enthralling, and viscerally realised. It is
one of the most entertaining novels I have read of the times we
live in'
Chigozie Obioma, author of *The Road to the Country*

'A beautifully observed portrait of self-discovery and uncertain love'
Natasha Brown, author of *Assembly*

'Tender and spell-binding, *Okay Days* breaks you all the way open'
Annie Lord, author of *Notes on Heartbreak*

'Fresh and sharply observant . . . one of the most intriguing
books I've read in some time'
Elaine Feeney, author of *How to Build a Boat*

Jenny Mustard is a writer and social media influencer, born in Sweden but living in London. She has over 600k followers, and more than 50 million views on YouTube. Jenny and her work have featured in the *Observer*, the *Independent*, *Vogue*, and elsewhere. Her debut novel, *Okay Days*, was published in 2023.

Also by Jenny Mustard

Okay Days

WHAT A TIME
TO BE ALIVE

JENNY MUSTARD

Sceptre

First published in Great Britain in 2025 by Sceptre
An imprint of Hodder & Stoughton Limited
An Hachette UK company

1

A CIP catalogue record for this title is available from the British Library

Hardback ISBN 9781399740876
Trade Paperback ISBN 9781399740838
ebook ISBN 9781399740845

Typeset in Bembo by Hewer Text UK Ltd, Edinburgh
Printed and bound in Great Britain by Clays Ltd, Elcograf S.p.A.

Hodder & Stoughton policy is to use papers that are natural, renewable
and recyclable products and made from wood grown in sustainable forests.
The logging and manufacturing processes are expected to conform
to the environmental regulations of the country of origin.

The authorised representative in the EEA is Hachette Ireland, 8 Castlecourt
Centre, Dublin 15, D15 XTP3, Ireland (email: info@hbgi.ie)

Hodder & Stoughton Limited
Carmelite House
50 Victoria Embankment
London EC4Y 0DZ

www.sceptrebooks.co.uk

To my parents
and to David

I REACH MY hands around my back to unhook my bra.

'Before you do that,' Hanna says, 'there's something I should maybe tell you.'

I pause but don't remove my hands from the clasp. Hanna is behind me on the bed and I am facing her wardrobe. 'What's that,' I say to the row of clothes in front of me.

'Well. I might be bi.'

'Oh. Okay.'

'I'm not sure yet.'

My wet hair drips cold water down my spine. My arms are goosefleshed. Tentatively I say, 'But it's not got anything to do with me right?'

'God no. I mean, no you're not someone I would be attracted to.'

'Then I don't think it will make a difference,' I say and hook off the bra and drop it onto my waterlogged sweater on the wooden floor.

On our way to Hanna's Östermalm apartment we got caught in a rain so heavy it was hard to look through, like a veil, and now she is lending me clothes. Her bedroom is huge with a double bed although she is the only person sleeping here. One of the walls is made up of five floor-to-ceiling wardrobes.

'What about you?' she says.

I think for a moment. 'So far I have only been straight.' She says huh. On a chair next to me is a thick cream towel. I dry my arms, chest, and back, still in my soaked jeans. Then I knot the towel around my head.

'Take whatever you want,' she says. She has already changed into a loose shirt and black leggings with a small hole on one knee. Her bleached bob is tousled and the brown roots of her midpart look almost black now when wet.

I consider my options. Her clothes are not colour co-ordinated or organised in any perceptible system. I flick through the hangers while the rain drums the windows.

This is the first central Stockholm apartment I have been inside. It is quieter than expected. I feel her eyes on my naked back and now I wonder if my undressing is appropriate behaviour. This is not gym class, we are adults, maybe I should not be so naked. My heart feels a little fast. Among her expensive garments, a black cotton t-shirt seems the safe choice.

I hold the hanger in front of me and turn around. 'Is this okay?'

'Wow Sickan. Of all the clothes in that closet you go with the black t-shirt?'

I put it on over my towelled hair and say, 'I also eyed the Chanel jacket.' She chuckles.

'I won't have any trousers your size.' She stands up and opens a drawer and hands me a pair of grey sweatpants and matching zipup. 'These have drawstrings.' She sits on the bed again. I peel off my wet jeans and my skin is red and cold. I put on the sweatpants and pull the string and tie a bow and hope they look nice as oversized on me and not clownlike. My underwear is wet but borrowing something seems too intimate for a first social call.

She plays music out of speakers I don't see. The kind without instruments, I don't know the genre. It is nice and I move my shoulders to the beat and flip through her clothes again. She lies on her back with hands laced under her head and talks about class. 'Konrad is such a specimen, teaching tech but dressing like some history professor.'

'I like Konrad a lot.'

'Me too,' she says and I'm confused.

I stop at the Chanel tweed and finger the fine beige threads and wonder what it would feel like to own this wardrobe. There is a brown stain on the jacket. I lightly scrape it with my fingernail. 'It has a stain.'

'Does it? Well it happens, even to Chanel.'

'Shouldn't we clean it?'

'That's fine, just leave it.' She yawns. 'It's not mine anyway.'

I hang it back but this feels stressful, almost criminal. 'Whose is it?'

'Most of it is my mother's. She buys new things and gives me her cast-offs from the nineties. I'm sure it's meant as a hint of something.'

Looking at her splayed on the bed it is not so hard to guess what the hint is. Hanna Mellberg is repellent in attitude and appearance, is the truth. Her hair is always oily at the roots and if she wears makeup it is the angry kind. Also her teeth are large and yellow and she shows them a lot. Not like they look rotten or anything, but they are decidedly more yellow than normal. None of her clothes seem to fit her body or be worn with a specific result in mind. She is muscular, round shoulders and racehorse thighs. On another person this would look powerful and attractive but on her it comes off as intimidating. Her appearance says: don't touch me.

Altogether this makes me surprised to now find myself in Hanna Mellberg's fin-de-siècle Östermalm apartment. In a lineup I would never have picked her out as a friend prospect.

I collect my wet clothes from the floor and say, 'Where should I?'

She says hang on and disappears towards the kitchen. With the clothes bundled under one arm I remove the hair towel and dry the wet patch my clothes have made on the herringbone. Hanna comes back and lifts an eyebrow and holds out a white plastic bag for me. 'That's nice of you.'

For some reason this makes me shy and I don't know how to reply but then Hanna says are you hungry and I say yeah yes, very.

BEFORE TODAY I have not had much interaction with Hanna Mellberg. I study software development at Stockholms universitet, second year, and this spring we share some classes with the technological psychology students which means Hanna. It is March and I have seen her in the lecture halls twice a week since January. She is easy to notice because of her look and her way of talking to teachers without raising her hand. She doesn't sit next to the same people every class but neither do I.

You become who you socialise with, so I am careful when choosing company. I have been in Stockholm for a year and a half and have still not made a close friend. I get general invitations from my classmates to things like the pub and I sometimes go to panel discussions where I see people from class but I have yet to make one-on-one plans with someone. It always happens that something simple like the pub becomes an insurmountable effort by the time I have to leave my room in the student corridor. I often cancel and stay inside and watch Buffy series five and feel disappointed.

Socialising is an activity that drains me both before and after the event. Before is the struggle to leave home with all the nightmare scenarios of things going terribly playing inside my head. Returning home after I feel bulldozed, skin tense from aggressive smiling. The morning after, I get the hangover, an anxiety so acute as to be lifechanging, methodically going over the evening's word-for-word dialogue. The faults I find in my behaviour, I will convince myself to be apocalyptic, ruining any chance of me ever being liked or beautiful. Accepting a social invitation will invariably lead to this chain of mental acrobatics, so although I know humans need company, it is much easier to simply stay home.

I have met people at universitetet who behave like the person I want to become. Kind, smart, with easy manners and nice taste in clothes. But so far I have been too timid to ask anyone out. Going home with Hanna though, is not choosing company carefully, it's the opposite. She is the antithesis to the person I want to become. She seems kind and smart yes, but has neither easy manners nor a nice taste in clothes.

One day after class when I was walking through the hallway there was a loud shout. I jumped from fear and turned, then realised the shout had been my name, Sickan. Hanna was rushing towards me. I took a step back.

'Your scarf,' she said and waved the navy knit fabric. 'You left it.'

'Oh. Thank you!' I accepted it and she smiled with her large teeth. I calmed a little. It was nice of her to hurry all the way down the hallway. And also it meant she knew the scarf was mine. And also that my name was Sickan.

Once, I met her on my way out of the library, a large building with exposed brick walls where every whisper becomes a hush mingling with other hums and murmurs. Libraries are my favourite because of this sound quality. The quietest air can get without being void of human noise. I have never attended a sports game but I think this would be my least favourite. Also books are a welcome break from the screen because I do worry about my eyes.

I had borrowed a book on software and societal advancement because I sometimes lose study motivation when code doesn't connect to off-screen human evolution. Hanna stopped me in the doorway, by the electronic gates detecting book thefts.

'What did you pull?' she asked. She scratched her hair with rasping nails.

'Pull?'

'Did you borrow a book?'

'Oh. Yes I did. One book.' I didn't want to show her because it was not part of the syllabus and also maybe it was weird. My elbow pressed the tote bag shut.

'Are you not going to tell me which one?' She laughed a little as if this amused or confused her. I picked up the book to show her because now I had no choice. 'Yes, that one's quite good, it has these nice tangible examples.' And then she said, 'I think you'll like it.'

What surprised me was not Hanna having read it because actually she seemed like a person who would. What surprised me was her view of me as someone who would also read this book, and enjoy it. I knew it was not allowed to ask what had given her this impression so I put the book in my tote and went home and started reading it immediately as if for clues.

I've seen her now and then at school things or in some beer café or by the ground-floor kiosk of our department building. One time she bought a huge green apple and bit into it right there in front of everyone. A violent bite with those teeth and seeing this my saliva glands stung from the imagined acidity. But mostly she buys a kaffe and cinnamon bun combo for twenty-five kronor to bring to morning class. She doesn't unroll the cinnamon bun from the outside in like you're supposed to. Instead she bites straight in as if impatient for the gooey core.

I never buy anything in the kiosk but I will fill a small kaffetermos at home which helps keep me warm in the eternally cold classrooms. I hate being cold but it is my destiny it seems. Hands and feet like ice, nonstop. My parents' home is always cold so maybe growing up there had damaged my circulation?

Most of our lectures are held in a mid-century building with large halls and orange brick. I like picturing the students in the sixties sitting in these exact chairs. Nail-straight hair and flared jeans. Back then you could light up a cigarette right there in class if you felt like it. Incredible.

At class this morning Hanna had not eaten a cinnamon bun, she had rushed in just as Konrad closed the door and she seemed flustered but in a good mood. It was a cyber-psychology lecture about developers mostly creating services with only able-bodied users in mind, but how in recent years more effort had been put into disability-proofing apps.

'Like people with colourblindness, carpal tunnel syndrome, autism, how will they interact with the app?' Konrad said. 'Actually if there are any dyslexic or partially paralysed or bipolar students in this class, you should put it on your CV for added value.' I couldn't make up my mind if him saying this was despicably cynical, or quite the contrary, apt and compassionate.

Soon we were discussing crypto because somehow all lectures still led to crypto and Konrad talked about the psychological intricacies of establishing a digital currency which the owner believed to have value but which the intended adopter often viewed with scepticism or reluctance. Without raising her hand Hanna said, 'So basically like dick pics.'

I laughed.

The rest of the class was quiet and someone even sighed, maybe because Hanna often interrupted Konrad. I was the only one who had laughed. I could feel people looking at me. The hair on my neck bristled and my heart quickened. Hanna turned around and smiled, a large toothy grin. I looked down at my notes and let my hair fall forward to curtain my face.

Afterwards in the hallway Hanna was waiting for me. 'Hey,' she said, 'do you have afternoon class?'

'No. Not today.'

'Me neither.'

We exited the building together and walked south towards the city, which didn't make sense since I lived in the student corridors north of campus. It was chilly and I pulled my scarf tighter.

'They are such serious people, our classmates,' she said.

'Hm. I think this is to be expected of coders? We're used to laughing inwards or with our fingers.'

'Fingers?'

I mimed typing ha ha on a keyboard.

She chuckled. 'That's true, but I like laughing outwards.'

'Yes, me too.'

She pointed things out as we walked, strange Stockholm landmarks related to celebrities and scandals in the past. I felt that she knew the city in a way I as a southerner never would. Some of the celebrities caught doing coke in McDonald's toilet stalls, I'd never heard of. I wished I had, so I remembered the names to look up later. Even if a Skåning by birth I desperately wanted to be a Stockholmare. I was actively losing my southern accent.

It started raining when we crossed Humlegården. The March grass was brown and the branches bare. Now with the needle rain it certainly looked bleak. The drizzle intensified to a downpour and Hanna said we should take shelter at her place. 'It's close, Artillerigatan.'

'Artillerigatan?'

She scoffed. 'Don't look at me like that.'

THE BUILDINGS ON Artillerigatan are in soft creams and apricots. Some apartments, like Hanna's, have a small balcony overhanging the street. Hers has white cast-iron chairs with navy blue cushions, quite well-worn. It is still raining but the chairs are roofed by the balcony above.

Hanna hands me a blanket, then places a second one on her chair, before going back into the kitchen. I tuck in my legs and stomach. Looking through the windows across the street, I recognise a Murano glass chandelier, just hanging there as if normal. This is possibly the most out of place I have ever been.

Hanna's apartment is staggering. It used to belong to her grandmother, now dead, and it seems when moving in, Hanna updated only the bedroom. In the other rooms everything is dark and layered, Persian rugs, a Charlotte Perriand chaise longue. Three stuffed birds in the sitting room: owl, crow, hawk. In the hallway a claw-footed upholstered sofa. Things like that. The rooms don't have doorways, they have entryways. I wonder just how rich Hanna is because I have no frame of reference.

Besides Hanna's bedroom there is a study, a sitting room, a TV room, and a kitchen with a dining table for ten. When she took me on the tour her voice sometimes echoed.

'Bon appétit.' She puts two pasta bowls on the balcony table. Tortellini, the kind with a hole in the middle, is steaming underneath a dollop of crème fraiche. 'It's chive and garlic, just storebought,' she says and looks at me expectantly.

'It smells so good,' I say because it does. We mix the tortellini until glistening with crème fraiche and Hanna grinds salt and pepper on hers so I do too.

The spinach-filled pasta pillows are chewy and the smattering of rain makes me think of summer. It is cold on the balcony but I am always cold anyway and I have wrapped myself tight in the blanket. I hold the warm bowl in my hands.

'You know what I love?' Hanna asks.

I shake my head.

'Smoking while eating.'

I look at her. 'No, Hanna that's terrible! Don't do that.'

She leans through the open balcony door for a pack of cigarettes on the windowsill inside. 'Try. It's decadent.'

She lights one cigarette and hands me the pack. I reluctantly accept to be polite. Then we take a mouthful of tortellini each and smoke through the chewing. The smoke in my lungs tastes like garlic. 'This is a strange sensation,' I say.

'I know.'

'I think I prefer to keep eating and smoking separate.' I carefully extinguish the cigarette on the rim of my bowl and place it on the table.

She shrugs and says to each their own.

After I finish the tortellini I am nice and full and I reach for the lighter to restart my cigarette. Hanna lights one too. I am shivering, very cold now, but don't want to leave the balcony. The rain has eased to a drizzle and my hair and underwear are almost dry.

'You look good when you smoke,' she says.

'You think so? I have practised.'

She laughs. 'Have you really?'

I tap the ash pillar into my empty bowl. 'One time when I smoked a girl told me I look like an amateur because I hold all my fingers upright, like this, not just the index and middle finger, like this.' I illustrate and inhale smoke and feel the kick of nicotine. 'I hadn't realised you could look bad at smoking so I practised in front of a mirror later.'

'You're funny,' she says and then, 'Well it paid off.'

This makes me feel at ease and languid and I look up at the sky and I hope it won't stop raining just yet.

WHEN I FIRST came to Stockholm a year and a half ago, it was Sunday and school would start that Tuesday. I went straight to the student corridor, my new home. It was a small room with a shared kitchen but at least I had my own toilet and shower which was lucky because not all corridor rooms did.

There was a single bed, a pine bookcase, a pine desk with a swivel chair, one armchair, and a Formica coffee table. I didn't know who picked it but this furniture was ugly. I put my rucksack and two suitcases on the floor and breathed in through my nose. It smelled clean, floor soap.

There were two windows looking onto a big lawn with a footpath straight across like a scar. Many four-storey buildings with student corridors like mine were on the grassy hill. I could see all this, and touch the walls and everything, but still it didn't feel real. I had counted down for years, and now I was here. Stockholm. All sorts of things could happen.

I drank water from the tap in the toilet and then I took a bus to the army surplus store. There I bought the cheapest version of everything. Bedclothes, cleaning products, kettle, bowls and glasses, survival food. On my way up from Skåne I had decided that I would be a real student, do all the things. I had never been a real schoolchild so I was adamant about not missing out on the student experience. There was catching up to do! This was my time! That's how it felt.

I already knew some of the student paraphernalia from movies and books. So at the surplus store I bought quick noodles, the curly kind with the flavour sachet, six fifty each. I also bought instant coffee and a cheap pair of yellowlight glasses for fifty-nine kronor, because I didn't need reading glasses but thought that sitting at a desk annotating a textbook with glasses on and a knee drawn to my chest was a very nice image indeed.

Back at the corridor I put on pink rubber gloves and cleaned the shower room. There was a stain in the bottom of the toilet bowl so I soaked it with bleach and then scrubbed with a sponge and then steel wool but still it wouldn't come out. The scrubbing made me sweat so I took a shower and somehow the shower now felt more dirty, not less, after cleaning it.

I made the bed with my new sheets, plugged in the kettle, and prepared student noodles, mushroom flavour, to eat on the bed. The noodles were packed with flavour enhancers and I thought I could eat them every night. I streamed baking shows until I fell asleep. I had yet to see the kitchen.

I STARTED UNIVERSITETET that Tuesday. Because of nerves I didn't talk to anyone all day. I wore a long-sleeved black shirt and jeans because I thought wherever you go in the world you can wear jeans and a black shirt and no one will react. It seemed to me the other students all knew some-one else but that was highly unlikely. More likely they were not crippled by timidity and so made small talk. But this was the first day, my only duty was to make it through without doing anything insane. So sitting silent, looking like an average person in my clothes, was more important than making contact.

At one point two girls behind me in the auditorium started laughing and I blushed and looked down. This was a reflex of mine, expecting any laughter to be directed at me, even though I logically knew it was not. Back in school I had tried to never listen to laughter but since then I had forced myself to and this way learned that whenever someone laughed, on the street, in class, on the bus, it very rarely had anything to do with me. I had become self-centred that way, but was working it off.

When I got back to the corridor that first day I was exhausted and smelled of sour sweat. I hadn't said a word to anyone. But now I knew the lay of the land, how the classrooms were systemised and where to go for kaffe and toilets, and spatial awareness always made me more socially courageous.

I checked my phone. My parents hadn't called since I left Skåne but grandma had, the night I arrived in Stockholm, and I described the ugly furniture in an amusing way until she tssk'd that way she does. I then texted my parents and they replied *Good that you have arrived!* I didn't call them now about my first day, instead I ate some cereal and my eyes grew heavy already at nine thirty in front of the laptop.

Then there was a scream.

I jumped out of bed and stood still in the middle of the room.

Another scream.

My nerves bristled. I swallowed. My screen said 22:00.

Then another scream, closer, almost next door. More screams, close and far. I moved slowly to the window and looked out. There were lights in many windows with people hanging out of them screaming their lungs raw. Students like me just screaming. It lasted less than two minutes and then stopped completely but even so I couldn't go back to sleep. I lay awake wondering what would make people scream like that.

In the morning I searched Stockholm students screaming out of windows why and so found out it was tradition for students to scream at 10pm every Tuesday to let out their anxiety. It made me worry what student life was going to be like if there was a need to scream the anxiety out of you. Before the following Tuesday I bought earplugs at the apotek.

THE BASS HITS my chest like a second heartbeat. We are in a club that plays only hip hop which is my favourite to dance to. Hanna is here on the dancefloor, almost as tall as me. She is dancing and it is surprising because she is good at it. She has a bulk about her, due to her height and muscularity, but more because of her heavy footsteps and abrupt movements, as if trying to take up more space in the world. But she isn't abrupt now, she is sort of, fluid. And what I like is that she is very into it. Sometimes she closes her eyes and leans her head back towards the ceiling and flashes her throat like that. It's tremendous.

The large dancefloor is encircled by a wraparound balcony for talking and looking at the mass of people. Dancing under the influence is the one time my aversion to sounds flips like a switch. Now I want the music to be loud, to pulse right through me and make my ears pound.

I am likely not a good dancer but with Hanna I don't much care. She is having fun. A drop of sweat runs from my neck down my chest, tickling my skin like an insect. Hanna makes a cigarette gesture and I nod and she takes my hand and we move towards the exit.

My head is floating because we have been drinking for hours. We were walking around Södermalm since it was a sunny day with no wind when Hanna asked if we should go into a beer café on Katarina Bangata and I said hm. I wanted to get a drink but a night in a bar was something I couldn't afford. I don't know how sensitive Hanna is to budgets but maybe she understood my dilemma because she said, 'Or we could buy beers to drink in the park?'

In Systembolaget I bought four beers and Hanna bought a screwcap Sauvignon. By the time we entered Nytorget the sun was almost done but children were still playing. Some other adults were drinking kaffe or beers, scooted up against the fence where the sun still reached and we joined them, sitting on Hanna's scarf on the ground. She took off her sunglasses, leaned her head back, and closed her eyes to the sun. The skin on her face was so strikingly pale I worried about UV.

'So why did you choose software?' Hanna asked and screwed the cap off the wine. She took a swig and handed me the bottle. 'I've tried to peg you but the more I see, the less tech you seem.'

I sipped the wine. 'I'm good at it. It's easy for me somehow.' I didn't say I prefer the predictability of code to the vagaries of human behaviour but that would also have been true. 'And you?' I asked.

'Money.'

I sucked on my lip. 'Really? Money?'

'Okay, independence then. A good job and never talking to my mother's bank again.'

I was thinking that with money I would not buy independence, I would buy an apartment. Good clothes, healthy savings. I would buy forgetting the noxious taste of money problems. 'Actually I am also doing it for money,' I said, and so admitted it for the first time.

'Knew it.' She tilted her head back to the sun. 'You couldn't care less about code.'

'I care.'

'You don't.'

'I'm good at it.'

'Not the same as caring. It's the good girl syndrome, the perfectionism. You know, people-pleasing.'

I blinked and didn't say anything and she talked a while about how women now are expected to be good at both the traditional male things like education and money, but also the female things like aesthetics and social grace.

'And you think I have it, the syndrome?'

'Yes, you're textbook. You won't prioritise.' Her smile was teasing but not unkind.

I squinted.

She said, 'So you're saying you don't want to both have a career and make lots of money, but also be pretty and know how to decorate?'

'That's true. I do feel I should be good at both.'

'It's like we're supposed to be both expert women and expert men.' Leaned back like this, her nose made a curved silhouette. 'I figure you only get to choose one, otherwise you're spreading yourself too thin? For me, it's money and success.'

I wondered if her obvious lack of aesthetics and sociability was a way to take herself out of the running, be beyond critique. If her apartment's messiness and her unwashed hair was a way to visibly opt out. Maybe I really did have the syndrome because sometimes in her messy flat I became fidgety, that's how much I wanted to sort it out.

I tried to rank my own priorities. I thought of the status given by money and success but also the violent urge I had to be pretty and sophisticated and well-liked. 'I don't think I'm ready to skip anything,' I said and she laughed and said, 'You're trying too hard.'

And yes, I did wonder at what point hard turned into too hard.

It was dark now and my whole body was stiff but still we didn't leave the park. Hanna seemed to prefer outdoors to indoors even when cold. I breathed on my hands.

She said, 'Can you imagine how much money we'll have to give away once we get tech jobs?'

I grinned. 'It will be fun for us, giving money instead of getting it. I like this idea.' And I thought about someone's tax money now putting me through school and that some-day my tax money would put another young person through school. It seemed tidy.

Then someone shouted Hanna's name and a girl left a group of people and walked up. 'What are you doing, are you crazy? It's like five degrees out,' she said.

Hanna stood up and they hugged. 'Sickan, this is Lottie.'

'Charmed,' Lottie said and kissed my cheek, once. I almost kissed her twice but took my cue from her. I had never pictured Hanna with other friends before now.

Lottie had a short-cropped afro and dressed all in black, her upwards-nose and freckles softening the severe clothes. 'We're getting falafels and then going dancing.' She jigged her shoulders and pinched Hanna's arm. 'Come on.'

Hanna looked annoyed like a younger sister kind of dynamic. She turned to me and raised her eyebrows.

'I want falafel,' I said.

And so we were all going dancing and I was not going home alone to the corridor.

EVER SINCE TORTELLINI on her balcony I have been doing things with Hanna. Not so much at school because I always sit in the back and she sits front row. But after class she finds a reason to talk to me. Sometimes she follows me to the library and sometimes she takes me to a café she likes.

The first time I saw her drunk was at a faux-Irish pub around Odenplan and this was when I realised she had the best laugh. I knew she was funny because she told me dry jokes all the time. But when she drank alcohol her face went feral and when she laughed you could see her chest move. I tried allowing my own laugh its full depth too. Now I always look for ways to make her chest move like that.

It was surprising, the first time I found myself searching for her after class, wishing she would ask me to hang out. I thought maybe our classmates looked at Hanna the way people had looked at me back in Skåne and this made me terrified of being associated with her, but also it spawned sympathy in me. Maybe I wanted to study her to learn specifically why a person was looked at that way, because so far it had eluded me. Or maybe I just liked her company. Whatever it was, I gradually grew unable to think about much else other than Hanna. Like an eclipse, that way.

SHE FILLS TWO glasses of water and we drink until they are empty. We are in her kitchen at Artillerigatan and the tiles are cold under my hot throbbing feet. It is quiet here and the ghost of club music is in my ears. The only light is streetlamps coming in orange and metropolitan.

We danced with Lottie and the others until early morning and then Hanna and I walked home. Now I don't want to count how much money I have spent on drinks, but even less do I want to count how many of my drinks Hanna paid for. I will eat rice and lentils for a month.

When we got our coats and bags from the cloakroom she said I could sleep at hers because the night bus back to the corridor would be cold and boring.

'No I can't, I have to study tomorrow early.'

'Don't you have your laptop?'

My laptop was in my bag. And I did feel irresponsible then, for leaving it like that in the cloakroom all night. Hanna said we could eat breakfast and study together because it was more fun that way. I didn't agree because I could not focus with someone else in the room, but she had a point about the bus being boring and cold.

Now she is in the bathroom brushing her teeth and I am changing into the t-shirt she has laid out for me. I climb into the double bed, left side, and the sheets are stiff and cool on my legs. The hair around her face is wet when she comes back and her skin glistens with moisturiser. She is holding a blister pack. Once on the bed she sits cross-legged and asks if I'm tired and ready for sleep. I am, I am very tired and say, 'Yes, I think so.'

She holds up the blister pack. 'Okay because these are for sleep and once I take one I have to fall asleep within thirty minutes.'

'Or, what happens?'

'Or I stay awake but almost like I'm dreaming anyway? Like in between awake and asleep.' She looks serious. 'It's fucking scary.'

'I can imagine,' I say although I really can't.

'So, should I take one now, are we done talking?'

'Yes. Okay. Goodnight.' I smooth down the duvet next to my thighs. She swallows the pill with some water from her night table and gets under the covers.

We are quiet for a moment and it is maybe a little awkward. I am not used to falling asleep with someone and I am not sure if you're supposed to stay quiet as if the other person is not in the room? I can hear her breathing.

Maybe it is intense for her too because she says, 'I'm happy we're friends.' She turns towards me, her head on her elbow.

'Yes, me too.'

She looks at me, her face lit by orange streetlamp. I say, 'Do you really not care about being popular, or well-liked?'

She breathes out. 'I don't know, usually I don't.' She lies on her back again. 'But actually, sometimes I do.' She sounds a little shaky, her voice agitated. The bed creaks under us as she adjusts her position. 'Sometimes with friends I get paranoid they don't actually like me at all and I convince myself they have some ulterior motive, which is stupid I know, but I convince myself until I feel sad, or like upset. And who knows maybe I'm right.' She clears her throat. 'Maybe I'm really not very likeable? Not even my mother, but whatever I don't like her either. I mean it's normal to hate your mother I guess, but I don't think she's supposed to hate you back?'

I don't say anything. I feel the onset of nausea, a bad taste on my tongue. The atmosphere changed so quickly I can't adjust. We were having a good night dancing and being fun but moments later it has got very dark. I don't know what to say. I wonder if it is taboo, what she has told me. We are not touching each other but it feels like we are. Her anxiety seeps out, threatens to soak me too. I want to shake my hands, I feel weird.

After a while she says, 'I think we talked too long.'

'Oh no, the pill?'

'Yeah I've gone over.'

'Are you sure?'

'Well,' she says, 'I am looking at the ceiling and it's covered in macaroni, so I think I'm fairly certain.'

'You are scaring me now Hanna,' I say. 'Should I call the ambulance?'

'Jesus. No, just hand me that book.' She waves her arm towards the night table on my side. On it is a bruised copy of *Fullmetal Alchemist*. I give it to her and she clicks on her phone's flashlight, places it next to her on the bed, and turns her back to me. 'Goodnight,' she says and then all I can hear are the rasps of turning pages.

I stare at the ceiling but can't see the macaroni. My pulse is loud and I worry she feels it through the mattress. It is shocking that Hanna is the friend I have made, the careless-ness of it. Clearly this is the advanced level of friendship, she is not someone you learn the basics from. I promise myself that if I lie still here until morning, I will not have to hang out with her again. Sleeping seems impossible in this bed but somehow it is possible because I wake from Hanna tapping my arm. 'Sickan. Wake up.'

The room is light now which is disorienting. Hanna looks worn, like she's been shaken too hard. 'Your phone is vibrating,' she says, although it is quiet now. 'Someone's called twice so I thought maybe it was important.'

'Really?' I say and reach for my phone. And yes there are two missed calls. From dad.

Without looking at Hanna I tiptoe out of the bedroom, close the door behind me, and go to the balcony. It is freezing outside and this wakes me up. Dad answers on the first ring.

'Hello, Siv?'

'Yes it's me. Hi.'

'I didn't wake you did I?'

'Dad, what's wrong?'

'It's your grandmother. She died.'

Maybe it is the cold air but I feel no emotion.

None at all. I am blank.

Instead there is only pragmatism, and what I am think-ing is: I'm done for.

THE CLOCK OUTSIDE the Södertälje petrol station says 05:30. I took the bus here from the student corridor and I am wide awake, the morning nip making me hop on my toes. Every car filling up on fuel I scan, holding my thumb out for any suitable candidates leaving the petrol station onto the motorway going south.

I have one sacrosanct rule when hitchhiking: to only enter cars containing an adult woman. I never go in cars with a single male or males plural. Unfortunately cars containing single males or males plural are usually the most willing to stop and let me in.

The dew is slowly spreading in dark circles on my canvas shoes. It is only April so no fresh grass yet, but some daredevil flowers have arrived, white or sometimes yellow. My clothes are loose-fitting and I am wearing makeup because I don't want to look too young. I am standing by the exit, bag on the ground beside me. This is quite an easy hitch-hike. Either the E4 inland all the way down to Helsingborg, or the E22 on the east coast towards Kalmar and then Kristianstad. If you go early you find the long-haulers. After reaching one of the bigger cities you have to take a chance on the smaller roads or pay for a local bus to Åhus, my Skånska hometown.

A middle-aged woman in hijab closes her petrol cap and gets in the driver's seat of a grey Ford. She stops by my thumb and I am lucky, she is going all the way to Kalmar. She is wearing bootcut jeans and a blazer and the car smells clean. The funeral is the day after tomorrow. I check my phone, no notifications. I turn it off and place it in my bag.

I FIRST CAME to Stockholm by hitchhiking. My parents said to take the train up and even offered to pay for the ticket. I checked what a ticket to Stockholm would cost and decided I'd rather have that sum in my bank account. Mum transferred me the ticket money and although it was not the first time I lied to her it didn't feel good.

They drove me to the station and followed me onto the platform. Late August, high thin clouds. The wind made mum's eyes water.

'You don't have to wait,' I said. 'The train will be here soon.'

'We'll wait Siv,' dad said. 'To see you off.' He was wearing a cap that he held in place whenever the wind threatened to take it.

'Seriously, you can go, I'll manage.' I felt stressed so I took mum's shoulders and hugged her. Her cheek was damp with wind tears. I didn't mistake them for real tears because the wind always made her cry.

'Okay, if that's what you prefer?' dad said.

'Yes, let's not drag it out.'

Dad and I hugged stiffly and then they left with some encouraging words about taking over the capital. When the train arrived at the platform, I was already in the carpark outside looking for a female driver going north.

It was my first hitchhike and it was a great success. It took an awful long time to reach Stockholm but I went on two scenic routes and the thrill of it all made me want to go on forever. Some drivers played loud rock music and some said bizarre things and one bred expensive kittens and it was wild in a brand new way. Also, my bank account was six hundred kronor richer. I thought that if I was to become an altogether new person in Stockholm I needed something to signify the metamorphosis and at that moment nothing felt more symbolic than a new name. I became Sickan Hermansson that day and left Siv behind somewhere around Vaggeryd on the E4.

IT IS ONLY 5pm when I step onto my parents' driveway. The Christian couple taking me this last stretch from Kalmar wanted to drive me right up to the door. I asked them to drop me one street away and waved as they drove off. Listening to their strong Skånska accent with the rolling rs and the surplus of vowels transported me back to my childhood when I had believed every Swede talked like that. When I had talked like that myself.

I rarely hear the thick southern accent in Stockholm and now to my ears it sounds fake. I have worked hard at losing mine and I think it is pretty much gone.

It has been a while since I visited, last Christmas blaming schoolwork and staying in Stockholm. This had not been a good idea, spending Christmas alone. But now it is

April and my parents have an apple tree in the front garden that looks like it's about to sing.

As always I get a little disoriented by the house, and can't quite believe this one-storey seventies brick villa housed me from infant to nineteen. It seems like I should feel some affinity or nostalgia. Like I should call this coming home, not visiting parents. But standing in the driveway about to open the front door, I don't feel much more than a neutral familiarity. Like yes, here you are still.

I fit the key in the keyhole and open the door and recognise the unoiled squeal the hinges make and again time is reversed.

'Hallå, dad, mum? Malin?' I shout down the long hallway. I hang my jacket on the overfilled coat hanger and place my shoes neatly on the rack. Malin is the first to greet me. She chatters a little as she jogs towards the door, then she jumps up on the hall table and I touch her soft grey head and play with her tail which annoys her. Malin is turning seventeen this autumn and this is not something I like to think about. I have looked up world record old cats. Someone called Sally has the record at thirty-eight. I would settle for thirty. I kiss her head and she smells like herself.

'Mum?' I shout again.

'Here, coming.' Mum appears in the hallway and gives me a quick hard hug and says, 'and the trip was fine?' before reaching for my bag and walking ahead of me to the back of the house, my old room. She is wearing her beige age-old cardigan over her clothes. Only fifty-three but she looks older, grey in her braid, shapeless clothing, a slight hunch in her spine. Seeing her braid swing right and left across her hunched shoulders heading down the hallway, it kills me a little bit.

She places my bag on the floor in my room, though from the cat hair on the bedspread, it is clear this is now Malin's room.

'You freshen up, I'll make tea.'

I wash but still feel unclean after the long drive so I change into a fresh t-shirt and black leggings which Malin's light grey fur will ruin shortly.

Mum is humming and I enter the kitchen to the smell of Assam. It is chilly in here and I know that if I touch the heaters they will be cold. I sit at the table. She hands me my cup but doesn't take a seat. I blow on the tea.

'What time do we have,' she says and looks at her wrist-watch. 'Five twenty, okay. We didn't know exactly when you would arrive.' It looks like she is calculating. 'I just need to finish up some work. Maybe you want to take a walk around town? See the old places? And the new café! And then we can all have dinner. Dad will be home at seven thirty if you text and tell him to.'

I stay quiet for a second until I am able to talk in a casual tone of voice. 'Sure. I can text dad. Dinner at seven thirty.'

Malin jumps up on the table and I stroke her head, my fingers finding her sweet spots by reflex. 'She is happy you're home, the old girl,' mum says. Then she moves to the door, cup in hand.

'Mum, wait.'

She stops and turns around.

'How is dad?' I ask.

'Dad? He is fine. You mean about grandma?'

I inhale slowly and my voice might shake. 'Yes. About grandma.'

'Well. You know how he is.' She pauses a moment. 'Actually, I think you could ask him? How he is doing about grandma.' She gnaws her bottom lip. 'Could you?'

'Oh. Yes, maybe I could ask him.'

'Okay then. So see you at seven thirty.'

'Seven thirty.'

I COLLECT MY hair in a low bun, and push it through the opening on the back of my cap. I hope the cap makes me more incognito but it could also make me less.

From my parents' house it is a five-minute walk to Åhus town centre. I move briskly and don't look around because there are many childhood landmarks and I don't want the memories. I walk past the sandbox and my eyes sting. Then the lamppost on Dragaregatan I held on to very tightly that one time. I shake my head and look at my feet as I move forward. The landmarks are one thing but seeing someone from school would be something else completely. I have no choice because I looked in the fridge and there was only cola light and cat food, jars of long-life things. The freezer was filled with one-portion dinners, mostly lasagne and fish gratin. One family-size pizza, capricciosa.

I order takeaway tea in the new café which is nice, then walk with my cup down to the sea. I turn a corner and it is there, like always. I taste salt and the wind sprays my face. Today it is overcast so the sea is grey and the sand is pale and the stranded seaweed is ink-black, scattered like a scrawl along the beach. This is my favourite sea, the cloudy one.

No one is here except an old woman with a Labrador so taken by the waves and the spray she is actually skipping. This is nice to look at and the hot tea is warming my fingers. The wind here is relentless. First thing that comes to mind when remembering my childhood is the wind. The tinnitus-like shoosh, the tug on your hair, the dizzying feeling of getting inside and closing the door to an abrupt stillness.

I say hello to the woman with the dog as she passes and she says hej hej. The dog rushes at me, then stops shy and sniffs my fingers with surprising timidity and this seems somehow human to me or maybe it is animal. I walk back towards the ICA supermarket and try not to look up at sounds. I buy ingredients for dinner without eyeing a single face in the shop aisles. The cashier doesn't know me.

I cook potato wedges, vegetarian schnitzel, and béarnaise sauce, unsure of what food is appropriate when your grandmother has just died but sensing it should not be colourful. The baking potatoes smell terrific and my stomach is hollow, but it is just hunger. I still haven't felt any real sadness about grandma, only guilt about my lack of feelings. The oven is slowly warming the kitchen. I whisk the béarnaise, fry the schnitzels, and quarter a lemon. For the vitamins I peel and cut carrot coins. At seven twenty I knock on the door to mum's study.

'I have dinner almost ready.'

'Yes I can smell it!' She is typing while talking and hasn't looked up from her screen. 'Is dad home?'

'No. Not yet.'

'Okay, give me one minute.'

The front door opens and closes right then and I hear dad talking to Malin. I hurry out into the hallway, my socks skidding on the tiles. 'Hi dad,' I say a little breathless and the look of him, as always, makes my heart ache.

'Hej, hej you. Come here, let me look.' He takes my shoulders and leans back to see me better. 'So that's why Malin's so chirpy,' he says, and then in a booming voice, 'because the favourite daughter has returned.' He gets like this, mock-pompous, whenever there are strong emotions around. Although the pompousness is put on, I have come to recognise its backhanded authenticity since it only surfaces to mask real, overwhelming feelings. Or maybe he doesn't experience large emotions and this is just his approximation of human behaviour. But I prefer the first alternative. 'How are you dad?'

'Oh you know,' he says and there is almost a catch in his voice.

'I'm sorry,' I say and the awkwardness is too much for him even though I haven't mentioned grandma.

'Why be sorry. You're here, mum's here, Malin. I got all my girls for dinner, and isn't this a treat on a Tuesday.'

I roll my eyes.

At dinner the only anomaly is that neither of them shoo Malin off the table when she approaches the béarnaise sauce.

I USED TO wish I had a sibling but now I don't. Back in school I would picture an older sister who would teach me things and how to dress. Or a twin to share a secret language with. My prepubescent bookshelf was filled with novels on this theme and I felt that twin sisters were the luckiest, even if a lot of those books were about one of the twins dying. Or about one of them being popular and the other one not.

It had seemed that sisterhood was the closest two humans could be and I ached for it. Maybe being siblingless is always hard but I think probably particularly hard in my parents' house.

Back then, they often said I was precocious, my parents. And the fact that I had immediately looked this word up proved their point I guess. I think they believed I was born that way, just an abnormally mature child, and not an effect of our three-way dynamic.

I don't have any memories of mum and dad telling me they love me but I know they do. And I am mostly sure they're oblivious to the fact that they are unsuitable as parents.

My mother is a physicist. Not just by occupation, physicist is an identity. She is not on social media but if she was her bio would state physicist first. Louise Hermansson, physicist, wife, mother, Skåning. She loves her days in the study and she is very lucky to be paid by different universitet to do just that, sit at her desk and think. She only comes out if forced to, really.

Dad is a biologist and spends most days in the field studying moths, butterflies, that kind of thing, and him being away all hours and her being shut in the study is how they prefer it. They suit each other perfectly. They make almost no money because sometimes they are between grants and they only take on projects they get a kick out of. Neither have career ambitions so things like tenure or salaried positions mean little. They are paid researchers most of the time, unpaid researchers working on their own in between, but they don't need hobbies and they don't travel except for work.

I always thought we were working class because we were so poor all the time and it wasn't until my late teens that I understood my parents are academics and that mum is very respected in her field. It was a strange realisation because it meant our financial situation was by choice, and they could have used their degrees to make more money and live better and afford nicer clothes for me to wear to school. Although I tried not to, I hated them for this for a while, which made me feel horrible because I also loved them so much.

I was eight or nine when I started picking up some of the slack, making grilled sandwiches, recycling newspapers. I learned that asking them about work made them stay longer at the table. That they loved their work more than me made me insanely jealous, but also I envied them having studies to escape into. I wanted to disappear into my head like that and since schoolwork was not very challenging, the result was my steadily growing book collection. And later, losing myself in source code.

They were not wrong, I was precocious. But I was also painfully childish, naïve to the point of stupidity, and almost never knew what the other girls meant when they told jokes or spoke badly about people's bodies. I don't know if my parents' social inability was passed down to me genetically or if I was just untrained. I still don't know. Maybe their awkwardness is a combination of their genes and their culture. I don't think they would be socially comfortable or physically affectionate anywhere, but I do believe growing up in pre-internet Sweden exaggerated their reservedness to the extreme.

I was always happy they had found each other and were content, it seemed almost miraculous to me. But back then, oh how I wished I had someone, a sibling, a buffer. Someone who shared the exact same upbringing and would always understand, even as adults, what it meant to have parents like ours.

So I read the books and wished for a sister, and though I still long for that closeness, I no longer wish. Because it would mean someone I loved also having had this child-hood. I don't think I could bear that.

AFTER DINNER WE have kaffe and schackrutor in front of the TV. Then mum says goodnight and goes to bed. I look over at dad. He seems quite normal. If I didn't know his mother had just died I would not have guessed. I think about what mum said earlier, asking him how he is doing.

Now would be a good time.

But I don't.

Back in my room I remove the bedspread and tiny Malin hairs fly around. I make the bed with childhood sheets, white flowers on purple. They are soft from many washes and smell like lavender.

The next morning dad has left for work when I wake up and mum is in her study with the door closed. I knock and walk in.

'Hallå,' she says and looks up from her desktop. 'Sleep well?'

'Yes,' I say. 'Just, about tomorrow, is everything planned and ready?'

'Yes, mostly I'd say. But we thought maybe you should have some input as well?'

I feel a rapid wave of unease. 'You mean, as in, talking to the funeral home?'

'If you want. If you have a psalm or something you want in the service.'

'But you have been there already, with dad? You have already talked to them?'

'The funeral is tomorrow Siv, of course I have talked to them.'

'Okay. Yes, sorry. Sure I can call them on the phone.' But the unease is still there. I get the disturbing sense that no one has taken care of grandma since she died, but of course they have. She is in a clean cool metal box with a tag around her toe or maybe she is cremated, I don't know.

Mum says, 'The number is on the fridge.'

When I call the funeral-woman Berit Sandemo she only says oh good, as if she is expecting me, and asks me to come in at 2pm. And for some reason when I put down the phone I feel like I am about to cry.

MY PARENTS ARE not orderly people. Mum's study and dad's office nook are filled with things in chaotic systems. The rest of the house is dirty yes, but more so it is neglected and messy. After moving to Stockholm I asked them to get a cleaner because I didn't know what state the house would end up in. They said yes good idea, we will see, which meant they thought it a waste of money they didn't have. They must occasionally hoover and dust the shelves but are likely never-minding about the intense things like cleaning the fridge or clearing hair from the drains. I suspect they don't even notice.

It is only 9am so I put on mum's sweatpants and t-shirt and slide my feet into rubber slippers. I start with the fridge because it is the worst place but easy to clean since it is almost empty. I remove jars and wipe each shelf and the repulsive water collection pocket in the back. Then I spray the oven door on the inside and clean out the grime.

It is disgusting, all of it. But also satisfying to clean something this dirty, the improvement so radical. I finish the kitchen, the filthy spice rack, on top of the kitchen fan. I wring out the dishcloth and the water is brown and gritty every time. The white suds smell of lemongrass and look like freshly shovelled snow. I fold the cloth over the tap. Then I take a break and make myself a pot in the kaffe-kokare. I have worked up a sweat. My hands and arms feel dirty up to the elbows.

After the coffee I walk around the house with two paper bags, filling one with rubbish and one with recycling, mostly newspapers and old empty envelopes and also handwritten notes filled with scribbles I here and now decide are not important. I conquer the bathroom and hoover under the sofa cushions without looking too closely.

When I am done I put the paper bags outside and tour the house. It smells fresh and I picture how nice they will feel next time they open the fridge or put the capricciosa in the spotless oven. Then I shower and try not to think about the curly hair I twenty minutes ago picked up from the drain. I rub my arms with soap so many times they start itching. After I have dressed and played with Malin I push my bun back through the hole in the cap and go to the funeral home to meet Berit Sandemo.

THE TRUTH IS I can't say what type of funeral my grandmother would have liked. Maybe she had a favourite psalm, I don't know. This does not mean we weren't close. We were, in our own way. It was nice when grandma came to the house. She liked to cook and even bake, and she taught me useful kitchen skills like cutting broccoli horizontally instead of vertically. She was not physically nor verbally affectionate, but the thing about my grandma, she knew my favourite food. She took interest in my schoolwork and my reading, and I guess what I am saying is that although I didn't know much about her, she knew me. As a person. And her saying things like, that sounds like Siv alright, or, why do you always have to do this or that, gave me a sense of being a little person with an already distinct personality. I felt she was a backbone to our family. Without her my parents and I will be three disconnected limbs, flailing on the floor.

She knew enough to realise I needed money. Every Christmas and every summer graduation she would hand me an envelope made of thick paper and in it would be twelve thousand-kronor bills, crisp from the bank. It used to be three bills but after I left home there were twelve of them, two for each month until the next envelope. Combined with my student loan this is how I put myself through school and covered the expense of living in Stockholm without a job. My parents never knew, grandma and I were culprits. With her gone, I have lost more than the family backbone. I have lost the means to support myself.

A WOMAN IS standing outside the funeral home with a cup of coffee, leaning into the sun. She looks surprised to see me.

'Berit?' I ask. 'Sorry, I might be early.'

She smooths her hair brusquely. 'Siv, I'm guessing. Apologies, I didn't mean to greet you like this, coffee in hand.' There is something of the cafeteria lady about her.

'No no, it's me who's early.'

'Well, come in and we'll have ourselves a chat.' She pulls the door hard and holds it open for me, then walks ahead through the reception, into the first room on the right. 'Tea? Water?'

'No thank you,' I say and she gestures for me to sit opposite her at a large table. She opens a laptop and scattered on the table are pamphlets and catalogues and a small square box of something. Horribly I wonder if the box contains ashes but of course it doesn't. I dry my hands on my thighs.

What Berit Sandemo then tells me is that there are quite a few decisions still to be made and that this is extremely last minute and hearing her say these things makes me feel completely and incurably alone. She runs through a list and I can't make sense of half of it. Before she is done I interrupt. 'I'm sorry but I'm having a hard time. Are you saying none of these things have been decided?'

'Yes, that's what I'm telling you.'

I don't think I can stay in the room any longer with its grief pamphlets and respectful carpet. I wish I had asked for some water.

She folds her hands on the table. 'Okay then Siv, let's take this one step at a time. I will walk you through it.'

'Can we, I mean, is there like a standard funeral service? With psalms and everything?' I umm. 'What I mean is, I haven't been to a funeral since I was very small and I don't know how it should be. I just want like a very normal service.'

Berit Sandemo nods her head once. 'There isn't one standard template as such, but I have planned many funerals in my years here.' She clicks her laptop. 'Why don't I make a dignified service suggestion for you, and you tell me if you want to change anything.'

I exhale until my lungs are completely empty. 'Thank you,' I say and my voice sounds young.

'You will have to give me a moment.' She nods again and starts tapping on the keyboard with her nails.

I look around the room and try not to picture what could be in the box that isn't ashes. Surprisingly soon Berit Sandemo twists the laptop so we can both see the screen and then she talks me through the programme and bluntly hums each psalm so I can recognise them.

'Now is there any other psalm you want to use instead?'

'These are the normal ones, for funerals I mean?'

'Yes. These are the normal ones.'

'Thank you, yes these will be great,' I say and then I add, 'I like them,' which surely is not an appropriate thing to say.

She asks me about some logistics and mostly I don't know how to reply so she gives me suggestions that I readily accept. Some things have different costs and I never choose the cheapest alternative but often I choose the second cheapest.

'That's the bulk of it,' she says. 'How about I finalise this and email it to you for approval.'

'That will be good, thank you.' We both stand up and move towards the door. 'I'm sorry my parents, I mean, that this has been so last minute. I hope it hasn't caused you a lot of stress.'

She stops by the doorway and looks at me. 'You know, I've worked here a long time and I have talked to many many sad people. And I can tell you one thing,' she takes hold of my wrists, 'we all grieve differently. And I have seen it all. That's it.' She squeezes my wrists, then lets go.

I wish I could say something but my voice would be ugly, so I simply nod and walk through the reception and what I am thinking is that this woman Berit Sandemo, I love her a little bit. Outside around the corner I exhale a few times and shake my hands to get rid of the tingle.

IN MY JACKET pocket are the keys to grandma's flat. I take a local bus from the funeral home, then press the door code and walk the stairs up to floor three. She has always lived in the flat, and grandpa too when he was alive. When I open the door I know the smell immediately, earthy and something like blackcurrants. I love this smell. Her coats are still on hangers in the hallway. There are even some of grandpa's coats although he has been dead a decade.

I leave my shoes and bag in the hallway then walk around the rooms and touch things. There is an old CD player in the living room and I turn it on, curious to hear the last piece of music she listened to. Nick Cave. This is wild to me. Her faux-Persian rugs are everywhere and I take off my socks to walk barefoot.

In the wardrobe is an unbelievable amount of clothes. All grandpa's shirts and trousers and jackets are still here. I wonder about this. If maybe she was lonely. If his clothes, his things, are the source of the earthy smell and getting rid of them would leave her with only blackcurrant. I open her drawers and there are sensible bras and underwear, many pairs of stockings. It seems almost brutally intimate, seeing her underwear folded there, empty.

The flat is not large and nothing in it is valuable. They were frugal and lived without fuss and every time she gave me money I knew she had saved up, but this didn't make me feel bad about accepting the twelve thousand because her face would radiate such dignity handing the envelope over.

It has always been a comfort visiting grandma's flat, how nice it smells, how tidy it is, and even sometimes almost pretty if the sun comes in or when it is snowing. She managed this without much money, and that is what comforts me.

I fill a glass of water from the tap in the kitchen and I wonder what will happen to all this. Her things. I can't see my parents going through the underwear drawer. They are not sentimental and will not want anything to keep. And I won't be here. Who does that leave, the landlord? Dumping her things at the recycling station to make room for new tenants? Grandpa's things she had found so important to keep. I smooth a hand over the countertop. It feels likely I could cry now finally. There is a thickness in my throat and my eyes sting. I drink some more water and hold on to the counter. And yes there are tears. A cramp like a sob from my stomach. I don't like it so I don't go on. Nick Cave is still singing so I go to turn him off.

Back in the hallway I flip through the coats and try them on, one after the other, and this makes me soft, warm-hearted. Grandpa's double-breasted overcoat sits like a perfect navy box on my shoulders, ankle-long and heavy. I keep it on.

On a small table by the door are keys and lipsticks and coins. In the top drawer under an address book is an enve-lope with many different-sized bills. I count to twelve thousand, then fold the wad of cash and deposit it in the chest pocket of grandpa's navy coat. I replace the rest in the envelope in the drawer and then I walk out, locking the door behind me. I don't feel bad about taking the money because I am certain grandma would have approved. One final act as family backbone.

On the bus to my parents' house I bring the coat lapels to my nose and breathe in and yes, it has the smell, earthy and something like blackcurrant.

LATER THAT NIGHT, the night before the funeral, I bring my laptop out on the veranda where dad is sitting with a cup of tea and a tablet. Mum is loading the dishwasher in the kitchen and the radio is on. Talk radio, not music. I sit down. 'Dad can I check this with you?' I show him the screen. It is the final version of the funeral programme. He stares longsighted at the screen and when he realises what it is he winces.

'Yes yes, I'm sure that's all fine,' he says and looks away and calls, 'Malin is that you girl,' in the direction of a rustling sound in the garden.

I allow myself a long breath and then I say, 'Oh, and dad, maybe I could ask you, I mean maybe you don't want to talk about it but I want to know if you're okay? About grandma.'

He rubs his nose quite ferociously. 'I'm fine. Yes I'm fine.' Then he sighs. 'It doesn't feel real, does it?'

'No. It doesn't.'

He keeps his eyes on the twilit garden, maybe searching for the cat. 'One thing that does feel real.'

'What's that?'

'I feel that she had a good life.' Now he turns towards me and his eyes land on my knees. 'And you are one reason for it Siv, you know that.'

The words are unnatural in his mouth. Still I am grateful to him for saying them.

'Yes. I know that.'

TOMORROW WILL BE the funeral. It will be overcast, the service will be dignified, neither mum nor dad will cry. Mum will look like she is focusing on displaying correct behaviour but dad squeezes my hand and holds it for the duration of 'Härlig är Jorden' which is embarrassing but nice and when the psalm finishes he whispers, it feels more real now don't you think?

I TOUCH MY phone to check the time. Seven fifty. So far we have mostly met up after class so I don't know yet if Hanna is very punctual. My guess is punctual but stressed, like in school, often rushing in just before the classroom doors close.

I pour myself water from a carafe in big clunks and scroll my phone by the window. There is a lit candle and a bowl of peanuts on the small table, beer in the miniature fridge under my desk. Now and then I look out to search for her on the footpath below.

Except for small talk in lecture halls, I have not seen Hanna since I slept in her bed. She hasn't asked to hang out so maybe she has noticed my subtle withdrawal. I do not feel nice about it. Also, I miss her. On the drive up after the funeral, when picturing Stockholm, I thought of her. She is fun and I am alone, a domino tile reaching no other if tipped. If it's the same for Hanna, I don't know.

Three minutes to eight she materialises on the lawn below, flustered with hair flying and a long-strapped bag banging her hip as she advances on the building. My abs contract as if steeling myself for the intensity.

'SORRY I'M LATE,' Hanna says loudly and flashes her teeth.

'Oh, no actually you're early.'

She wrestles her bag over her head and drops it on the floor. Her hair is static. Her lips are pink. As are her cheeks.

'How are you?' she asks, eyes big.

'Yes, good.'

'Nice. What are you up to?'

'Nothing really.' I point to the almost empty water glass by the window for some reason.

'That won't do.'

I get two bottles, glasses, and bottle opener and sit down while she pours the beer for us. Looking at her there in the chair I am suddenly awfully pleased I decided to invite Hanna today. She is just, like, kind. She doesn't seem to disapprove of things I say and this quality has proven a Stockholm rarity. Her humour is never mean which is the most impressive type of humour. She can be quite critical but I have never seen her intentionally cruel. The cold glass chills my hand. There is thick froth on top.

'Skål,' she says and clinks my glass too hard.

We drink.

'This is good beer,' I say.

She looks at the label. 'I had my first intoxication on this stuff.' She takes a handful of peanuts and chews loudly.

'Mine was on witchbrew stolen from mum's bar cabinet.'

'Ah, I had forgotten about those parties with the witch-brew. Almost as nasty on the way down as on the way up.'

I shudder and sip and don't say that my witchbrew wasn't drunk at a party but alone at home when my parents were out. But yes, I agree, nasty on the way up. Then we talk about class and it is like her anxiety in bed last time never happened. I wonder if she regrets telling me. She is her funny self and makes many risqué remarks on professor Mikael and his tight jeans bulge. I get tipsy although the brown bottle says only four point nine percent.

'You look nice today,' I say.

'Why?' she asks midchew, her open mouth full of peanuts. I look away.

'I've never seen you in lipstick.' I nod. 'It's good.' And it is. Her hair is washed and her clothes sort of match, as if she's made an effort.

'Thanks. Now stop it.'

I can't tell if she wants appearance-based compliments or not. I often find myself thinking of ways Hanna could improve her appearance. It is horrible of me but completely involuntary, like I'm subconsciously stressed by her failure to adhere to beauty standards, and itching to apply my adjustments. It is an unwelcome reminder of my own vanity.

Hanna walks around my small room. This is the first time she has visited and I try not to imagine her thoughts. By the desk she picks up one book then another. 'Are you running for office or something.' She holds up a slim paperback about the dismantling of borders.

'Oh no. I can't have faith in politics. I tried but it was awful.'

She turns to me and puts the book down. 'Why?'

'It's just, I think I prefer pragmatism.'

She sits again and pulls her legs up on the chair. 'What does that mean?' She holds her knees and raises her eyebrows expectantly and I feel a ridiculous responsibility to deliver.

I bite my lip a few times and then I try saying things about human nature's inherent selfishness, the mistake of making morality the basis for change, there not being enough compassion to go around. About a video I saw following this Dutch woman creating an EU-sanctioned algorithm that calculates where to best build refugee homes based on factors like school system, same-language communities, unemployment, hate-crime rates. It had struck me as such a neat way of using technology to override populistic politics. And I became interested in software after that. Hanna has not seen the video but offers similar nice stories as reinforcement.

'So I think I believe in technology more than human decency is what I'm saying.' I have been speaking quickly and now I need to breathe.

'Do you really think that?'

'Oh, I don't know. I'm sort of working it out as we go.'

Hanna chuckles and scrunches up her nose. This is the most I have spoken in a long time and I feel winded and a bit self-conscious, laid bare but not alarmingly so. I get us more beer from the fridge.

Hanna's phone vibrates on the table. She glances at the notification then turns it screen down.

'Something wrong?'

'No no. Just my mother checking in.' Hanna looks small now, her shoulders rotating forward.

'My mum never just checks in,' I say.

'That's nice.'

'Yeah.'

It seems like she has told me something private although she hasn't. I want to give her something in return, like I owe her an intimacy. Maybe tell her about grandma?

'Anyway,' she says and fills her mouth with beer.

I say, 'I'm very happy you came over today.'

She smiles. 'Softie.'

I tssk and kick her leg under the table.

'You know what,' she says. 'This place is a depression.'

This startles me. I feel ashamed. It is not a nice room but up until now I have never thought of it as a depression.

'Sorry, but sharing a kitchen?'

'Yes well,' I say, and I think we don't all have a dead grandmother's apartment and an overflowing bank account. Hanna is the richest person I have ever met but I am not sure she knows this, or even reflects on it. Maybe money is like sex, you only obsess in case of lack.

LIKELY I AM emboldened by how things are progressing with Hanna because this morning between classes when I heard Astrid and some others talk about going out I simply walked up and asked, 'Can I come too?'

They looked a little surprised but not averse and Astrid just said, 'Sickan, of course you can. Fun!'

I don't know what to wear to a poetry reading because I have never been to one so I look at images online for suggestions. It seems many people at poetry readings dress rather strangely, but I am staying safe, classic. Black turtleneck, black cigarette trousers, black loafers, velvet headband. Very winged eyeliner. I don't own a beret, so the braver beatniked version of this look is not something I even need to consider.

I stare in the mirror and I know I am overthinking but merely knowing you are overthinking never helps, which makes that advice, stop overthinking things, really quite toothless because how?

I would like to be a person who regularly attends poetry readings so this morning it had sounded exciting. But now, twelve minutes before I have to pick up my bag and lock the door, I only feel dread. Not a high-pulsed sweaty dread but something like exhaustion. Like there is a risk my thighs might not carry me all the way to the bus and then down the stairs to the Gamla Stan wine café. I am not surprised to feel this tired since I always do before a social event.

And this morning I had known I would tonight feel this way, but I still made the plan. Because I had hoped this would be one of those times, the lovely times, where the excitement turns into exhaustion, but then turns again, into gratitude, to myself for forcing my thighs out to one of those glorious nights, when moods soar and people are nice and you fall a little bit in love with everybody.

It doesn't happen often to me. With Hanna it does sometimes because we tend to drink a lot and she is easy to talk to. So likely yes, I have been emboldened.

Still. To leave this corridor right now feels like a punishment. In my mind I picture a night at home: a pot of Assam, my softest cardigan.

I know I'm just convincing myself to stay in. I look at Astrid on my phone and what I want is to cancel. But I have never been out with them before and I am pretty certain it will be a bit much to both invite and uninvite myself in the span of nine hours.

Bag. Locked door. Bus to Gamla Stan.

I don't spend much time in old town. It is a maze of tight alleyways and slow tourists, and independent of weather conditions, it's always windy. The centuries-old grey stone houses look thick like prisons and forts. Medieval, claustrophobic. Who lives here?

I am too cold in my clothes, my coat thin and my ankles exposed. Arms around my shoulders, I press into the head-wind. My eyes tear. I am not allowed to think I should have stayed home. Instead I remind myself who will be there and details about their lives I can ask them about. Astrid's mother is in the military. Karl likes watches.

The reading is in a damp cellar with cobbled floors and rugs. The chairs and tables have been removed, and the bar is tucked in a corner. I pay one hundred kronor for a green stamp on my wrist. Astrid and Karl and the others are over there and I am pleased to see they are wearing similar clothes to mine. I walk over and say hej and try to look at ease and happy, and they say hej, great, you made it, and point out the bar as if it wasn't very visible to everyone.

I buy a glass of Cabernet because I have decided beforehand that red wine will be my order tonight. Thinking on the spot is not my best skill in new situations. I take my time at the bar, wanting the reading to start and put an end to rigid small talk.

When I return to the group they are already seated on the floor so I join them and we toast and right then, blessedly, a person clears her voice into the microphone and introduces the first reader.

I have never done poetry before, neither writing nor reading. So I decide to take the poems at face value without trying to judge the quality, out of respect for the poets who will know what they are doing. I can't say I understand much, or find the evening profound. But some moments are good, some phrasings reverberating off the stone walls quite beautifully. I am sure there are ways to tell if a poem is impartially good or bad but I think few people on this planet will be qualified to make the distinction.

I am getting bored. Now I want the reading to end.

Some people are coughing gently or shifting position so I don't think I am the only one.

Then it is over. Afterwards we all stand around in clusters and discuss the poets who move around the room like satellites, their objective unknown to me. Maybe they are in pursuit of a publisher if publishers bother coming to these very studenty evenings. It seems romantic, this scene of people actively looking for art. Pretentious of course but who cares when it is also so completely benign.

We are talking about my favourite reading and I want to say something intelligent so I venture a kind of speech on the beat and rhythm and alliteration of a certain poem, which to my ears does sound intelligent enough definitely. But Astrid laughs a little and says, 'Sickan, I swear I sometimes wonder if you're even a girl at all,' and this stops me cold and I search back through what I've just said, trying to identify anything that might come off as overly masculine, but what does that even mean, to talk masculinely about alliteration and rhythm, so I come up short. 'What do you mean? I'm a girl,' I say. 'I mean I identify as girl.'

'I mean, I, identify, as, girl.'

Astrid has just mimicked me. That really happened. I feel nauseous. She laughs good-naturedly. 'You always talk all cut up like that, I love it, like a robot from the future.'

The others laugh a bit too, saying oh yes actually that's true, and although I know she is not being mean, she is just making conversation, what happens is that that word, robot, it sparks a memory.

IT WAS SOMETHING like November, because there was no snow but still I was cold in my täckjacka walking home from school. The trees cast long shadow fingers. Fallen leaves had turned to orange pulp that made my feet skid. I was twelve.

Although school was bad for me, the walk home was worse. In school there were rules, we had to be in specific places at specific times and could only speak when given permission. But that stretch of street, between the safety of home and the order of school, was dangerous. In the mornings I left the house too early to run into anyone, arriving when the halls were still only semi-lit. But walking home, I had to make a call. Hurry out the classroom to be the first to leave, or stay until everyone left but risk them lying in wait.

That Tuesday I went to the library to delay. There had been a bored tension in class that day, the sad weather and dull lesson pulling down spirits. Boredom was not good, it meant they would be looking for thrills. I waited in the library for forty minutes. Forty minutes late I could explain. Mum was working from home, and my class schedule was taped to the fridge door.

A soft drizzle darkened the asphalt as I left the school building. I could see no one and thought everyone would be indoors in this weather, but I was wrong.

Minutes into my walk home, by the playground, I saw four of them.

They told me to sit on the bench so I did. They asked me questions that I replied to with either yes or no. Fear made my body shut down. My body and brain had been here

before and they would no longer take part. My hands heavy
on my thighs. My lungs too small for air. I rested my eyes on
a forgotten tractor in the sand. Yes, yes, no, I don't know.

How come humans can close their eyes but not the ears?
I hate it. If I could, I would keep my ears closed almost all
the time. And there was already too much, at twelve, I
wished I'd never heard.

I listened when he asked if I was a real human. If I had
a hole down there or was smooth as a robot.

No.

He asked me to prove it. Show them the hole.

No.

One was behind the bench. He held my arms, I couldn't
stand up. The others stood close, their legs brushing my
legs. They seemed to consider, should they do something,
or not? I thought maybe I should scream, or kick as hard
as I could, something.

But I knew it was useless. If they wanted to see the hole
they could see it, I could do nothing, no control over my
body or their bodies.

Walking away from the playground I forced my feet to
slow because the urge to run was so large my chest was
exploding with it. But I had learned to not run or look
behind me. It made it worse. Sometimes they came after
me again. But this time I could tell they were done. When
the excitement turned into a sort of disgust, as if my weakness was suddenly offensive to look at, that meant they
were done. Even so, knowing it was over did not convince
my legs and arms. My ears pounded. I was freaking out, I
needed to calm before reaching home.

I planned how to hide what had happened from my parents. The shoulder of my täckjacka was torn but the worst thing was my hair. It had been completely soaked in mud. No other part of me, just my hair. A torn jacket could be explained. My lateness too. But not the hair.

There was nothing more important to me than them not knowing. It would break me. It was shame of course, but guilt was worse, much worse. The pain it would cause them if they had seen what happened in the playground.

I opened the front door with my jacket turned inside out to mask the tear. I kicked my shoes off and jogged upstairs shouting, hej I'm home, I'm taking a shower, before locking the bathroom door and washing my hair in hot water for a very long time, then I dressed and slowly walked downstairs to the kitchen where my dad was cooking dinner and my mum sat at the kitchen table reading the TV supplement.

The kitchen wall clock was ticking. The radio was off.

I sat down opposite. My hair dripped on my back. Behind me dad fried blodpudding. The blood smelled sweet.

No one questioned where I had been the one and half hours since school finished but mum said, 'Did you have a nice day?', and right then, in the overwhelming normality of that kitchen, I lost my mind.

'You're shivering, Siv, do you have a fever?' She reached out to touch my forehead but I reared back as if struck. She looked shocked.

I wanted to tell them then, shout it, and for it to be acknowledged, finally, that this was my life. That someone else was seeing it.

I felt hot. I kept breathing and breathing and then the moment passed. My shivering slowed and eventually stilled.

Mum gave me the thermometer and I obediently put it under my tongue. I didn't have a fever.

When dad placed a plate of blodpudding before me I said, 'I'm a vegetarian,' and so decided to make my life non-violent.

Dad said, 'Oh,' a little unsure of next steps, and mum said, 'Truly Siv, you never cease to amaze.'

I TELL ASTRID I am going to the toilet but I don't, I go home. The nights are still shockingly cold and the wind is awful. Walking to the bus stop there are some people out, a group of men. I walk steadily, fast but not rushed. When there are drunk men around and it is late I know to look down. If I wear a short skirt I don't pull it. I hunch my shoulders slightly. This no longer takes conscious adjustments, it is a learned behaviour, automatic. I am not twelve and disgusting anymore. I am now just as sexualised as other women, and I have been alive long enough to know how to slow my steps, not look back, and never run, no matter if my ears pound and my chest is exploding.

OUR FOOTSTEPS ECHO in a way that seems excessive. Especially Hanna's shoes which sound like high heels, but are in fact white worker boots. The cobblestones have been here who knows, centuries, and the streets are narrow like tunnels. It is moody in this moist April weather, the sky just waiting to release its hail. We have no real plans. Hanna is looking in small shops and showing me places.

We are on Södermalm, the southern quarter, and everything is surrounded by water. I didn't realise this about Stockholm before moving here but it's all just a cluster of islands isn't it.

Up here in the hilly part, the houses are very old. Some are eighteen-hundreds stone, grandiose with checkerboard marble vestibules. But my favourites are the low-ceilinged red wooden houses. The workers' quarters. This area of Stockholm has a specific accent, saying eeeh, when other Swedes say aaeh. Instead of caring they say kehring, which nowadays signals wealth but used to sound poor. Strange how that goes.

Hanna doesn't say kehring because she is old money, meaning Östermalm. On Östermalm they say a pinched-up kind of iiih instead of eee. Hanna says triiihtop instead of treetop. I'm from Skåne so my accent is much stronger but I have almost worked it off.

Up and down there are street-level or lower ground-level shops and restaurants. All the tiny subterranean shops seem a bit weird, as if they have stayed too long, losing all measure of relevance. Children's toys, tea and incense, real fur coats, picture frames, who would buy these things?

'But how do they survive?' I ask.

'I don't know, I think the rent is so obscenely low they don't really have to sell anything?'

'Well, I hope they do, survive.'

'Me too.'

'Except the fur.'

She takes my arm as we make our way upwards in the moist headwind. 'There's fur in my wardrobe you know.'

'No. Not seriously.'

'Yes, and endangered animal skins. Mostly from my grandma but some are my mother's. Probably some blood diamonds too. But I wouldn't know how to check.'

'Hanna!' I stare at her. 'Get rid of it!'

She laughs. 'Fine I will.' She shakes my arm a little. 'The fur at least.'

We go into a shop that sells secondhand lamps and glass. We lift things up to the light to watch the gleam. I look at the price tags. It's not so bad.

There is one thing in the shop I love at once, a white ceramic candlestick with five arms on one foot. One arm in the middle, four arms in a square. It is a simple, very traditional Swedish piece and I think my grandparents had the three-armed version in their living room. I can picture this in the middle of a dining table, lighting up the faces of dinner guests. But when I imagine it in my student room I get a little sad. Like Hanna said, the room is depressing. I put the candlestick down.

'A classic,' Hanna says and picks it up and scrutinises it for flaws. 'You like it?'

I shrug.

'You know when I visited your place I was going to bring a housewarming gift but I forgot.'

'I've lived there almost two years.'

'Still, it's new to me.' She walks up to the counter where there is a pensioner with steel-wool hair. 'Hello,' Hanna says to the lady.

'Hanna please don't, there's really no need.' I feel flustered now and I absolutely don't want her to buy me a candlestick. She is too generous with her money, it makes me uncomfortable because I can't pay her back.

'Would you have bought it for yourself otherwise?' Hanna asks.

'No.'

The pensioner says, 'Well you can't really want it then can you? Next to nothing the cost of this one.'

'My grandmother just died,' I say before realising she hadn't asked about my financial status. I make an um sound. The pensioner looks confused, waiting for me to continue which I extremely don't want to do.

'My grandmother is dead too,' Hanna steps in as if at all helpful.

'But Hanna. When your grandmother died you got her apartment and all those things.'

She turns to me. 'What, you didn't get anything?'

'No nothing,' I say and feel horrible. 'Well I took twelve thousand out of a drawer but that's, anyway, what I mean is she used to help me every semester and now she's dead.' I can feel my eyes sting which is mortifying. 'And now it sounds like I'm only upset because of the twelve thousand but that's not it, I'm upset she is gone in general too. Although I do feel like, if your grandmother is going to die, at least you should get some money out of it?' And now it is audible, the sadness shaking my voice. I can't even look at the pensioner who is standing completely still.

Hanna says, 'You stole money from your dead grandmother?'

I nod. 'Yes.'

All of this is shocking. I look up at Hanna, blurry through my wet eyes. She looks very serious but I can tell, she wants to laugh. It is a bizarre situation.

'Seriously,' she says. And yes, Hanna does start to laugh then, and yes I sort of laugh too even though I was tearful a second ago, because it is lovely to talk about grandma even in this bizarre way. Hanna says, 'Good for you,' and I say, 'I took grandpa's coat too,' and hold out the lapel to show her. She fingers the material, 'Nice,' and shakes her head and sort of slams my back and says, 'God you're such a weirdo.'

The pensioner says, 'Okay calm down now girls,' and looks so appalled I am abruptly taken out of the laughter-crying, realising we have overdone it and been scandalous and that this ordinary pensioner wants us to leave now, we are making her uncomfortable. Once again I have failed to control my outbursts, which is a thing that seems to happen quite a lot with Hanna. I can definitely not go into this shop again, and thank god this happened in front of just a stranger. Then it dawns on me that maybe the pensioner is herself a grandmother, and we have not only reminded her of her mortality, but also introduced the idea that her grandchildren will only miss her for her money. I back-pedal with intensity. I turn sombre and polite and firmly pull Hanna's sleeve to exit. Hanna, unflustered, buys the five-armed candlestick without rush, to the sound of my rattling impatience.

TWO STREETS SOUTH there is an underground crêperie, down some stone stairs and through a low door. The floor is made of rough tiles and the wooden tables are so rustic they smell sort of damp. Hanna orders an assortment of crêpes and iced tea, and I ask for just the iced tea. As soon as the waiter leaves I say, 'I'm sorry about that.'

'What?' She takes off her sweater.

I feel too stiff to lean back in the chair. I sit on my hands. 'For crying. And laughing too much.'

'I don't think it's possible to laugh too much?' She honestly looks confused, like she hasn't registered that we just made spectacles of ourselves. I try so hard to not be a spectacle I am ceaselessly looking for signs of it, but maybe Hanna doesn't mind it or maybe she has given up. And it is true, although she called me the weirdo there is no deny-ing she is even weirder. At least she hides it less. I have never had this role before, being the sound and sensible.

And with her, listening to her tall anecdotes or outlandish opinions I feel, in fact, ordinary. Boring even. Sometimes, especially if a little drunk, I find myself trying to up my eccentricity, match her offbeatness.

Looking across the table at her now, thirstily drinking her iced tea, I feel almost lightheaded with relief. There will be no repercussions for losing my composure in the shop. She won't even mention it again. And I wonder how far I can take this, how loose I can get, before I outweird her. Maybe I can't outweird her. The thought of that.

I taste my tea. Tart. I want to go out tonight. 'Let's go out tonight.'

She laughs and says okay then.

When the waiter returns with her crêpes, he nods for us to move the brown paper bag with the candlestick out of the way. As I carefully place it on the floor I thank her again.

'You don't really have anywhere to put it though,' she says.

Once more I picture my bleak student room, the sad pine furniture, the stain in the toilet bowl, the sex sounds through thin walls, people screaming their anxiety out of windows. I don't want the candlestick.

Then Hanna says, 'You know the other bedroom in my flat?'

'The study?'

'I've been thinking of renting it out. Doesn't feel decent keeping it empty.'

I am wondering how she'd find someone our age who could afford it.

'What's your rent now?' she asks.

I don't want to say. 'Three thousand nine hundred.'

She whistles. 'A disgrace. Would you want it for an even three thousand?'

I look at her, dumb.

She cuts a crêpe and puts it in her mouth even though it is too hot. She exhales loudly and steam comes out her mouth. 'The exshtrah hedroom,' she says, mouth full. 'Or half the apartment I mean. Sharing with me.'

'As in, move in? At Artillerigatan?'

'Why not.'

I might have known this was her reason for insulting my student room and it is euphoric picturing myself walking barefoot on her herringbone floors and although I should think about this and not say something I can't take back I extremely don't care. 'Yes. For three thousand I would.'

She grins at me and I am already mentally moved in and I hope this is not a conversation I will grow to later regret.

I ORDER A cappuccino and open my paperback. Strindberg's *Röda Rummet*, a Stockholm classic. Not quite May yet but the weather is nice so I sit outside. I stay in the sun since the shade is still on wintertime, scooting my chair as the sun travels across the sky.

Strindberg is funny but the prose is in old Swedish with the weird spellings so the going is slow. I know the general consensus is he's a woman-hater so I look for signs in the text but so far it is not so bad. Didn't Ibsen write *A Doll's House* as a feminist reimagining of Strindberg's *Miss Julie* or did I make that up? I check on my phone and it seems like no, it was the other way around! *Miss Julie* a sexist reimagining of *A Doll's House*. I decide that maybe I don't have to read more Strindberg.

Three people sit down at the table next to me. Three girls in beige clothes and fresh faces and understated sunglasses which they are all now removing, squinting at each other.

They are not speaking in hushed voices like people sometimes do in public spaces, so I can make out their conversation and it is sort of intriguing. From my cotton bag I remove my black notebook. A4, two hundred lined pages, almost empty. I flip to the next empty sheet and click my mechanical pencil. I smooth the page.

The group is gossiping and I have to concentrate. Apparently there is a fourth friend who recently made some poor social media decisions and now the others are worried their names will be tarnished by proxy. The quandary is to balance loyalty for their friend with reputation damage control.

Remarks and comments that stand out I write down verbatim on the left-hand page. After some minutes, the page is three quarters full. I bite the tip of my pencil and read it over, now tuning out the group. I sip my cappuccino. The sun on my face is even warmer than the coffee and I have plenty of time before the shade will reach my table.

After putting down the cup I rewrite the same dialogue on the right-hand page, finding the clichés and intensifying them until they're borderline absurd. What I want is to find the exact wording that signals the beige Stockholmness, the quintessential Östermalm expressions and tone and fillers. The eeehs instead of ummms.

This takes a little while and is mentally demanding. It is my favourite mode of meditation. Also it sharpens my ability to read interactions and understand subtext, the real meaning under all those niceties, and how to deploy this polite vagueness myself. Even though it makes my bag heavy, I bring a notebook most places.

I STARTED THIS habit of filling notebooks with absurd overheard conversations when I was twelve. In mid-December there was a school disco called the St Lucia dance although it was just a standard disco in the music room with chairs lining two of the walls, one line for girls opposite one line for boys. I always attended these school discos although they weren't obligatory. But staying home would make my parents notice so I went. I made myself invisible in a chair by the snacks table, alert to sudden movements.

Kids are cruel, adults said. Just ride it out, hang in there, you'll love university, they said on TV when someone was friendless in school. Being misunderstood, this was a concept I especially liked. As if I was wrong in time or maybe place, not in person, and one day I would find other people in some other place. No one told adults how to dress and no one cared if you spoke slang as long as you were kind and paid your bills. I could manage that. So I was counting down. Years and months, until I would be old enough to go to universitetet and meet people who didn't know me but who would like to.

The discos always ran from six to ten. It was a blessing when the lights came on.

Our winter jackets hung in the cloakroom and I had memorised exactly where mine was to find it and exit quickly. The others were lingering and chatting in the hallway, getting dressed slowly to make the night last. I opened the heavy door to the carpark and icy air welled in. There was a crowd of cars, some of them with head-lights on. Parents were waiting, impatient in the cold. Big lazy snowflakes floated downwards. The air was still and black.

I looked for my parents' blue car. And I saw it, parked two rows down. Mum was leaning a hip on the hood, staring at the snow by her feet. She was dressed badly. Dad's shiny red winter jacket, green leggings with sag around the knees. Hiking boots that she hadn't bothered lacing. White tube socks. Crazy hair. She looked sloppy, odd.

A few cars away, closer to me by the school doors, a group of parents talked and laughed quietly. Katrin's mother and some others. I didn't need to hear to know they were talking about mum. Although I tried not to listen, as I walked past I picked out the words 'no really, it's sad'.

Mum didn't notice me until I reached her. 'Hi let's go,' I said, wanting to get her in the car, cover her up, before the rest of my classmates exited the school. It was a chronic confliction in me, this being so painfully ashamed of them, then feeling guilty about the shame.

Inside the car she put the key in the ignition, and looking at her a thought occurred to me: school must not have been fun for her either. I thought, she was also twelve once, doesn't she remember that everything, precisely everything, can become a taunt, and couldn't she have made just the smallest fucking effort.

This was the first time I thought that word about my mother. It was upsetting. I bit the inside of my cheek.

We drove in silence. She asked if I'd had a good time and I said yes it was fun. Then we were silent again. She had the wipers on at the slowest setting, making a rubbery squeak every eighth second, I counted, clearing the large airy snowflakes off the screen. Her headlights caught flakes in the air, illuminating them like so many minuscule moths. Gradually I calmed back down to normal.

A gnaw started in my stomach during that drive, a gnaw that persisted for days. Because I had seen in that carpark that it doesn't matter if you are an adult. If you didn't behave like an ordinary person and dress in clothes that signalled sanity, you would be shunned. What I saw was, adults hate abnormality just as much as children do.

There was no countdown to graduation, no suffering through. If I didn't learn to behave and dress and talk I would be stuck on this schoolyard forever, at forty-three with saggy knees being laughed at by other adults.

Some days later when we went to the big supermarket I stopped by the notebooks because I thought perhaps I could study this like a school subject.

MY CAPPUCCINO IS finished and my chair is in the shade when I look up. I hadn't noticed the Östermalm girls leaving. I click my pencil and close my notebook and replace both in the cotton bag.

I DRY MY hands on my dress. It is not warm in Lottie's kitchen but my skin is a little moist. We are sitting at the round dining table, eating pretzel sticks and drinking awful highballs.

Lottie picks up a card from the deck and says pass. Hanna reaches for a card, then places three Jacks from her hand on the table. 'Three Jacks, suck on it.'

I am not entirely certain of the rules of this game but I do my best. It might be a drinking game but so far no event has prompted any drinking. Hanna changes the song to Swedish forties music, Ulla Billquist. Lottie raises an eyebrow.

'What?' Hanna says. 'It's Valborg.'

'Okay but please no boy choirs,' I say because actually I really do like Ulla Billquist.

It is April thirtieth, Valborgsmässoafton, the official end of winter, mostly meaning rampant drinking with other students in whatever closest park. Some even wear the white hats and everything.

Card games at Lottie's is a pre-party, but pre what is still undecided. Hanna seems pleased either way, if it was up to her we would just stay here, the three of us, card games and getting drunk and all the nonsense. I also kind of want to stay here, I'm so relaxed I feel heavy. But even more I want the rampant park because I've never been to a Valborgs park party and I want the experience. Though it seems Lottie finds this unsophisticated, a party only worthwhile if selective, invite only.

Lottie is not as easy to read as Hanna, but from what I can tell she seems okay with me coming along. Her body language is mostly lax as if slightly bored and indifferent to what happens to her. But she smiles a lot so I think she is having a good time, the indifference just a personal panache. This is my interpretation.

'Kris is out in the country so it's a no-go there,' she says. She has a low voice which is attractive. I take a swig of highball and quickly put three pretzel sticks in my mouth to cover the taste. The salt grains are large and crack between my teeth.

'What about you,' Lottie says to me. 'None of your friends throwing a Valborgs?'

I freeze. Then I cover my mouth and chew demonstratively. I make the pretzel last. Then I swallow and say, 'Most of my friends live in student corridors anyway.'

Hanna slaps her thigh. 'Park it is.'

I try to hide my enthusiasm. She looks at me and grins.

Tonight I am going to my first park party and I have two friends to go with and the highballs might be disgusting, but they make things fun. I am even partaking confidently in the confused card game when Lottie says, 'Whatever happens, I am making out tonight.' We laugh at this, then she holds her palms up in a gesture of announcement. 'Girls, listen up.' She pauses for effect. 'I'm starting a pod.'

Hanna groans and rolls her eyes but I genuinely think it is the best idea. 'What about?' I ask.

'Sex. And strange people.'

'There are enough of those already though,' Hanna says. And I'm thinking that really, I've been missing out.

I MOVED INTO Hanna's grandmother's apartment on Artillerigatan last week. It was a Saturday and I rang the doorbell with my rucksack, suitcases, and two large black rubbish bags filled with things. Hanna opened the door and slowly said, 'Welcome, to Jurassic Park,' and I said oh dear and she seemed sped up with energy. We carried my bags to the study. She had cleared out her things and placed a thick mattress on the floor. There was a small wardrobe and a chest of drawers just by the desk. Judging from the smell of new wood, I guessed she had bought the wardrobe and the chest specially. She seemed a bit shy, watching me take in the room.

She put on the kaffekokare while I unpacked. Then she walked me around the flat, coffee cups in hand, showing me where she kept towels and which of the two bathroom cabinets she had cleared for my toiletries and there was ample space for my serums, creams, exfoliators, cleansers.

Strolling about, taking it in, it felt unreal that I would stay here now, wouldn't go back to the corridor tonight. I wouldn't cook my pasta to the sound of aggressive computer games from the common room, wouldn't sleep with earplugs to block the drunk sex sounds of my neighbours. Amazing, how you can end a whole chapter of your life by simply lifting a rucksack.

We only grew shyer as Hanna showed me more storage spaces she had vacated for me. It was a novel feeling, someone considering my needs this way, merely because she wanted to. By the half-emptied shoe rack in the hallway, my heart swelled. Left side for her, right side for me. 'Hanna, you didn't have to go to all this trouble.'

'No stop, it's fine. I thought maybe you'd feel like a guest otherwise and I want you to feel like you live here.'

'That's kind of you.' I could hear it sounded a little formal. We still got caught in these shy moments, because I had the brutally irritating tendency to flip from light-hearted to instantly serious.

She shrugged. 'It's important to get the dynamic right from the start. Guests always think you'll cater for them, so I should manage your expectations.'

'Smart.'

'I don't even own an ironing board, so you know.'

There was one worry. When I had accepted Hanna's invitation to move in I had miscalculated the money. Even though I paid less per month now than in the corridor, there you didn't pay rent over the summer. I had secured an internship at a large video streamer, but it was unpaid. It had seemed reasonable at the time because without rent and with the twelve thousand from grandma I could survive just fine. But now I had rent to pay and no grandma, so I was a little bit screwed.

After coffee Hanna went out and I was alone. I told myself I wasn't doing anything wrong opening and closing cupboard doors because this was not just Hanna's home, it was mine too. I had left the cheap kettle and miniature fridge in the student corridor as a tribute to the next student but I had brought my bowls and glasses. I carried them to the kitchen and opened a cabinet. Next to Hanna's china my army surplus bowls looked plastic. I carefully pushed her plates to the left and stacked mine on the right.

WE HEAR THE people in the park before we see them. As always near large crowds my senses are jittery. The sky is not completely dark yet and the wind makes fun of our hair. Lottie and Hanna and I cross the old stone bridge to Djurgården island, with its theme park, zoo, museums.

Smoke is rising from a large open park in between the tourist sights. Although Valborg celebrates winter ending, we somehow do this by lighting an enormous bonfire to scare off witches back to Blåkulla where maybe the devil lives. I am sure this all made sense at one point but the logic is now lost. I am wearing a white cotton dress, ankle-length, with many buttons at the back, even though everyone knows not to wear white on Valborg, the soot will ruin it. Putting it on, I had vowed to stay clear of soot best I could because it is my only nice dress.

It is late now so the fire has been out for hours, more for the kids than anyone else. But there is still light in the sky, cobalt straight above, electric at the horizon. In every lagging sunbeam a cluster of midges congregates. Watching the Mayfire as a child, I thought it magical. Orange blaze, startling heat, young men singing old songs in passable harmony and suit jackets. Mum would buy me a doughnut from the stand which was a once per year thing so maybe that's where the magic came from. Freshly made, still warm, sugar and cinnamon. Every time, she challenged me to eat the whole thing without licking the sugar off my lips. I never could do it, it tickled too much.

Hanna hands me a plastic bottle, the type you take to the gym. I drink from the nozzle and it feels decidedly wrong to taste alcohol out of this container. Leaving our pre-party Lottie had mixed more highballs, poured into two water bottles. Hanna and I share one.

As we approach, we see silhouettes of hundreds of people. My pulse is high.

We skirt the crowd looking for something, I'm not sure what, maybe a way in. Then Lottie screams and runs off. We follow and try not to lose her.

'Pernilla, as I live and breathe,' Lottie shouts to a short girl with long red hair.

'You hag, it's been ages,' Pernilla says. They hug tight, jigging from side to side. Then Lottie introduces me and Hanna.

Pernilla seems to belong to a group of about ten people. They are standing too close to the ash pile for my liking but I knew the dress was a risk when I buttoned it up. By now I am quite drunk anyway so concepts like permanent staining and dry clean only have little meaning.

Lottie asks, 'Who are your serious friends?' and points at four boys in slim suits.

'They're in a band,' Pernilla says. 'Britpop soundalikes. Quite good actually but maybe not good good.' She swoops her hand across the remaining five or so people. 'The rest are like randoms. I came with Noor and they're all uni friends of hers. Humaniora or sociology or something, so you know, a bit yuck.'

But they don't look yuck, they look lovely. Nice clothes, very Stockholm but without the precisely tied belts and neck scarves. As if fitted to each other's company, a crew. One is large and wide. He is talking to a short one with black curly hair wearing a huge beige sweater. The way the short one laughs at the large one makes me feel sweet.

A girl detaches herself from the group and comes over. She has long dark hair and bangs, a thick cardigan buttoned up over smoking trousers. There is a cigarette between her fingers and I am thinking that she should own a Vespa.

'Welcome to my little shindig,' she says. 'Make yourself at home but please, everyone, shoes off.'

I laugh and consider taking my shoes off to partake in the joke but I don't. It is my first park party and above all, I'm not being weird.

'Noor, this is Lottie and,' Pernilla looks at me and Hanna, 'and I already forgot the other names but I am sure they're lovely people.' Pernilla's meanness makes me uneasy but no one reacts so probably it is intended as fun, maybe even charming. I want to relax and enjoy myself but there is a lot to take in and my eyes dart around of their own accord.

As per tradition, this Valborg night is stinging cold. The ash pile still radiates half-life heat and the crowd keeps moving closer, packing us tighter and tighter which also helps against wind. Most teenagers drop off to meet their midnight curfew.

Hanna pinches my side and it tickles and things are hilarious for no reason which means we are drunk. 'Look at that guy,' she says and nods to a blond making large, confident gestures. He is crowd-hopping, interrupting whomever as he goes. He seems to know no one but to be unbothered by this. We watch his progression for a while, thoroughly entertained by the evasion efforts of his victims.

I don't know how it happens but amazingly our group meshes with Noor's. I am almost close enough to hear what the two guys are joking about. Lottie has already called dibs on a band member with a bowl cut. He looks young but I know Lottie leans towards cute. She can have all the dibs on this one.

Hanna is in deep conference with Noor and I look away when I see Noor hand her a pill. I want to stay out of it because I have no information on good pill manners and I don't think I want to decline a pill and I definitely know I don't want to accept one. When I turn back, Hanna is talking to the large guy, the four of us now in a circle, the short one right next to me. Without meaning to I smooth my hair which is such a tell.

The large guy offers Hanna a cigarillo which she accepts. I, on my side, decline.

'Good for you,' the short one says to me.

'Oh yes. The smell is vile,' I say and make a face. We are of similar height so our eyes line up. A few specks of ash fly between our faces. A moment passes. He smiles, licks his lips. They look a little dry, as if he's been standing too close to the fire. 'Were you here when it was burning?' I ask.

'Yeah. It was a giant.'

'Scare many witches?'

'I reckon enough fire damage has been done to the community.'

I laugh and click my tongue. 'Did you come up with that now?'

'To be honest I did try it on someone else earlier.'

'What's your name?' I ask and again without meaning to, I fuss my hair.

He screws the lid off a metal flask. 'Abbe,' he says and hands it to me. 'Vodka?'

'Thanks.' The liquid is cold and hot down my throat.

'What's yours?'

'Sickan.'

'Really? Short for?'

'Siv.'

He grimaces. 'Wow, okay. Better with Sickan, I agree.'

I take this insult in my stride and interpret it as easy teasing. I want to come up with something smart to ask but my brain is lulled by the highballs and also I am distracted by the fact that his eyelashes are as curly as his hair. I am scared he will turn back to his large friend if I don't speak now.

'What are you two on about anyway?' someone says, and like so the blond crowd-hopper has made our duo a threesome. I'm so grateful I could laugh.

'Not much, not much,' Abbe says and chuckles. He moves closer until we are hip to hip, turned towards the blond.

'I swear everyone in this fucking place is so boring.' The blond pulls a hand through his hair then wipes his fingers on his trousers.

'Not having fun?' I ask.

'What a joke. Even my day job is more fun.' His voice is slurred but perfectly intelligible.

'Oh yeah?' Abbe asks.

I hand Abbe the vodka. He takes a swig and passes it back to me. I lean a little closer and easy as that, our upper arms are touching. First a layer of thick knit, then his hard shoulder and round muscle. I get a thrill to my stomach. He doesn't move away.

The blond says, 'Yeah that's right, I fuck for a living, what do you say about that?'

'You're an escort?' I ask, suddenly invested.

'No man, are you joking? I'm in porn.'

I tilt my head. 'I wouldn't have guessed.'

'Yeah I don't see it,' Abbe says.

The blond sways and pulls at his sleeves. 'I'm a celebrity in porn, you must have seen me.'

'Well,' I say. 'I'm sure you're very talented.' A wind is being nasty so I get a sweater from my bag. When my head comes out the collar, there is a phone screen right in front of my eyes.

'Look,' the blond says.

On the screen three people are having sex, closeups on genitals. I don't look to see if the blond is one of them. I push his arm away and I feel nauseous. I swallow and can hear my own ears. This was a bit too much for me. I search the crowd for Hanna but can't see her right now.

Abbe says, 'Alright nice talking to you bror, have a good night now okay.' He touches my elbow and angles us both away from the blond.

'Yeah I'm actually talking to her,' the blond says and steps in front of us.

I say, 'You were talking to me but now you're done,' and amazingly my voice doesn't vibrate.

'Yeah mate, you're good.'

'Hey what the little prissy snob fuck,' the blond says to Abbe and pushes his shoulder, hard enough for him to reel back. Abbe finds his balance and steps forward but I go between them and put both hands on the blond's chest and press him backwards. 'Back off.' My voice is calm, my heart is not, violently beating my skin. The blond grabs my hair, a thick chunk of it. He pulls and my head jerks. My scalp is splitting. Abbe reaches for the blond's wrist.

'Hey is there a problem?' someone says. Abbe's large friend. The hand holding my hair lets go. Abbe breathes heavy next to me. The adrenaline makes me dizzy which is familiar. But now it is over. The blond wanders off and I touch my scalp.

I see Hanna over there and the sight of her is such a comfort it makes me tear up. She is walking towards me with a deep line between her brows. She asks am I okay and I say yes yeah okay as the four of us join the others and Noor asks what happened and I listen to Abbe tell the story while gesturing with one hand and pressing a cold can to my head with the other. My brain is fevered and I am still dizzy. Calm down now, it all went okay. I take the can and hold it in place, cooling my scalp. Abbe does a good job of the retelling.

As I listen to him, I see how this is new. Abbe and I had teamed up, two against one, protecting each other. I have never done that for anyone, and no one has done it for me. Then Abbe's friend had made it three against one. I have experienced three against one, but I've always been the one, never the three.

Abbe telling the story, I can't keep my eyes off him. The can on my head feels nice. 'And then Sickan pushes him backwards and says, back off, in the coldest voice, I swear I got chills.'

The band member next to me slaps my back appreciatively. We all agree it was a good team effort and that the situation had been dealt with satisfactorily. I smile at Hanna and her brow line smooths and I can't wait to talk to her alone and hear her opinions. My throat still tastes sour and I am a little shattered but all in all it seems to be a successful first Valborgs park party. Soon Lottie kisses the bowl-cut band member, which sort of cements the meshing of the two groups. I look at them kissing and I also want to.

WHEN I WAKE up it is the first of May and I have a terrible hangover because of all the highballs. I get up. Hanna must still be sleeping. I make microwave popcorn and sparkling water in Hanna's carbonating machine. On channel two is a gameshow with experts on art, classical music, and literature competing in teams. I listen to snippets of Mozart and watch the experts place them in order of year.

Almost always when hungover I get anxiety for no apparent reason and I think this is one of those times. Around my diaphragm is a pressure, I can't take full breaths. While humming along to Requiem in D minor I go over the night in my head to find cause for worry or remorse. I want my anxiety to change from general to specific. Finding the specific faux pas, I can teach myself not to repeat it, and so feel proactive about future hangovers.

My head hurts. There is a sore patch where the blond ripped my hair.

The anxiety seems centred around this part of last night. I think I am a mostly rational person. But I know that women are often labelled overemotional, hysterical. This is something I am quite scared of. I really don't think it would feel good to be perceived as hysterical, bothering other people with overbearing emotions. That would make me very uncomfortable.

I touch the sore patch absentmindedly and eat most of the popcorn. I have oversparkled the water so drinking is a bit stressful.

By the Mayfire, interacting with the blond, I wasn't sure if I had managed to keep my emotions in order. I had been scared. But I had also been very angry, and that's the least attractive feeling for women to show. When you are drunk it is harder to keep emotions in check. With Hanna it's fine, because she never minds and I don't think she would even deem hysterical that bad an insult. But last night there were many new people, and I had been the only one to show strong emotions. Okay, so here it is, the specific source of my anxiety. This I can dissect to make sure I don't repeat. Although I have to admit, the chance of my hair being pulled by a porn star again does seem rather slim.

But, being mistreated by an unsober man in a public space doesn't. That's a when, not an if.

This thought makes me bite down. Him behaving that way, and here I am the one worrying about my reaction being sufficiently feminine.

I wonder what Abbe makes of this. We were in sort of cahoots and it had seemed he appreciated my involvement last night but maybe today he looks at it soberly and finds me odd. Last night he kissed me on the cheek and said, maybe I'll call you sometime, although we didn't exchange numbers. It seems like a missed opportunity, the whole thing. I could have asked for his number myself but I know it's not good in these situations to come across as eager.

The popcorn is long gone and I am wetting a finger to fish up salt flakes from the bottom of the bowl when Hanna walks in. On the table she places a container of green grapes, just rinsed, drops of water on their skin. I put one in my mouth and it is almost rudely strong.

'Why are you watching this?' she says and sits down next to me.

'It's okay.'

'It's boring.'

'It's not so boring.'

'What, you're that keen to learn the difference between Monet and Manet?'

'Yes sure. It would be nice to know.'

'Really?'

I shrug my shoulders and eat another grape.

She laughs a little. 'I swear to god you live your life as if forever ticking off a list.'

I consider this for a moment. 'Sometimes I think things are more fun if they're also ticking off a list. Because otherwise the entertainment has to be entertaining enough in itself to be worth the time investment. That's a lot of pressure.'

She folds some hair from my face. 'Hey. You look a bit harassed.'

'Do I?'

'Did that scare you, last night?'

'It's not that, I don't think. I have some hangover anxiety.'

'Why? It seemed like you were having a good time. I mean, mostly.'

'He said he might call but I didn't give him my number.'

'Oh, him? He's just some boy, forget it.'

There is not much point talking to Hanna about these things because I have come to realise she doesn't have the romantic sensibility. 'What about you, did you see anyone you liked? Noor is pretty.'

'Yes. Too polished.'

'What about the friend, the large one.'

'Pontus? Oh, he's an oaf.'

And I think but you're also an oaf and it is shocking to think this about my only real friend.

In an attempt at repentance I say, 'Do you have time to cheer me up all day today please?'

She smiles wide then and slaps my thigh three times. 'It's the first of May, we should march. Let's go, get up.'

FROM THIS VANTAGE I can see all of Stockholm. I lean forward and below is the harbour with the cruise ships to Finland or Estonia. To my left is Södermalm and to my right the archipelago and then the sea. It is the first time I have seen the city like this.

At the table behind me is Hanna and her mother, Iréne. We are having lunch in a restaurant on the twenty-second floor with glass walls on three sides. Even though I want to look out the window some more, I sit down and we open the menus.

Iréne is the legal owner of the flat on Artillerigatan and she has asked Hanna to bring me to lunch since effectively, I am her new tenant. Hanna didn't want me to meet Iréne but said we had to do it if we wanted to live together. Personally I am curious about Hanna's mother so although I am a little nervous I am also fully invested in this lunch.

I don't know what I expected but it's not this. Iréne gives the impression of a very normal woman in her fifties. Considering the hand-me-downs in Hanna's wardrobe I thought she would be dressed extravagantly but the woman in front of me is slight, medium blonde, dressed in a green cashmere jumper and small pearl earrings. Her lips look filler-free and she has lines on her forehead as if left natural. Now next to Hanna there is no hint of a resemblance. I keep searching for it but, nothing.

'What looks nice?' Iréne asks and nods at the menu. Since Iréne is paying I look for inexpensive.

'Maybe the forest mushroom risotto?' I say.

'Me too,' Hanna says. At some point since sitting down, she has scooted her chair towards mine, leaving a larger gap to her mother's.

Iréne signals to the waiter. 'Three mushroom risottos, two green salads to share, one glass of the white Beaujolais, and two large bottles of mineral water. Tack.'

Hanna says, 'Three glasses of the Beaujolais, tack,' and Iréne smiles and says nothing.

While we wait for the food we taste the wine. It smells like overripe fruit but maybe that's the intention. It is my first Beaujolais so I don't know.

'I hear you come all the way from Skåne,' Iréne says and then she asks me many questions about my studies, my parents, what they do. I find myself describing my parents' work in a way that makes it sound important and prestigious. I leave out the dirty fingernails and long hours of silence and the repeat-wearing of the same threadbare clothes. I want her to think renowned scientists, not the mad kind.

Iréne smiles politely. 'It sounds impressive! I can barely tell the difference between physics and chemistry myself.'

I consider telling her the difference, but don't. I wonder if I should ask what she does for a living but maybe she doesn't do anything and it would be rude to bring it up. By now I am deadly curious to find out how Hanna is so rich but I have yet to ask.

I am sure the risotto is great but I am too focused to taste much. Iréne is telling a sweet mother–daughter childhood story and she places a hand on Hanna's wrist on the table but Hanna pulls her arm away. Iréne looks like nothing has happened and continues her story.

And then she asks for the bill. We take the elevator down and say goodbye. Iréne gets into a taxi. Hanna and I walk north. It was an utterly normal lunch, despite the expensive menu. I was expecting something more to happen, now I'm not sure if I'm relieved or disappointed.

'Don't say it,' Hanna says.

'What?'

'She seems fine to me. I know you're thinking it.'

'I'm so sorry Hanna but yes, she seems just fine.'

WE WALK UP the city and through the door to a konditori off Birger Jarlsgatan. Although not warm outside, the sun is bright through the windows and the armchair is hot to the touch. The lady comes to take our orders and Hanna asks for a café au lait and an äppelmos doughnut and I order just a Ceylon tea because the pastry in this part of the city costs a lot of money. I angle my head to the sun and my face begins to thaw.

'This is what she does though, she acts like the ordinary caring mother but she did actually send me to boarding school, let's not forget.'

'You went to boarding school?' Before this moment I had felt boarding schools only existed on television.

'Yes, the one with all the hazing. You know it, it's a tabloid scandal every year.'

'Oh true, I know it!' And now I am thinking that no matter how strange my upbringing was, it will never compete with Hanna's. 'Was it horrible?'

'At first it was quite bad but then I started to like it and that's when she brought me back home again.'

The lady places coffee, tea, and doughnut on the table. I lift the porcelain cup to warm my hands. It is too hot to drink still. Hanna slurps when she tastes her coffee. It has a lot of foam on top. Then she says, 'And also she's constantly favouritising my sister.'

'Hanna! You have a sister?' I stare, eyes wide.

'Yes, Viveka. But seven years older so we didn't really grow up together.'

'This is a very big thing not to tell me.' I put my cup down so not to spill.

'I mean.' She picks up her coffee spoon and starts cutting her doughnut down the middle. 'You're not jealous are you?'

'No, not jealous.' I think for a second. 'Maybe envious?'

'Here, lift your cup,' she says and when I do she places half her doughnut on my saucer and licks her fingers clean of sugar. 'What's the distinction?'

'I think, I'm not jealous of you two being sisters specifically. But maybe I do envy you the experience of having a sister.'

When she bites into the dough the sticky applesauce squeezes out. With her mouth full she says, 'So you're saying you wouldn't want to be my sister, specifically.'

And I think I definitely do not want to be Hanna's sister. When I picture this it seems disastrous and very intense. 'No. I mean, we're friends.'

'Yeah well, having a sister is not so great. It's like a permanently ongoing competition.'

'Oh. Yes. That doesn't sound so nice actually.'

The sun is behind her head now and floaty strands of hair light up and move like tiny antennae when she talks. 'What do you think of old-school kollektivs?' she says.

'You mean like, hippies living together?'

'Well yes. Or like, people with similar worldviews choosing each other as family. Instead of just keeping their original one.'

'Do you really think so? That you get to choose your family as an adult?'

'I just don't want family to be based solely on genes.'

I rake my bottom lip. 'So you don't strongly feel Viveka's your sister?'

'The other day she out of the blue asked me to go to London with her for a week. It's something she does, inviting me to things whenever she remembers she has a sibling.' The chair scrapes the floor as she sinks deeper, arms on armrests. 'But I can't go anyway because we have that essay on VR.'

'Which topic did you choose?'

'Addiction.'

'That's exciting.' And it does sound much more fascinating than neural development which is my topic.

The coffee machine hisses and when it stops I say, 'You should go. To London. I'll help you with the paper, we can do it together.'

She looks like a devil and says, 'Will you write it for me?'

I am fairly sure she is joking. 'Um, no?'

'Sickan, I will give you two thousand to write it for me.'

I bite into my half of the doughnut and I try not to lick my lips free of sugar but it tickles so much that I have to. 'Yes okay,' I say and feel scandalous, 'for two thousand I'll do it.'

I PICK UP the phone. 'Hallå?'

'Hi, it's Abbe.'

'Oh is it Abbe?' I stand up from the desk and go to the window and scan the street below as if he might be there.

'Yes, how are you anyway? You sound strange.'

'I just had a cold.' I open the window and close it again. 'I coughed so much I lost my voice. Sounds a little disgusting I know.'

He chuckles. 'You sound like a boat engine.'

'Yes.' I resist the urge to clear my throat and instead I go back to the desk, close my textbook, and turn off the desk lamp, astonished I can perform these tasks with Abbe now calling me on the phone. 'It took you a long time,' I say.

'To call?'

'A month.'

'You knew I was going to?'

I walk around the room, just walking around, because there is too much energy. 'I didn't know but I hoped.'

'Is that so.' He tssks. 'You could have called me.'

'You said it would be you who called. But now it's been so long so I wasn't sure.' The phone feels warm against my ear and I hear him perfectly, like he is in the room. Although I'm glad he is not in the room because I think it would have been too much. Also my hair is unwashed.

'I could blame it on not having your number, but that would be lying because it wasn't so hard to find, I've had it in my phone since the day after we met.'

'You have? How?'

'I just asked Noor who asked Pernilla who knew that Lottie had your number.'

It is hard to process, Abbe putting this chain of people in motion to get my phone number. I almost want to hang up to just lie down and think about it. 'Sometimes it's easy to forget that this city is not very big,' I say and pick up a pencil from the desk. 'So why didn't you call until now?' I enfold the pencil in my hand.

'Honestly, I didn't want to complicate things.'

'Is that what we are doing now, being complicated?' My hoarse voice comes out as a breath.

'Depends.'

'Very cryptic.'

Again he laughs. 'Okay, so, I thought calling you might give the wrong idea. Because I'm not looking for anything serious, or even like casual.'

'Oh. Why?'

'Actually, I'm moving next summer. To Mexico City.'

'Mexico. That's quite far.'

He tells me his mother's uncle's stepdaughter owns a design studio in Mexico City with some employees. And she has promised that if he wants it, she will get him the visa and give him a job.

'So, that's why I don't want to start anything, since I'm moving anyway.'

'But you're calling now.'

'Yes well. I had to thank you.'

'What for?' I lie down on the bed and look at the ceiling which is featureless and white.

'For saving me. From the porn star.' He clicks his tongue. 'You swept down like some vengeful demi-god.'

I laugh, my throat hoarse like a caw. 'Don't tease.'

'I'm teasing but I am serious, so thank you. For stepping in. You shouldn't have done that.'

I close my eyes. 'I could see he was going to hit you. And I was sort of banking on him not hitting a woman, which is ridiculous when you think of it. I mean, men do tend to beat women much more willingly than other men. Statistically.'

'Were you scared?'

'Yes very.' Even now, just talking about it brings a sour taste to my mouth.

'I could tell.'

'Weren't you?'

'Not really,' he says. 'I was just going to let him clock me once and play dead until he left.' A relaxed moan as if he is lying down. 'But anyway, you saved me a black eye.'

'I'm happy you didn't get, clocked.' The word sounds strange in my mouth and he laughs. 'But actually it wasn't me who saved you, it was Pontus.'

'He is handy that way.'

And I am once more disoriented by the fact that body size still is the most valuable commodity in a modern technological society. 'It lessens my motivation to study sometimes,' I say. 'I mean what's the point of an educated brain if I still have practically no control over my own physical location.'

He makes a huh sound.

'If I'm walking on the street,' I say, 'someone bigger can just pick me up and take me somewhere else without my education or intellect mattering at all.'

'Wow, okay. Do you really think like that?'

'Well it's just, how evolved can we be if I'm still getting dragged by the hair?'

'Fuck,' he says. 'I'm sorry it happened. And you know, I bet our porn star is totally unbothered. Like here we are reevaluating our worldview and to him it was just another Thursday.'

'Only because he has the physical advantage. And I feel like, being a woman, one of the saddest things about grow-ing up is going from equally strong to much less strong.' I wave my hand. 'In general.'

'You mean, as in, that fact alone makes the world scary?'

'I don't know about other women, but yes, I'm scared almost all the time.'

'Jesus. Although I hear what you're saying because I am, I mean, I'm not Pontus. I'm not big. But also I think there's power in not letting it affect you? Like showing you're not scared of a beating. It sort of, dislocates the dynamic?' He pauses then says, 'Non-violent resistance and all that, governments have been overthrown.'

This is a nice thought but ultimately I am not optimis-tic. 'It's depressing being a pacifist when no one else is.'

'Yeah,' he says and this conversation has taken a strange turn and now I don't want to talk more about violence.

'Are you in bed?' I ask.

'Yes, I am.'

'Describe it for me.'

'Calm down.'

I blush, hard.

I know in these situations that I should play hard to get but even though I probably could pull it off, I feel reluctant. I just can't stop seeing honesty and guilelessness as the worthier pursuit. Playing hard to get seems to me not only morally poor, but also highly counterproductive.

I say, 'Your room I mean. So I can picture it.'

He describes a room with a large bed and beige wallpaper and one potted plant, the kind you don't have to water. It is a student flat, not a student room, which means he has a kitchenette, lounge, and his own bathroom. 'That's fancy,' I say and mean it. His mother contributes a little in return for him coming over once a month to do her bookkeeping. 'But I think mostly she just wants to hang out,' he says.

'What's her name?'

'Fernanda.' He pronounces it in Spanish not Swedish and the sound is thrilling.

'Teach me some Spanish.' I open my palm and look at the pencil still there. Warm and moist, I put it down.

I GOT A job. Two nights a week I tend the bar at a lazy inexpensive side-street place selling mostly a big-strong, meaning a nondescript pint of whatever cheapest lager.

The clientele is young, students who sit outside and smoke in the June sun.

I can wear what I like and no one orders complicated cocktails or expects me to juggle bottles. Basically my job is pouring big-strongs and holding out a card reader.

Next to me in the bar is Ingela. 'You have to flirt,' she tells me. 'I'm sorry but that's the way it is.' She says this as if my embarrassing contribution to the tip total is due to some principle of mine, too feminist to flirt. I don't disenchant her. I prefer her interpretation over the truth, me simply not having the skills.

Even so, I very much prefer my nights at the bar over my internship. The streaming app's offices are trying too hard, that's my opinion. People wear their casual outfits very seriously. And my allotted tasks are numbingly unchallenging but exhausting in number. But this is to be expected and I don't need it to be fulfilling, I need it to grace my future CV. The internship is unpaid but I still have some money from grandma and with the bartending I might just be able to afford rent and an occasional big-strong.

I wrote the paper on VR addiction for Hanna, besides my own essay, so she could go to London with her sister. We got an A on mine and A– on hers and she grumbled but in a way I interpreted as light-hearted. She paid me the two thousand and I hoped this transaction would not affect our friendship in some way.

A week before summer break I stayed after class to talk to Konrad about my academic progress. We walked through the hallways and over the grass towards his office and I helped carry some papers. I gathered courage to ask him straight out how I was doing. 'What do you mean,' he said. 'You already know your grades are excellent.'

What I wanted to know was not how excellent my grades were per se, but how excellent in the context of other grades. I didn't know how to ask this without sounding crude so I just said, 'I would like to know my placement, in class,' and so accepted the crudeness.

He stopped and raised an eyebrow. We had reached the asphalt path running through the grass, which had turned a bright summer green. Although it was cloudy the grass made me wish for sunglasses, that's how bright it was.

'Don't worry Sickan, you're my best student. Top of the class.'

I felt hot. 'Oh am I, really? Top of the class?'

'Don't tell anyone.'

I handed Konrad back his papers and he smiled in a way that made me think he considered placing a hand on my shoulder. Walking to the station all I wanted was to call Hanna. It was sad I couldn't tell her this news, because Konrad had asked me not to, and anyway it would not make her happy because she was also a frenetic student like me.

When I reached the dark hole of the station entrance I decided to walk home instead of taking the tunnelbana. The weather was warm and my legs had energy to use up. His words were on repeat in my head, like when you get stuck on a song. My best student top of the class.

The streets were clean, there were dandelions and some other flowers with other names. Almost everywhere you looked there was a child with a softserve ice cream. We were in the long exhale of a Stockholm summer. Almost two years in now, I felt like a resident. I was home here. In the city at large, but also with Hanna at Artillerigatan. I was a young person with a friend living in central Stockholm. It seemed my counting down the years and months as a schoolgirl had not been so stupid. Because here I was, at ease, at home.

I called Skåne. Dad picked up and I asked him to get mum. When they were both on the phone I repeated Konrad's words, best student, top of the class.

Dad said, 'Oh that's nice Siv.' Mum said, 'We're not the least bit surprised,' and dad agreed. And I didn't say why are you not surprised, there are many smart people in the class. Instead, I ended the call and walked through all of Östermalm feeling sick with myself for still turning to my parents for praise or emotional sustenance.

'HEY, ARE YOU hungry?' Abbe asks now on the phone.

'Yes, I am.' And I realise I really am. It is nine thirty and I haven't eaten since noon.

'Me too. Do you want to eat something?'

'I have student noodles, the curly ones?'

'Really?'

'Yes. Mushroom flavour.' I swing my legs out of bed and go barefoot to the kitchen. We have talked for well over an hour and my hoarse voice is by now a monotone whisper.

'I used to eat those all the time after school,' he says. 'You've made me nostalgic now.'

I shake the packet so he can hear the curls.

'What are you having?'

His voice strains as if getting up from bed. 'I can microwave some pasta leftovers.'

'That sounds nice,' I say and fill the kettle and flick the switch. Hanna is not home and the lights are off but the flat is light from the June evening sun. At 2am it will be almost-night but then at three the sun comes back again. Still they're not even scary when dark, these rooms. It is always warm and the parquet creaks conversationally. I like it best when Hanna isn't home and it is dark. As if the flat is napping.

He talks about his friends and reminds me what everyone is called. I ask if Abbe is short for something. 'Abrahan,' he says, Spanish pronunciation.

I silently try it with my tongue. 'Is it Mexican?'

'No, Chilean,' he says. 'Mum's from there, dad's from here.' Then, 'Sickan is sort of a great name. Like a forties pilsnerfilm.'

'Yes, better than Siv.' I hear his microwave ping as I pour boiling water on my noodles and stir the mushroom powder around with two chopsticks.

'Siv. It's like your parents actively wanted you to get bullied,' he says and I know it is a joke but still I freeze and let go of the chopsticks. The water continues to circle.

'Are you there?'

'Yes.' My voice is almost gone now. Just air, no tone.

'Hey, you weren't actually teased for being called Siv, were you?' he says carefully.

'Oh no, you don't ask stuff like that on the first phone call.' I try sounding flippant. The noodles soften and swell.

'Anyway, sorry, I shouldn't have said that.'

'Where are we eating?' I ask.

'In bed?'

I take the hot bowl with me and sit lotus on the bed with an A3 notepad as a tray. I can hear him chewing under his words, blowing on the food before each bite. Now I am regretting the noodles. Between my hoarse voice and the sucking sounds of noodle soup the unsexiness of this phone call will likely kill any remotely romantic prospects.

'I didn't think this through,' I say. 'The noodles. It will slurp.'

He chuckles and I feel he is almost constantly amused and I am not sure if this is a good thing or a bad. 'Let's hear it,' he says.

And yes, it slurps. I am grateful he called without video.

'Actually it's not bad,' he says.

He tells me he has bought new speakers. I ask him to play me a song and he says that the greatness of the speakers will not translate well through the phone. I say I don't care and he plays me a song. I hurry eating during the music and I drink the last bit of stock from the bowl, then I put the bowl on the floor and lie down on the bed again, staring at the ceiling. It is confusing to be so relaxed and insanely nervous at once. My stomach is full of warm food and sticks out even though I am lying on my back. I place my hand on it and it goes up and down when I breathe. I wish I could fall asleep like this.

The music changes and he lowers the volume until it is no more than background noise.

'Anyway, I have a question,' he says. 'Henrik, one of the guys in the band, he's having like a party on Friday.'

'That's exciting,' I say.

'Want to come? Noor will be there too.'

'Oh. Yes I want to come.'

'Okay then, Friday. I'll text you the address.'

'And this isn't like, being complicated?'

'Well, I mean. I was going to ask if it's okay to be, you know, just friends. I like you, so it's stupid not to hang out.'

'Hang out, just as friends,' I say. 'We can do that.' And it is better because this summer, between my internship and the bartending, I have exactly no time to date anyone. It will be a nice thing, calling him my friend and talking like this on the phone, maybe without so many nerves because we are not dating. 'So no sex then, right?'

He is laughing now. 'Um, I mean do you usually have sex with your friends?'

'No.' I don't say that my only confirmed friend is Hanna and the thought of having sex with her is too outrageous to consider. 'I've never done that. Have you?'

'Oh no, you don't ask that on a first phone call.' He yawns and I like picturing him there, sleepy on his bed with an emptied plate of pasta. Hand on shirtless warm skin. I badly want him to come over.

'So what are your plans for tomorrow?' he asks.

'I don't know.' I close my eyes lightly. 'I have work but maybe I will call you after.'

'Maybe?'

'If I have something good to talk about.'

'Well. Maybe talk to you tomorrow then.'

'Okay. Hej då.'

He hangs up and I place the phone next to me on the bed and then I pick it up again to doublecheck that the call really is ended before I clear my throat loudly up at the ceiling. I have just spent two hours with Abbe on the phone. I said many things and he laughed almost all the time. I grab my arm and squeeze it hard.

I get a text. *Your voice is sexy like this.*

My phone says 21:58, Tuesday. If I was still in the student corridor I would have opened the window and mingled my scream with the others.

WE ARE IN the smaller of two sitting rooms and Henrik is playing us a song from his band's new EP. Abbe is right there next to me on the sofa facing Henrik by the CD player, because the EP is four real tracks on an actual disc. He hands me the cardboard cover, an image from above of four pairs of feet standing on grass next to a sign saying *Don't walk on the grass.*

'Now, listen now,' Henrik says, and plays air drums.

It is clear our attention means a lot to Henrik so we sit still and listen, me staring at the cardboard cover, shy from Henrik's expectant glances. I like the music. It is the cute type of pop that sticks to your brain and makes you hum the melody over and over.

'Can I have one?' I ask and wave the cover and then regret it. Maybe it is rude to ask. But no because Henrik says for sure. He sticks his hand into a box on the lowest bookshelf and hands me an EP.

'Do you have a pen?' I say. He looks at me blankly. 'For signing.'

'Oh right.' He opens a drawer and finds a thick felt pen. Then he disappears into the other room shouting the names of the other three band members, and so Abbe and I are alone.

'His first autograph signing,' Abbe says, as if it had been a smooth-talking act on my part, which it hadn't. 'Well, I liked it,' I say and turn to him on the sofa, my knee now touching his. Neither of us moves.

We have been in Henrik's parents' Södermalm flat for about an hour. I am a little drunk and feel spunky. Henrik's parents are in the summer house so he is having a party. The flat has two sitting rooms, a kitchen, and four bedrooms. I have never known anyone who grew up on Södermalm and this makes me scan Henrik's speech and manners, to see if the enviable postcode has imprinted on him.

His parents have decorated the flat in mismatched flea-market finds, but designer. Apparently the mum is a dentist and the dad is an ad man with a trust fund. I wonder who all these other people are and what their parents are like.

Despite Henrik having learned how to walk among the deliberately haphazard furniture on the oak parquet, he seems completely normal and not a snob. Maybe it has made him right-wing, I don't know, because blessedly no one has brought up politics yet.

'Hey, in here,' Henrik shouts from the other room. Abbe rolls his eyes. I smile and we stand up. He places a hand on the small of my back as we walk through the doorway and I wonder if this is something just friends do. After he lets go, a warm handprint lingers on my tailbone.

I walk up to Henrik and his band members in the kitchen as Abbe goes to the fridge to refill our glasses. One band member, the bass player, hands me the EP and they have all signed their names on their corresponding pairs of feet on the cover.

I take it and say, 'Not to be ungrateful or anything, but if you get famous I might have to sell this at auction.'

'Not if,' says the bass player. 'When.' And he looks so surly I can't tell if he really is upset with what I said or just riffing. I feel a little confused but no matter because now we move towards the sofas in the larger sitting room where there is a small group of people and I sit on the floor by Abbe's legs. I shake my head to refocus. The band members are now full of bravado and take turns playing songs they try to convince us are 'the perfect piece of music'. Together we all judge each song's perfectness by a show of thumbs up or down. Most often I feel inadequate judging if perfection or not, so I wait for the other thumbs and go with majority.

After seven played songs, Aretha Franklin's 'Chain of Fools' is in the lead, followed by The Smashing Pumpkins' '1979'. I drink a mighty vodka sour and hang as casually as my body lets me on Abbe's knees. Once, he puts his hand on my head for a moment and my skull prickles.

'Your turn,' Henrik says and hands me the phone. I freeze. I had not expected to be required to contribute. This is not something I am good at, picking songs or saying movie titles or recommending TV. I scroll up and down aimlessly. Not a single artist comes to mind, every song is embarrassing. But even more embarrassing is to take this long. I feel the tension growing in the room, soon someone will cough. To my horror, I tap a song and immediately, ruthlessly, the intro fills the room. Those first few guitar notes and then the very noughties beat.

The room stays silent. Furrowed brows as people try to identify the song. I don't look at Abbe. I feel clammy and want it to end. Finally a girl named Simone shouts 'oh haven't heard this in absolute ages', and pulls up another girl from their sofa. They start dancing. 'Lucy Pearl right?' I say yeah, and have maybe never been more grateful to a person.

The bass player shakes his head. 'Sorry but this is actual garbage.'

'Hey now,' Abbe says but he is smiling.

'Alright, let's vote,' Henrik says. The two dancing girls turn their thumbs up. The bass player's thumb goes down. Two others down, and then Henrik thumbs down too. But Abbe's thumb goes up, maybe out of solidarity or pity. My song gets a respectable fifth place which is so smack in the middle it couldn't be more inoffensive. The song changes to some music I don't know but everyone seems to love and some other people start dancing too so the spotlight is off me. Abbe gets up and looks at me but I shake my head and he says you sure? and joins the dancers.

I finish my drink, leaning on the sofa where Abbe's legs used to be. I wonder what he is thinking and what is going on in general terms. We are touching and I am flirting as much as I can. He looks like he is enjoying himself and uninterested in talking to other people.

Abbe's friends are good dancers. I feel like I am their audience watching like this. My theory is that Simone is into Henrik but that he is gay. Now Abbe is dancing with Henrik and although it is meant to be silly I can tell Abbe is a good dancer. His movements are quite small and subtle, but natural. Seeing Abbe like this, his confidence, I'm attracted to him of course but even more I want to be him. Yes, I wish I were him dancing with Henrik and Simone, being silly, having someone look at me like I am now looking at him.

Sometime later most of us are packed inside Henrik's bedroom. They are all teaching each other about something and I am half lying on the bed, quite drunk and relaxed. I worry about being too relaxed but then tell myself to give it a rest, please, anxiety tomorrow. A thin blond boy walks in with some silver ampoules and a clear plastic bag. 'Who's having a laugh?' he says.

I look quizzically at Abbe, sitting by the foot of the bed. 'Laughing gas,' he says. 'Want to try?'

I am terribly tempted because I do love laughing but the last bit of intelligence in my soused brain shows me a mental image of me laughing uncontrollably in Abbe's face and I firmly decline. As does he. The others take turns inhaling from the bag, breaking another ampoule, inhaling again. I am very curious to see the effect, which soon becomes apparent as the inhalers start laughing even at boring things, even at serious things. They discuss religion with voices that have gone weirdly deep, giggling all the time. It is a bit unnerving really. Abbe smiles at me and shakes his head. I am glad neither of us inhaled.

He touches my leg. 'You having fun?'

'Yes.' I sit up and look at him. 'But maybe should we go to another room?'

'Oh. Okay.' He stands up and gives me his hand. 'Come on.' He signals something to Henrik who only grins in reply which to me seems very suggestive indeed.

I'D NEVER HAD sex before coming to Stockholm. Twenty seemed a shameful age for a virgin but I was terrified of my first time being with someone that mattered, like a schoolmate or a friend's friend or someone who might talk about me afterwards. I wanted my first lover to be completely detached from my life. I had watched porn of course but I knew porn was not like real sex. Besides, studying is not the same as practice.

When I had been at universitetet for three months, I dressed up one night. I used makeup to look older and wore a long-sleeved black dress and stockings but not heels because I was already tall enough. In a nice hotel on Strandvägen I sat at the hushed bar and looked around. I had three requirements: nice looking, kind, and foreign.

I finished one glass of Sauvignon and ordered one more to get up the courage to talk to anyone. I was terrified. I heard my heart in my temples. But fortune favours the bold. And I couldn't stay a virgin forever.

The first man was attractive, mid-thirties, Dutch. Though after talking to him he did not seem kind so I excused myself and waited in the toilet for fifteen minutes until he gave up, paid his bill, and left.

The next man was very kind, but not as attractive. Early forties, Estonian. I had sex with him in his hotel room and it didn't hurt much. There was no bleeding although I had expected some blood. I was disappointed, like the red stains on white sheets was a rite of passage I had somehow managed to miss. When I told him it was my first time he smiled and said 'yes of course' like it was a game we were playing. Afterwards he became hesitant and awkward, and

I worried I had done it wrong. Then I realised he was wondering about payment.

'No, it's not like that,' I said, appalled. 'This was just for fun.'

'For fun? You're sure?' He squinted at me. 'I don't mind giving you something.'

I considered for exactly two seconds.

Then I said, 'I'm sure,' because although I certainly needed the money, I had just lost my virginity moments earlier and was probably not mentally ready for this extraordinary development. Also, if anything, I should be paying him! I was the student, he the teacher, and yes, I felt I owed him.

The man went back to Estonia I guess. His name was Koit or something like it.

THE ROOM IS strange. Narrow, single bed, dark floral wallpaper. A walnut nightstand with framed photographs, a tissue holder, and a wastebasket underneath. And then, in the corner, an empty wheelchair. We are in the one-bedroom flat next to Henrik's parents'.

'Who lives here?' I ask.

'Henrik's grandmother. She doesn't mind me using it when she's in the summer house.'

'You've slept here before?'

'Sometimes, if too drunk to go home.'

I walk over to the wheelchair. 'Won't she need this in the summer house?'

'Um. I don't know. Maybe she has a spare?' He sits down on the edge of the bed.

I touch the armrest, the worn pleather. 'What's wrong with her?'

'Just old I think.' He clicks his tongue. 'I have to admit I don't find the subject of Henrik's grandmother to be all that intriguing right this moment.'

'But, you didn't expect me to ignore a wheelchair in the room?'

He picks up his phone and chooses music. 'Okay but soon maybe turn your focus back on me?'

'I know this song,' I say.

'Denise LaSalle.'

'It's in that vampire film, Only Lovers Left Alive. Jim Jarmusch?'

'Oh is it.'

'Is that what you want?'

'What?'

'Me to focus on you.'

He smiles shyly and looks to his left. 'Yes. Yeah.'

'Because we are friends.'

'Right.'

I take two short steps closer to him on the bed. He sips his drink and the music is nice and slow. 'So,' I say, 'since we are just friends, what kind of things should we do together?'

'I don't know. Hang out.' He leans back on his hands and looks at me.

I come closer until my legs touch his and say, 'Can we do this?' and run my fingers through his hair.

He leans into my hand and I can tell his breathing is off. 'Good friends can.'

'What about this.' I put one knee on the bed next to him, then the other, so I'm now on top of him.

He inhales. 'I think so.'

I can feel how warm he is. With my hand around his neck I pull him closer. He licks his lips in preparation and says you're funny, I like you, and then he kisses me.

AFTER KOIT THERE was a string of men. I went to another bar and seduced Hasse, late twenties. He had a flat in Enskede but I insisted on a hotel for neutrality and he said sure. He was not affectionate and it hurt quite a lot, not like with Koit. Then it was Ahmar from Gothenburg, who gave me my first third-party orgasm. Then some others. By now I was quite unapologetic about approaching strangers in bars. It was staggering to me, the power I had simply by being a passably attractive woman. I had never been sexualised in the normal sense, so now being looked at with desire, it was intoxicating. And the men thought they had lucked out, when so clearly I was the lucky one, walking around the city with this power to lay strange men with almost no preamble. I'd never had the upper hand in social situations before, and suddenly I was the orchestrator of satisfying sexual encounters. I was a player, that's what I was.

The last stranger was Rickard, mid-thirties, with hair cropped short and a smile wide as anything. I liked him, he was calm and I relaxed and that meant I could experiment without either of us getting too embarrassed. I took on the challenge with a student's zeal. He was a good sport. I enjoyed it thoroughly. Just like with the others, we met in a bar and went to a hotel. I appreciated the no–man's–land aspect of the hotels, the stiff white sheets, the smooth mini soaps, the thick carpet muffling our moans. There were no family photos or bathroom cabinets or sad refrigerators to jeopardise our social equality. I could have been anyone, what did he know?

Rickard adopted a laissez-faire attitude to my probing do you like this, what about here, would it feel good if, so I decided to see him again. He texted me ten days later inviting me to another hotel, and then the week after to his place. I don't know what I had imagined. Some gender-less, trend-nervous bachelor pad, Danish teak furniture and a best-in-test coffee machine. I don't know.

I do know that I had not expected the size 28 pink ballerina shoes and the yellow raincoat shaped like a five-year-old in the hallway. 'My daughter,' Rickard said. 'Emelie.' Then he told me that he and his partner had an open relationship and us sleeping together was completely above board. I believed him. And we had sex that time but there was none of the delight of our previous sex. I left afterwards feeling dirty. Not that I had done something dirty but that I had been dirtied by the actual flat, the child-proofed lack of sleep dishwasher tediousness of it. It bummed me out.

I didn't see Rickard again but that was fine because now I felt ready to take on men from my own social surroundings.

I AM ON my back and he is between my legs and we are kissing. He has pulled off my shirt and I am wearing only jeans. He is also only in jeans and I think we must match. We have not turned on any lights but the thin blue sky outside is enough. 3am and it will not get darker, already the earliest birds are awake and the trees outside are full of sounds. There is a chill in the room and both his and my nipples are hard. But he is warm to the touch, his stomach on mine, his breath in my mouth. It is so intimate I feel lightheaded.

'Hey listen,' he says and gets up on his hands, 'I can't, you know, do much more tonight.'

'Oh. Why?'

'I hurt my rib the other week. I can't, like, do that type of movement.'

I look at his stomach. A few dark marks that could be bruises. 'What happened?'

'It was stupid. Drunk football.'

'Which one?'

He sits up and touches a rib. 'This one.'

I run a finger across it, lightly. He winces but he lets me.

'It's not broken, just cracked.' He takes hold of the waist of my jeans, his fingers curved inside, directly on my skin. 'But that shouldn't ruin it for everyone.'

I don't breathe. He unbuttons my jeans, pulls them off, kisses the plate between my breasts then my stomach then just underneath my navel. When he starts taking off my underwear I put a hand on his shoulder. 'Hang on hang on,' I say.

He looks at me. 'What's up?'

What's up is that despite the string of men, I have never been licked before. I have done it to them, but not had it done on me.

'You don't feel like it?' he asks.

'I do. But, you're fine, your rib?'

'Yeah.'

I nod, like okay then.

His mouth is on my skin again and he takes off my underwear. I feel tense and awkward and worry I'll do something to reveal my inexperience. Then there is the first feel of his tongue and it is a brand new sensation. I marvel at it. It is like these two body parts are meant to meet. Like no two other body parts fit better together. I breathe out fully and lie back and stretch my arms tall above my head and touch Henrik's grandmother's headboard and I want to move my hips but I'm not sure if I am supposed to and then the movement comes anyway and it feels natural and he grabs my hips then reaches one hand for my breast and when he puts a finger inside me I come.

He stays down there a moment, wipes his mouth on the back of his hand which looks supremely masculine to me, before coming up to my face. 'That was quick,' he says.

'I'm like a fifteen-year-old boy.' I cover my face with my hand and when I remove it he is looking down at me. 'No you're not.'

I want to laugh because I am giddy, so I bite two of my fingers. 'Should I reciprocate?'

'Jesus.' He presses against me. 'That would be great. But I shouldn't. Next time.'

'Yes,' I say. 'There's no way you can do that once and not offer to again.'

He reaches for one of the cocktail glasses on the night-stand. I get up on my elbows. He moves the liquid inside his mouth for a second before swallowing. Then he leans over me. 'That was sexy,' he says and when I kiss him there is a bit of biting.

'Are you very frustrated?'

'Yes.' He laughs. 'Distract me.'

'Okay.' I let go of him. 'Tell me about your plan.'

He turns on his back. 'Mexico City?'

I nod. We are both looking up at the ceiling.

'It's kind of hard to describe. I mean it's so big and crazy it feels almost more like a whole country than a city. Anyway I've seen such a small part of it.'

'What does it look like?'

'Nothing like here. It's like the opposite of grey.'

'You don't like it here, do you?'

'I think maybe you appreciate Stockholm more if you're not born here, you know?'

'Too much history?'

'That's it.'

I raise my hips, slide my underwear on, and sit up. 'Well I like Stockholm a lot. Although I'm sure I would like Mexico City too.'

He laughs. 'You seem like someone who likes a lot of things.'

I think for a second. 'That's true, I do.'

'Any dislikes?'

'Mean people?' I say and immediately realise this came off too serious. I smile and snort to dismiss it or make it a joke but it doesn't work.

'I think everyone dislikes mean people?' He sits up too and places his hands on my thighs which makes it even more serious.

'Not the mean people themselves.'

'Yeah, kind of think they do.'

I pause. 'Then why be mean?'

He shrugs and smiles, and the seriousness is gone again. 'The human paradox huh.'

'Like you going down on people you're just friends with.'

'Tss. Friend, singular. It's not a habit.'

We sit opposite, me in underwear, him in jeans. His face is backlit by the blue window. We stay like this for a while and my skin is goosebumped by the chill in the room but his hands on my thighs are warm. I feel awake. I take in everything. He asks me questions about what I was like as a teenager. Difficult questions like when did you realise you're attractive and how come you don't have an accent and have you always been this straightforward and did you ever think you might be gay. As I try my best to answer these questions, all I can think is that after tonight, there is no single part of me that wants to stay just friends.

THERE IS ONE man among the string of men I don't like to think about.

We met in a bar and he was average looking, underwhelming. But for once he was the one walking up to me so I thought I'd give him the time of day. He put me at ease with his easy laughter and nice smell, and by telling me about his sister, a water polo player. He was the kind who, the more you talk to him, the prettier he gets. And soon yes, I did want to sleep with him. He touched my knee and I got chills up my arms.

It was too quiet in the hotel room. I regretted it the moment the door closed behind us because now he was serious, no more easy laughter. Immediately my nerves shot up.

We were on the bed. I could not understand the sex we had. His hands were hard and he moved my body without asking. We did things that I didn't want to do. I won't get into it.

I couldn't get wet so it hurt. I got tense and quiet but he didn't seem to notice or maybe he didn't care. I closed down to a cold remoteness I had felt before, but never when having sex. It was a relief, this detachment, because it made me not panic. I lay there thinking, this is also sex, how can this also be sex. How can we use the same word, for this?

When I got dressed he returned to his bar behaviour which made it clear he did not think anything untoward had happened. Easy laughter, nice smell. But I could not find him pretty.

Was it possible he thought this was sex? Maybe he was so misinformed he couldn't do it better, the real way?

Back in the student corridor I showered, then changed into leggings and sat on my bed, unsure of what to do or think. Should I react or was it nothing? I desperately, achingly, wished I had a friend, a person to call on the phone and tell the whole thing, for it to be seen by someone else. It was the loneliest I had been since coming to Stockholm, the lack of companionship making me feel exposed, skinless to the world.

What made me scared was that I hadn't seen any warning signs. I worried I didn't have the natural antennae to distinguish the bad ones from the good. I looked up what were these signs, then spent a good three hours reading the most harrowing testimonials. It seemed every girl on the internet had been through it. Of course I knew these stories existed, but knowing is not the same as reading the first-hand accounts.

They used the word rape. Not everyone did, but many. It felt huge to me this word, too heavy to carry.

Some of the stories were so confusing and revolting I became first nauseous, then overtaken with anger. The room was too warm, I took my sweater off, touched a cool hand to my forehead, my cheek. I didn't know what to do with the emotion. So I just sat there on the bed, reading the stories, filling my mind with images I did not want, in a madly depressing attempt at comfort in numbers.

I wanted company. That's why I kept reading so long.

Finally I closed the laptop. I put on slippers and went to the shared kitchen to cook rice. Just white rice with soy sauce. Waiting for the grains to soften my mind felt blank, scrubbed clean. I brought bowl and soy sauce back to my room, took my leggings off and got into bed. I realised, besides the anger there was another, gentler feeling:

Every girl on the internet.

It wasn't just me, no one had the antennae.

I blew on a spoon of rice, put it in my mouth, and exhaled hot steam.

ABBE AND I meet at a large department store in the city. We are on the escalator, next to each other on the same step. He is talking about something, a news story. I nod and try to listen but these escalators go up seven floors and there are many people around so the noise is quite overwhelming. My nerves do that bristling thing and my ears can hear my pulse. I shake my head a little and remind myself that these people are doing normal weekend shopping. No one will start looting. People will just pay with their cards in an orderly fashion. Nothing to get excited about. I wonder if this is the department store where that man stabbed the foreign affairs minister to death.

Someone taps my shoulder and I jump and turn around. Behind me is a woman trying to pass me on the escalator. Abbe takes my elbow and moves me sideways as he steps upwards so that he is now looking down on me. 'You okay?' he asks. 'You seem a bit, on edge?'

'No, sorry. Just sometimes I'm a little weird with noise.' I try a smile and shrug.

'Should we leave?' He still holds my elbow and I focus on just his face.

'No no I'm fine, let's stay.'

AMAZINGLY, ABBE AND I have been meeting up. It is not exactly like dating where both people present flattering facts about themselves, nervous to make a good impression. We are more like friends who have sex, very casual that way. I am nervous sometimes, but Abbe seems completely at ease.

Although I wouldn't mind dating and thinking up romantic gestures, I don't really have much to complain about because Abbe is both fun to be around, and also a nice person. And the sex is tremendous. We seem to enjoy it just as much both of us. We don't see each other all the time because we are busy with work but two or three times per week we meet somewhere and then I sleep at his place.

WE STEP OFF the escalator on floor five, designer accessories and outerwear. Up here are far fewer people than on the floors below with gift ideas and perfume.

I like the spongy carpet under my feet and the long dusky aisles with few customers but many members of staff. I wonder what it would feel like to simply walk in here and buy one of these handbags. To have that type of extreme money.

'Do you actually shop here?' I ask.

'Sometimes, if I really want something. My friend's sister works here, Sofia. She gets me staff discount, cost price.'

'Oh. That's handy.' I pick up a shoulder bag and open it then close it then put it back on the shelf. I couldn't afford these things even at cost price.

Although it is summer, Abbe tries on a ridiculously puffy jacket that shines in charcoal grey. He throws out his arms and moves them up and down. I laugh. He comes closer. I hold up my hands and back away and he embraces me until I am enveloped in puff, like standing inside a pillow.

He hangs the jacket back and says, 'The first thing I bought with Sofia's discount was a Stüssy sweatshirt, I remember I felt so cocky in school the next day.'

He tells me he was fifteen then and had just moved with his mother to a new house in a nice suburban area with a postcode that would get him into a college with a very good reputation and also a reputation for handing out undeservedly good grades, although Abbe already had deservedly good grades from his secondary school. 'She wanted me to go to a good school but it kind of backfired,' he says.

'Why?'

'It was a school for mostly wealthy kids, and I was like lower middle class with a single mum and also I wasn't white. Anyway, I tried fitting in best I could and it went alright.'

It is bad of me but this makes me envious. We had both tried our best to fit in at school but he had succeeded and I had failed. Still I am glad he has told me because I didn't know he had grown up feeling this way, about money or about being different. Maybe this is one reason we like each other. 'Was this after your dad left?'

'Yeah we moved right after. Mum wanted a clean start.'

'Was the breakup quite bad?'

Abbe hasn't told me anything about his father except that he left, but it seems like it was a tough time. He shrugs and picks up a hat and puts it on my head, pulling it down firmly. He grins and turns me towards a mirror. It is bright cobalt blue, between a beret and sailor hat, with a rubber Prada logo at the front. It fits my head-shape neatly and now I really want it. 'Oh,' I say.

'I know, you look great.'

'Yes, it's nice.'

'No yeah I really like it.'

'It's a bit eccentric,' I say to make myself feel good about not affording it.

'Yeah, maybe, but it fits you.'

This makes me a little uncomfortable, him thinking eccentric clothes suit me, but also I am happy for the compliment. The hat is three thousand three hundred kronor and even at cost price there is no way I could buy it. I put it back on the shelf and smooth my hair.

By one of the small tills is Sofia. Abbe points her out and there is no queue so we walk up and he introduces us. I can tell straight away she is flirting. I wonder, do they have a past? She is older than us and physically she is my opposite. Petite, long black hair, thick eyebrows, naked eyes, very red lips. She looks great and artistic.

She leans forward on the till with her elbows and talks in a low voice although she isn't saying anything secret. I tilt my head and watch their conversation, asking myself if she makes me jealous. And yes, likely I am because I realise I desperately want her to find me pretty. Also I hate her name, Sofia. It is an annoying emotion, jealousy,

in how it leads to these madly irrational thoughts. I mean
Sofia is a perfectly good name.

Abruptly I say, 'I love your makeup, I could never pull
off a lipstick that bright.'

Abbe turns to me, surprised. 'What do you mean, you
wear bright lipstick all the time.'

I hadn't calculated on him having an input. 'Yes, but
Abbe I don't look as nice.'

Sofia is smiling, high eyebrows.

'What about me?' Abbe says.

I look at him closely, trying to picture him in this shade
of red. 'I don't actually know,' I say. 'Maybe because you're
male and convention is sort of getting in the way of my
imagination?'

Abbe looks at Sofia who says, 'No I agree. I can't really
see it.' Then she reaches behind the till and produces the
lipstick. 'Shall we?' she says and with an incredible sense
for diplomacy she hands me the case. Abbe obediently
turns his lips to me and my hands only shake a little when
I screw the cap off.

WE LEAVE THE department store without buying anything
and on the escalator down Abbe says, 'I swear with you I
get into the weirdest conversations.'

He wants to eat something. Abbe orders the biggest
burger with large fries and I order a veggie burger with
large fries. We carry our red plastic trays to a table. He
opens two small pepper sachets and empties them in his
paper cup of ketchup, then he stirs with a fry. He must

have seen me looking because he asks, 'What, you don't do this in Skåne?'

'I don't know, maybe not.' I know my classmates used to bike to the drive-through on the motorway after school but I had only ever been there twice with my parents and neither of them put pepper in their ketchup. I copy him, two sachets, stirring with a fry and then putting it in my mouth.

'What about dipping fries in softserve?'

'Abbe stop! That's disgusting.' I am not sure if he is pulling my leg, but he says, 'No, it's actually good, let's get it next time.' I think about Hanna making me smoke while eating tortellini when Abbe grins and says, 'I can't believe how like, provincially clueless you are sometimes.'

I bite a fry in half and it is nice to be provincially clueless rather than just clueless. 'Did you ever sleep with Sofia?' I ask.

'Okay, wow, we're going there now?' He has a shy smile and rubs his mouth to cover it. 'Yes, yeah I did yeah. Does that bother you?'

'Yes, it does, a little. Isn't that funny?' I take a bite of the burger. It tastes like sugar and the pickles are warm from the patty.

'What exactly bothers you? Do you mind? I'm curious now.'

I think while dipping a fry in mustard. 'Well, I guess what bothers me most is that I know you are attracted to her and she looks very different from me. So it makes me wonder what your type is.'

'So, Sofia is my type I would say.'

'Oh.'

'But so are you because I see you as sort of the same type.'

'But. That's crazy. We are completely different.'

He holds the burger in both hands. 'No what I mean is, I don't care about height or hair colour and that, but I've always been drawn to like, art school girls?'

'Art school? Like alternative?' I think of Sofia and her naked eyes and ethereal face. 'But that's not me.'

'You're funny because you always think you're this normal boring person but you're not that at all.'

I drink Diet Coke from the straw and think how wrong he is, I have never once thought I was normal. And it is a bit devastating that despite all my efforts, this is still so obvious to everyone.

WHEN OUR TEACHER Pia asked us to get off we had been on the broken school bus for forty minutes. Despite the driver's fiddling and angry words, it wasn't going to happen. As the whole class paraded off onto the pavement, he was calling for a tow.

Outside was cold and very dark. When I breathed I saw smoke. I buttoned my denim jacket.

Pia told us we had to call enough parents to drive us home in cars. Yes she knew it was late and that we were two hours away from Åhus but what other option?

It was Thursday and we had spent the whole day since morning in the immense conference centre behind us, a field trip. Now, at almost seven, we would have to wait until nine.

As always when left to our own devices everyone clustered up. I went a little to the side to call home. My mobile was dad's old phone, one without internet. I didn't know for certain but it looked like I was the only one in class without a smartphone. I thought maybe it would occur to my parents that at thirteen I might need one, but at the moment they could only really afford cheap food like pre-sliced bread with tubed cream cheese, which was not nice. Truth is, I wasn't sure I wanted a smartphone, because I knew interactions were even more brutal online and I didn't think I could handle that so well.

Dad's old phone had a weak battery, I had to charge it and charge it. It still had two bars when I called home.

Mum picked up.

I told her the bus broke down. 'Will you come and get me, please?'

'Oh Siv, but you're hours away. I'm right in the middle of some work I need for next week.'

'Yes but mum the bus broke down.' I felt warm now despite the cold.

'Dad isn't home yet, not sure when he'll be home. But you can go in the car with one of your classmates, can't you?'

I looked over my shoulder at the clusters of people. There was no way.

'Mum I think it's better if you come get me.' I felt I might start crying, that's how much I wanted her to get me.

'Don't be silly Siv, just go in one of the cars. There's no reason for me to drive all that way.'

I closed my eyes. And I gave up. 'Okay, yes, I'll go in one of the cars.'

'Okay see you at home, have fun.'

She hung up. My phone flashed the one bar warning.

I walked slowly to Pia. She had only been my teacher for a month, since starting seventh grade. She seemed nice. 'Did you talk to your parents?' she asked.

'No I couldn't get them,' I said. 'But I was thinking, how, I mean, which car are you going in?'

'I'm not actually. My sister lives in Ängelholm, so I'll take the next bus.' She pointed at a bus stop.

Ängelholm was the closest town and I knew from there you could take a bus straight to Åhus.

She said, 'Should I ask which car has a spot free for you?'

'Okay. First I will try to call my parents one more time.' I went over to the bus stop and pretended to talk while I looked at the timetable. If the cars would get here around nine there were still two buses, 21:23 and 21:53, before the bus service finished for the night.

'I talked to mum, she is on her way,' I said to Pia back by the conference building and she said okay great, and then raised her voice to order us all indoors. We had already had a canteen dinner but there were pastries and chocolate balls and mazariner we could buy while we waited. I got a Fanta. Everyone was restless and bored. Someone had a deck of cards and someone a fashion magazine. The canteen staff wanted to go home.

The cars came with minutes between them as if the parents had all been waiting for the call. The last car only had one parent and three children so there was room for me. I could sit there in the warmth and go home.

I stayed where I was and Pia closed the door after saying bye thank you to the parent, and it drove away.

She came back to me. 'You're sure your mum is on the way?' She looked at her watch because it was a quarter past and I knew she wanted to get the 21:23 bus to her sister.

'I can text and ask.' I wrote a pretend text. After a minute of staring at my screen, 'She says she is ten minutes away.'

We waited together in the bus shelter. Pia was looking down the road, searching for my mother's car.

'There it is now,' she said, staring at the large red bus coming up the road. 'I'll just have to take the next one.'

'It's okay, you can go, she'll be here anytime.'

'No it's fine, I'll wait.'

'I can call and check.' I picked up the phone and pretend-talked to my mother. Still holding the mobile I said to Pia, 'Her GPS says it's less than two minutes!'

The bus slowed and opened its doors. Pia took a reluctant step up towards the driver. 'Are you sure?'

'Yes, Pia, I am thirteen, I can wait less than two minutes on my own.' I smiled a little as if to say don't be silly.

She nodded and said okay then thank your mum for me, and then the bus closed its doors and drove away.

I felt a little high from the swindle I had just now pulled off. I checked the timetable again. Half an hour, then a bus to Ängelholm, then a late bus to Åhus.

MAYBE MY PARENTS had texted to see which car I was in so I checked but no they hadn't texted. One battery bar. I opened my wallet and counted. Two bus tickets would cost some money, but how much?

I sat on the green metal bench and put my hands in my denim jacket. After a while the conference centre turned off its lights. There was only the thin overhead light in the bus shelter. I had new shoes on. They were a cheap copy of the black and white platform sneakers that were on trend. In the low-price department store you could find most trends for very little money, although the style was always a bit off.

Ever since the St Lucia dance last winter I had tried to learn how to dress. So far it had only led to ridicule but it didn't matter, really, since wearing untrendy clothes also led to ridicule. It was to practise and create a style before turning sixteen and going to gymnasium in Kristianstad. Where no one knew me. I had also bought some makeup from the sales bins and was experimenting with mascara and foundation. And lipgloss, but only at home. I would get better if I practised, I was convinced.

I sat on the bench and stared at my new shoes, tapping the toes on the ground to a beat. Time passed slowly but it did pass.

I had only a few minutes left to wait when I heard people. I looked towards the sound. Down the road came a group of six boys, maybe fifteen sixteen. They were being loud on purpose. I stared at my shoes. I wished I was not sitting under the thin light. Maybe if I didn't move at all.

But of course, they saw me. And then they were in the bus shelter with me. I had glass behind my back. I stood up.

They asked what are you doing and are you shy or something and why do you look so scared. I didn't say anything and I didn't dare to walk out so I just stood there, silent, dizzy with nerves. Why is everyone like this? Never leaving me alone! Do they smell it on me, something visible? Music was playing out of a phone and one of them came right up to me and started dancing, pressing against me in a sexual way. When I stepped back there was another one behind me and they were all laughing like this is a good time, so when I tried to get out they wouldn't let me and I couldn't get away from their bodies without pushing

so I pushed.

Then I ran. Up on the road. They were laughing, where are you going, come back why are you mad, can't take a fucking joke ugly come back, and I could hear them behind me but I didn't look, I ran, even though I knew not to run and make it a chase. My new shoes were not good for running. I tripped a little but didn't fall. I turned and saw them still back in the lit shelter. My ankle hurt. Then my stomach dropped. I saw the bus coming. The last bus for the night. It stopped and the group got on. It closed its doors and drove past me. Gone.

There was no choice, I had to call home. And I would have to tell them I couldn't get in one of the cars because everyone hated me so much.

I took out my phone and dialled the number. After two tones it went quiet. I looked at the screen which was black, out of battery.

I slowed my walk. I hugged myself. And I cried. Yes, I did.

My breath was jagged like it gets from running or crying. I just didn't know, now, what I could do. So I walked on and allowed myself to cry.

Then ahead I saw the lights of an ICA supermarket. Between it and me a person was walking. I wiped my eyes and saw a man in a green duffel coat carrying two plastic ICA bags. He stopped when he noticed me and tilted his head. 'Hey, you okay?'

I said, 'Yes I'm okay,' without slowing my steps.

'You don't look okay? Can I help?'

I hesitated. 'My battery died.'

'Ah. And you need to call someone?'

'Yes.' I felt very tired now, maybe I could sit down on the asphalt.

'Okay. Umm. So, you see that apartment building over there?' He pointed behind me. 'If you count three windows up, where the light is on, that's my flat.'

I found the light in the third window and it looked warm. I felt sad seeing that.

He said, 'You're free to use my phone if you want? I don't have my mobile on me but there's the landline.'

That put me on guard. I took a small step back. 'You don't have a mobile?'

He laughed a little. 'I mean I do, but I cracked the screen so it's being repaired.' I looked at him closer. He was an adult but exactly what age was hard to tell. He had soft lines next to his eyes. There was an *Aftonbladet* newspaper sticking up from his ICA bag and I could see frozen oven fries and a bag of premixed salad.

'How about this,' he said. 'I'll wait outside and you take my keys and use the phone while I stay here below on the ground. I'll stand where you can see me from the window.' Then he tilted his head that way again. 'I just, you know, I can't just leave you out here, like that.'

I stared at him, dumb.

'I mean, your face is a little . . . your makeup. It looks like you've been crying.'

My hands went to my face and it felt stiff and my fingers came back with black on them.

I knew the rule was to not go anywhere, with anyone at all, but my insides were telling me he was kind and also I didn't have a lot of choice because I couldn't stay out all night. If he stood below on the ground and I watched him from the window, that was a good plan.

'Okay, thank you, that would be good,' I said, and we walked together, with lots of space between us, towards his building.

'My name is Linus by the way.'

'My name is Siv.'

'You hurt your ankle Siv?' He nodded at my limp.

'I tripped.'

'Ah well, nice kicks anyway. My sister has those too.'

'Oh does she? Yes. Thank you.'

We reached the building and he stopped to get his keys from his pocket. His hands looked red from the cold and he sniffled. 'The phone is on the wall in the kitchen.'

He held out his hand with the keys, standing as far back from me as possible. I felt a little bad. I thought about walking up the stairs by myself and opening his door and finding the kitchen and taking the phone off its holder and calling my parents.

'You know, it's okay actually, you can come up too,' I said.

'No honestly don't worry, I'll wait here.'

'Thank you. But.' I held my shoulder. 'I don't want to go up by myself.'

'Oh.' He looked unsure. 'Okay, well yes, let's go up together then.' He held the door for me and we walked up the three flights of stairs, him first, me behind. It smelled fresh like lemon. He opened the door to his flat and walked in ahead of me, kicking off his shoes and going to the kitchen with the ICA bags which he put on the kitchen table. I took my denim jacket off and hung it on a peg, then placed my shoes on the doormat. My ankle still hurt but felt better than before.

It looked cosy, the kitchen. A sort of everyday familiarity, how Linus slowly emptied the food items onto the table. With a leek in his hand, he pointed at the wall. 'There's the phone. Do you want me to wait in the living room while you talk?'

It was nice and warm in the kitchen. My shoulders relaxed a little. Then I thought of mum picking up on the fourth ring and me explaining all of this to her.

'No it's just, I actually can't use the landline,' I lied. 'Because I don't know the number. Can I please charge my mobile in your socket instead?'

'Oh, uhm.' He looked at me maybe a little sceptical, then he sighed and nodded. 'Of course, sure, do you have a charger?'

'Yes.' I found it in my bag and unwound the cord. He pointed to a socket by the kitchen counter and I plugged it in.

'I was going to have some kaffe, if you want one while you wait?'

'Okay. Thank you.'

He made coffee in the machine, then stowed away his groceries and said maybe I should go take a look in the

bathroom mirror so I did. And I had black mascara everywhere. It seemed like such an adult thing, mascara on your
face from crying, like in a film? I washed it off with water
and a pump of soap. His bathroom was tidy. I turned off
the light.

He had brought out butter, hushållscheese, a new loaf of
limpa, and placed it all on the table. We made ostlimpa and
dipped it in the kaffe. I didn't like the kaffe. But I liked
slowly dipping the limpa and the way the butter melted. I
pulled my knees up to my chest and breathed, happy to
just sit.

'So, do you want to talk about it?' he asked.

I shook my head. 'No. Thank you.'

He squinted. 'Tough night?'

'Maybe, yes.'

'Parents giving you a hard time?'

'Oh no.' And I thought, this person Linus, I will never
see him again after tonight so I simply said, 'It's everyone
else.'

He raised his eyebrows. 'They're mean to you at school?'

I nodded.

'Why are they mean to you?'

I shook my head again and then I whispered, 'I don't
know.' The tears came back. Slowly they ran down my
face.

'But, this is stupid Siv,' he said gently and leaned a little
forward over the table. 'I don't get it, I mean you seem
smart, and kind, and you're pretty.'

I looked up. 'I'm not, I'm ugly.'

'Don't say that. You're not ugly.'

'But I am!'

He leaned back and was quiet for a moment. Then he said, 'Here, stand up,' and got up from his chair. I stood too. He placed light hands on my shoulders and angled me this way and that while looking at me. Then he stopped and looked straight into my eyes. 'Siv you are so beautiful. I'm not just saying that. I mean if I could,' and he put his hand softly behind my neck and then he said, 'would it be okay if I kissed you?'

My eyes went wide and I didn't know how to reply but I didn't have to because then his lips were on mine and although I didn't know how to kiss like adults it was fine because my lips somehow knew and made natural movements that fitted just right to his lips and then I could feel his tongue and it was happening, this kiss was right now going on, and I was one half of it, and the thing I noticed was how it felt so strange, so strange that my blood rushed too quickly and I got dizzy. I closed my eyes. I felt his hands on my arms. Then on my waist. Then he found the zipper on my hoodie and unzipped it. His hands were warm through my vest and then one hand was on my breast and his thumb moved over my nipple.

I moved back in shock.

This felt like a whole other thing.

He also drew his hand back, quickly.

I said, 'This is a little too much I think,' but he was looking at my breasts and I knew they were very small still, so maybe he was disappointed by their size because he just said,

'Siv, how old are you?'

We stood there in his warm kitchen, a distance between us, both our bodies heaving from breathing hard.

'Thirteen.'

'You're thirteen?'

'Yes.'

He stepped back. 'Jesus.'

This confused me. 'How old did you think?'

'Older, I mean, I don't know what, maybe I didn't?' He backed out into the living room and sat on the edge of the sofa. It was dark in there because no lamps were lit. I stayed in the kitchen.

'Okay well,' I said, not knowing where to go next.

'I'm so sorry.'

I said nothing, shifting my weight.

And then he made a sound. Like a sob.

He covered his face with his hands and he cried. Shoulders shaking. He looked small. I didn't like it.

'Please don't,' I said.

His breath slowed but he didn't remove his hands from his face. He just sat there, small and sad.

I didn't want to see him anymore.

'Should I go?'

He didn't answer.

'I will go.'

I turned around, unplugged my phone from the wall, then rolled the cord around the charger and placed it in my bag in the hallway. I used my finger as a shoehorn to put my shoes on. On tiptoes I went back to the kitchen and looked into the living room. He had turned his head and sat staring out the window, hands in his lap.

'Okay bye,' I said. 'Thank you for the help and for the kaffe.'

But he didn't hear me.

I backed into the hallway, took my jacket off the peg, and closed the door behind me softly as anything.

I walked towards the supermarket at a fast steady pace, a little disgusted and weirded out. I wondered if he could see me from the window but I didn't turn to look. I felt strange. I shook my hands.

The supermarket had closed at ten. The automatic doors didn't open.

I didn't know what to do now, it had all gone to shit. There was no one here. I sat down with my back to the doors.

But then the cold made me move. I just walked straight.

Across a large carpark there was a petrol station with a sign that said 24 hours. All I wanted was to get inside.

The door pinged when I opened it. A customer by the tills bought a pack of snus and went out to his car. The cashier didn't pay attention to me. I walked the aisles up and down, finding comfort in familiar brand names. The cashier was young, maybe eighteen, with one ear pierced and a name tag that said Ali. He was reading a newspaper and there was a TV on the wall behind him showing a horse race. I picked up a small pack of crisps.

'Just the crisps?' he asked and scanned the pack.

'Yes.' I cleared my throat. 'And also, I was wondering if you could check something?'

'Check what?'

'When the next bus to Ängelholm is?'

'Ah, you missed it did you?'

'Yes.' I blushed.

'It's nineteen for the crisps,' he said and then turned to his computer and clicked around. 'Four fifty-four in the morning is the first one.'

Four fifty-four in the morning. It was not yet eleven. I closed my eyes.

Then I opened them again and asked Ali, 'Could you also check how much for the ticket to Ängelholm please, and plus how much for a ticket from Ängelholm to Åhus?'

Later I was sitting on a stool by the window with the empty crisp packet, looking at lorries going past, when Ali spoke again. 'Aren't you hungry?'

'Oh I'm fine.' I needed the money for the tickets.

He pointed to the heat machine with the rolling sausages. 'Have a hot dog.'

'Thank you, but, actually I'm a vegetarian.'

'There are soy ones.'

'Really?' My stomach growled.

'Have a couple, I don't care.'

'Can I? Thank you.'

He shrugged. 'It's not my hot dogs.'

I made two, in bread, with ketchup, mustard, and fried onion, and put them on a paper plate. While I ate I stared straight ahead and zoned out, that's how good it was. Ali came over with a cup of tea and the newspaper he had been reading. 'You're better off in here, but there's the bus stop so you know.' He pointed further down the road. Then he went back to his till.

I turned on my mobile. If I had gone in one of the cars I would have been home now. There was no text and no missed call. I considered it, not sending a text, not telling them where I was. To see how long before they worried. But did I want to know? I felt tired, empty. I wanted to sleep.

I composed a text, saying I had gone home with Saga and would sleep over. We didn't have a Saga in class. I sent the text to dad.

Then I erased dad's number.

Then I found mum's contact and erased that too.

Sometimes someone would come in to pay for a coffee or a sandwich. Mostly lorry drivers but twice there were groups of drunk young people wanting food and cigarettes. It made me nervous every time the door pinged but when it was just me and Ali I felt safe. We didn't speak. I ate two more soy sausages and filled a paper cup with water. I leaned my head on my arms but I didn't sleep. Slowly the sky started turning.

At four fifty Ali cleared his throat because neither of us had used our voices in quite a while. 'You should go if you don't want to miss this one too.'

'Okay.' We sounded sleepy. I was unsure of how to say goodbye after this strange night together. 'Thank you for the hot dogs and for letting me sit.'

He shook his head. 'You need to learn to stay out of trouble, I swear.'

'Oh! I'm usually not in trouble, this is not what I do.'

He just waved me away and I went outside, and so heard the ping of the door for the last time.

On the bus I was the only passenger and after paying for my ticket I sat all the way in the back.

And then we were driving towards Ängelholm. I looked out the window at the fields and the new blue sky and it had been a whole night. I had done all these things. I had stayed out all night by myself and I had been kissed and I had been told I was beautiful which no one had said before, and I had found out about the bus, got on the correct one, and paid for the ticket.

AS THE BUS drove into town, the sun hit my face. It felt almost like being touched by a hand. Although I was travelling home it felt the opposite. Like I was going away.

I put a throat pastille in my mouth, then leaned my head against the sun, closed my eyes. I unzipped my hoodie. I placed a hand under my breast and moved my thumb over my nipple. You're so beautiful. I wanted to hear it again.

FROM A KITCHEN shelf I take three oval plates and put them on the counter. A moment ago the doorbell rang and a woman in a moped helmet handed me two paper bags with assorted sushi. Now Hanna walks in and says, 'We have better plates for that you know.'

'Hanna, let me choose which plate please.'

She shrugs and mumbles noncommittally. I ask her to put the things in the rucksack. Glasses, chopsticks, tiny bowls, paper napkins. In my tote bag I stuff a rolled-up blanket. I am wearing my bikini under my dress.

Although Hanna hasn't said so I can tell she is in a foul mood which is a pity since it is my birthday. And also because I have invited Abbe for them to get to know each other. If either of these things are related to her mood, I don't know.

Abbe has asked for the three of us to get together but Hanna has not once asked. They met at the Valborgs fire of course but since then I have not brought Hanna to any gatherings or beer cafés. Maybe this has hurt her feelings, but she seems uninterested or even opposed. Secretly I have been glad about her aversion, because I don't want the two of them to meet, is the truth.

I have reasons. Sometimes I sense Hanna wishes it were just the two of us. Maybe she interacts best one on one. I am sympathetic since I think I am that type as well. But it could also be her wanting to be my closest person and now with Abbe she is not so sure she is anymore. She says things about him sometimes that could be interpreted as ungenerous or critical, that's why I sense rivalry. This is a valid reason to keep Hanna from knowing Abbe but it is not my main reason. It is the other way around, I don't want Abbe to know Hanna. It is a strong feeling ever since meeting Abbe and I have tried to analyse it and my theory is that I am ashamed of Hanna. What her personality indicates about mine. As if Hanna is something you do in private only. While Abbe is someone you show off.

Hanna is openly eccentric. I can relax with her because she will never be appalled by anything I say or do but she will sometimes appal me, which is thrilling and a little scary. On the other hand Abbe is someone who will never appal me but who will often be surprised by things I say. He is smooth where she has edges. I am naturally edgy but in the process of smoothing. Putting the three of us in the same room will likely make all of this apparent to everyone.

I did invite more people for today, thinking they could act as a buffer. Lottie and four from class. All of them declined. Lottie had a clear reason, some festival up north. But the other four, Astrid and Carl and them, I think they didn't want to come. I got very sad when they declined, which maybe is an overreaction. I don't know, I had thought we were friends, that they might actively want to see me. Today is my birthday and I should be happy but two out of seven is not so nice a number. Embarrassing, this number. When I told Hanna she only said, 'I don't know why you invited them, it will be more fun just us.'

Abbe doesn't know I invited five more.

Outside the July sky is bright, twenty-four degrees in the shade. In the kitchen Hanna rips open a bag of ice and pours the cubes into a cooler. Then there is a ring on the door. I flinch. On my way to the door I glance at Hanna and she looks somewhat chaotic. She has not brushed her hair, bare feet and saggy leggings. But still, she is here, fiddling with a Champagne bottle. Maybe it will be okay?

Abbe smells like grass when I open the door. He says happy birthday and kisses me. He takes off his shoes. Wearing casual clothes, black t-shirt, navy shorts, he still seems dressed up. I talk about nothing and try not to drop the wrapped gift he hands me.

'Hanna is in the kitchen, let me give you a tour,' I say but he stops and whispers hey. I turn around, standing stupidly in front of him holding the gift with both hands. He squeezes my biceps. 'It will be great.'

'Even if she's being an asshole?' I whisper.

He laughs at this. 'She won't.' I inhale deeply and try to not be weird.

We go to the kitchen where Hanna is pushing towels into the tote. She doesn't look up. She just zips the zip.

Hanna suggested going to her sister's for my birthday picnic. Viveka and her husband live in a glass house in the archipelago with a private deck leading into the brackish sea. But I don't want to be in a space that's Hanna's, I want to decide a spot, no saying thank you for having us.

After a quick tour of the flat, soundtracked by Abbe's ah mans and herreguds, I put on the rucksack and Abbe picks up the cooler and Hanna takes the tote, then we walk the few blocks down to the water and the Waxholm boat. I have never been to Waxholm but I have walked the island on street view and it seems like we should find a picturesque enough picnic spot. Also the boat is a pleasure in itself. Sea foam, sun in your eyes, the smell of diesel. Seagulls shrieking like madwomen. Being rolled up and down by the benign waves. It is exhilarating every time the water sprays my face.

Abbe buys us brown bottles of pilsner in the boat bar and hanging over the rail I remind myself that this is my day. I ignore two out of seven and Hanna's sulk and let myself enjoy the wind trying to throw me overboard. My hair whips everywhere. I am twenty-two.

After walking the island with its snaking roads and weathered grey boating cottages, we find a small round cliff which seems nice but perhaps not as nice as a private deck. We unpack and I place each piece of sushi on the plates. The moist nori sticks to my fingers and smells like the sea. Or maybe it is the sea that smells.

Hanna peels the Champagne foil and pops the cork. We toast my increased age and Abbe makes small talk and then we eat the sushi. Hanna's favourite is the tofuhat sushi so I leave these pieces for her. Now she puts one in her mouth whole and says, 'It's your birthday, you can choose anything in the world to eat, and you go with sushi, the most basic food possible.'

My ears heat. 'It's not the most basic food.'

'It is.'

'What's unbasic food then?' Abbe asks and doesn't take sides. He does that a lot, asks questions instead of giving opinions.

Hanna says, 'I don't know, quick-macaroni and falu-sausages?'

'But that's, literally the most basic food in the country,' I say.

'That's my point.'

I just stare.

She sighs. 'You take any concept, like basicness, and turn the volume up high enough it will flip over into its complete opposite.'

I furrow my brows and glance over at Abbe. His jaw is moving as if trying to make sense.

Hanna says, 'A birthday party with quick-macaroni and sausages, you can't say that wouldn't be unexpected.'

'Okay, but that doesn't mean it works for any concept,' I say.

'Try me.'

'Cold,' Abbe says.

'If you turn water cold enough it will feel like it's burning.'

We explore this nonsense for a while. Left. Walk left long enough and you will circle the planet and return from the right. Things like that. We drink more Champagne and Hanna is quite ridiculous when she is grasping at straws. I do my best to argue against her but when she is like this I have no chance. Hanna and I speak quickly and interrupt each other a lot, groaning dramatically at each other's more ludicrous arguments. She refills everyone's glasses and I am enjoying myself tremendously. Then I look over at Abbe and maybe he seems perplexed.

I stop talking mid-sentence.

He says, 'What?'

'Nothing. Just, what do you think?' My face feels hot. Maybe Hanna and I have overdone it.

'Well I know it's your birthday, but sorry, I kind of have to agree with Hanna.' He taps his lips with his fingers. 'If you ask me tomorrow I probably won't anymore because it's a naff point you're making Hanna but you're making it so nicely I feel like agreeing with it right now. If that makes sense.'

'Oh I'm the same,' I say. 'I always end up agreeing with Hanna eventually.' I turn to her and smile.

'Then my work here is done.' She looks grumpy but I don't think she is.

'Should we open the presents?' Abbe says, and I think if any work has been done it's Abbe's.

HANNA SLIDES A white envelope across the blanket. Inside are two theatre tickets. *Annie the Musical*. When we saw the ads in the tunnelbana I had told Hanna how much I loved the movie growing up. The tickets are so thoughtful but I find it hard to express this because I am a bit drunk and there is a discrepancy between how I show excitement in front of Hanna and in front of Abbe. So I simply go over and hug her awkwardly where she is sitting. It is hot in the sun and her skin is burning. She sort of laughs and says alright alright stop it.

Abbe tells us he has never seen that movie.

'Shut up,' Hanna says.

'We should watch it together,' I say, and by we I mean me and Abbe but Hanna nods enthusiastically and this breaks my heart a little. The sun lotion is in my bag and I hand it to her.

Then Abbe pushes his gift towards me so I refocus. Black shiny paper and grey bow. The card says *Happy Birthday Sickan (don't worry, cost price)*. Inside the package is a cobalt blue sailor hat with a rubber logo. I touch it between my fingers.

'Put it on,' he says, so I do. The way he stares at me gives me a tingle at the back of my throat and I want to sit on top of him and lick his lips or do something wild.

'It's nice,' Hanna says and holds out her hand, 'let me try.'

I look at her unbrushed oily hair and I very much do not want to but I hand it to her anyway and she almost drops it in the leftover sushi mess on the plates. She puts it on and I take a photo and say super cute, then she hands it back and I pull it down on my head without looking inside first. Abbe places his arm behind me so I can lean in, and while Hanna starts stacking the empty plates I whisper I love it so much in Abbe's ear and then we don't talk any more about the hat.

Hanna plays Barbro Hörberg on her phone. The sun presses down the cliff. My sunglasses slide down my nose, slippery with sweat. I put the hat back in its box, then I stand up and take off my dress. When I slide down the seaweed-slick stone I hear Hanna behind me. I knew the water would be cold but still it's such a shock to my skin I gasp. Before I can reconsider I take five strokes straight out towards Finland. Hanna is right behind me shouting profanities and Abbe is calling us mental and mad.

I turn around and tread water to let her catch up. Already it is so deep my feet touch nothing. I stretch my legs and feel tall. Hanna reaches me and grins insanely. She dips her head back, swishes it left and right, and comes up with a wet backslick. I am thinking how good the brackish water must feel on her scalp. And yes she does look healthy, fresh. A bit sun-touched on her nose. I give her a quick kiss. Then I dip my head too. Abbe stays on the cliff despite our encouragements then taunts then threats.

With towels around us we are drinking beer straight from the bottle. I am becoming quite relaxed because by some incredible miracle the two of them are getting along. My hair is dripping and the chill is visible on my skin, my nipples so hard they hurt. They are talking about Orphan Annie and how annoying she is in the movie, and about how annoying children are in general. I think Hanna is surprised that Abbe is a bit witty and not so bland as she had thought or hoped. Also he is sharing quite personal thoughts which is surprising to me as well.

They discuss becoming parents one day when Abbe says, 'Maybe in another life I would have wanted to but now I'm not so sure.'

'Why?' Hanna asks.

'Honestly, I worry about not doing a good job.'

This is news to me. Even so, it makes sense. Hanna is gnawing on a nail and not arguing so maybe it's making sense to her as well. It is amazing people actually have children, and likely the three of us will too one day. Because of course everyone must worry about not doing a good job and also everyone who has been a child must be reluctant to put another small creature through the experience.

Hanna says she can't have children anyway.

'What, you know that for sure?' Abbe asks.

'Quite.'

I would be more stunned if I wasn't so used to Hanna throwing around big statements. 'How do you know?' I ask.

'Well first of all you must have sex to get pregnant and I am rather celibate. That's not a complaint by the way, it's a choice.'

Abbe asks why, as if this is outrageous.

'I don't know, don't you find it weird when you're attracted to a person because they make a nice and smart impression, and then once you're in bed this smart person turns into like a, thumping heap of flesh?'

Abbe is amused now, and he turns to me. 'Is that how you see me, a thumping heap of flesh?'

'Oh. Sometimes!'

'And still you want to have sex with me?'

I lean back, hands flat on the rock. 'More or less all of the time.'

He laughs and I am having fun.

'I doubt any of us will have kids,' Hanna says. 'I'm not having sex, Abbe you're worried about not doing a good job which means someone did a bad job on you, and Sickan you had it worse than either of us.'

'What does that mean?' I tense. The cliff is hard under me.

She looks confused, like it's obvious. Carefully she says, 'Well, you always sit with your back to the wall, like they do in prison, you know, to not get stabbed?'

I say nothing but it's true, my back is against the cliff right now. It is automatic. I flush and wonder what other revealing behaviours I show.

Maybe Hanna can tell I'm embarrassed because she says, 'Hey sorry, I just mean, I mean, we love you even if you're messed up.'

Abbe sniffles and squeezes the back of my neck with his hand. 'Let's get drunk,' he says. I blink and force a smile. Hanna opens three more beer bottles. Abbe lights a joint, and we take turns.

I hand Abbe my phone and ask him to play something nice. He taps the screen. Smokey Robinson sings about the tracks of his tears. Hanna scoops strawberry cake into bowls. We are all somewhat sloppy drunk but it only makes the cake better, the strawberries rudely sweet and moist. When Abbe goes off into some bushes I look at Hanna and quietly say, 'Did you really mean that, what you said?'

'What did I say?' she whispers back.

'That you love me even if I'm messed up.'

She grins. 'Oh hell Sickan, who isn't?' And I can't help it then, I have to laugh.

'What's going on?' Abbe says when he sees us there laughing and sort of punching each other. 'Just My Imagination' comes on and it is nice with its slow beat and

Abbe doesn't sit down, instead he pulls up Hanna and starts dancing. 'Come on,' he says to me.

'I can't,' I say and sway my arms, 'limbs too long.'

Hanna groans at me and then they dance. They look silly. Their movements are mismatched at first but soon they adjust to each other almost as if they're being serious. They just intuitively know how to do that, match their moves until they look sort of great together. I lean back against the rock and my hair is already drying.

It is after midnight and there are no streetlights here. Hanna and Abbe are silhouettes against the still-blue sky. There are mosquitoes and I wipe them off when they land on me. I try to think back to earlier birthdays but there are none I can remember individually. This one though.

MY NAKED FEET push into the soft rug under the table. It is early, just after seven, and we have slept almost nothing. I flip through a *Dagens Nyheter* on the table and Abbe is behind me by the counter preparing something to eat. Although it's only a month since my birthday it feels twice that, the days so long and many.

I have a hangover but not an annoying one, because somehow, blissfully, there is no anxiety. More that I am sleepy and thirsty and in the mood to be absolutely still. We came back to Abbe's at maybe four, the details are there but inexact. Last night was the first time we slept in the same bed without having sex and maybe this is significant.

'Kaffe? Orange juice?' Abbe asks.

'Yes.'

'Both?'

'Yes please.'

He places a cafetière on the table. Bread and things. When his timer beeps he presses the knob downwards and pours me a cup.

'This is my best hangover breakfast,' he says and picks up a piece of rectangular crispbread, the orange one with poppy seeds. He spreads oat cream cheese on the bread and taps his finger on the Herbamare salt on top. I copy him. The cream cheese looks fresh. We bite at the same time and the crunching sounds friendly. Smooth cream cheese coats the inside of my mouth and gets stuck. It seems a wholesome breakfast like something from a childhood. I could eat eight or nine. The radio is on and the hosts make inoffensive morning jokes and I drink the juice with both hands because my arms have a shake. I don't want either of us to move.

But Abbe says, 'I think I did something bad.'

I pause midchew, mouth full of crispbread.

'Let me just say it was by accident, but I do feel bad about it.'

I swallow the unchewed chunks, grating the back of my throat. 'What did you do?'

He exhales, hands on the table. 'Last night when you slept, I went to get water and saw this notebook on the floor that I didn't recognise and when I opened it the handwriting wasn't mine which meant it was yours.' The words come in one long take. 'And I was drunk, let's remember that, and I thought you wouldn't mind if I read some, so I did, the first four pages.' He rubs his hand over his eyes. 'And then two more pages in the middle. I'm sorry, it's a fucked up thing to do, I know.'

I stare at my hands and I want to leave this table and this whole flat. I can't look at him. I don't know what to say because I don't know what to feel. I should be angry but mostly I'm ashamed. They are so private those dialogues. Not because they are a journal or secret thoughts, but because they are my social inadequacy manifest, black on white. And all I am wondering is how reading them has affected his opinion of me.

'Why are you telling me?' I ask.

He frowns. 'I had to. Because I think you're always so honest with me and I really like that.' He smooths the table with his hand as if collecting crumbs. 'Also I wanted to tell you that I was surprised.'

My hands rest in my lap. I make myself sit still but my nerves are bristling. I want to go.

'No, not in a bad way obviously!' he says. 'I mean because I didn't know you could do that. Okay I was very drunk but still, I thought the dialogue was kind of great. And sounded like you. I could hear your voice when I read it.'

'I don't like that you did that.' I am trying to recall the dialogues, to know what exactly he has read.

'I'm an asshole. Always so curious really.'

'Yeah.' I pick up another piece of crispbread and spread cream cheese.

'But, also, I wanted to ask if maybe I could read the rest?'

'Oh no.' I tap Herbamare salt.

'So how does it work, I mean the two versions of the same dialogue?'

I consider not telling him. 'The first one is an actual dialogue I overhear.'

'And the next page is your parody of it?'

'I guess so, yes.' Up until this point I had seen it more as exaggerating regional and subcultural quirks, distilling speech patterns. But maybe that's what parody is.

'You know what it reminds me of?'

I shake my head and he tells me about this comedian who writes short monologues about typical LA people that she acts out. He scoots his chair over and shows me on his phone. She is cutting and precise and although I don't know most of the Angeleno archetypes, her writing makes them clear as if I have met these people. Most of all I am stunned this is what Abbe thought of when reading my notes.

'Would you ever act yours out?' he asks.

'Abbe don't joke.' I smack my lips. 'Can you imagine.'

'What about asking drama students or something?'

I push him off and say stop it now, and I am so shy it hurts, the idea of someone acting out my dialogues novel and strange.

He puts a hand on my thigh. 'Anyway I'm sorry Sickan, I do feel bad about it.' And he should feel bad. It has however been clear to me for some two weeks that I am brutally in love with Abbe, and I can understand that because of this I am unable to judge him objectively, now seeing his notebook transgression in a generous light which leaves him as guiltless and pure as ever. I think this generosity might be a dangerous thing, and I make a note not to take it too far.

'Can we stay here today?' I take his hand and lean my head in it. 'I'm dozy.'

'We can stay until like, six? I'm seeing Pontus. Playstation.'

And to me six feels like an eternity away.

'NO, IT'S ACTUALLY a nice area this,' Abbe says. 'Did I tell you I grew up just three tube stops from here?'

We are naked on his bed now and we have just had sex. It is midday already and the sun comes onto the bed and heats my shoulder and stomach. My body is post-orgasm defenceless and I am heavy, flat on my back, hands lax on the mattress. It is my favourite, waking up so hungover the front of your skull feels bruised and simply submitting to it, the tiredness. I detect none of the day-after anxiety. Abbe seems unaffected, he is talkative and moves around the two rooms a lot, goes to the kitchen to find new things to drink or eat. Maybe he is feeling guilty about the note-book. When we had sex I was too lazy to move and he did all the work.

We are both busy this summer but manage to sleep together at Abbe's three times a week minimum. We go out sometimes, but sometimes we go straight to his after work. It happens his plans change last minute because something came up and we meet later or another day, we are quite spontaneous that way. I am balancing my intern-ship, bartending, and Abbe. Which leaves very little time for Hanna but it is fine since soon school will start again and we will commute together every morning. I am think-ing kaffe in thermos cups that I can brew fresh for us since the walk to campus takes fifty minutes and in early-autumn sunlight it will be lovely.

The bartending hasn't paid as well as hoped so this summer I have eaten away at the last twelve thousand I took from grandma. The student loan starts again in autumn but likely I will still have to bartend. Life was cheaper before Hanna and Abbe because having a social life has proven to be expensive with all the drinks. It's stressful to think about because I want to excel at school and not waste time pouring lagers.

'Is it as green as around here, where you grew up?' I ask.

'Yeah. But the buildings are much bigger, like highrises and midrises and some are so long they sort of curve.'

'Did your building curve?'

'No it was straight. But long enough to have like ten doors to the street, and on the other side was another identical building again.' He gets up from the bed and puts on grey sweatpants. They sit low on his hips and I love looking at it.

'From my window I could see into the flat across the street and it was an exact replica of ours but mirrored and I used to find that so freaky.'

His hands are gesticulating here and there. My thighs relax so much my feet angle out. It is probably not so flattering, angled feet, thighs heavy on the mattress, and I wonder if us not having sex last night means we have now entered a stage where being attractive in appearance and manners is no longer the primary concern. 'What was there to do there?'

'Like for fun?'

'Mm.'

'There were playgrounds everywhere. I was quite the mountain goat, always up on those climbing frames.'

'Oh I can see that.'

He goes over to his desk and picks up a pen, clicks it, puts it down. 'When we got older we'd go swimming and eat pizza or play football and all that. There was an ice hockey rink just down the slope from the station and in the summer we'd sneak in to sit in the booth and smoke and hang out.'

'And just talk?' I ask, and prepare more questions in my head because I like listening to him describing growing up there in the midrise.

'I mean yeah, but like, under the pretence of playing some game. Like someone would bring a football. Or a deck of cards if it was raining, obviously.'

'Obviously.'

'And one time Ville even brought a frisbee but that's where we drew the line. I don't know what he was thinking.'

'What would you talk about?'

He thought for a second. 'I can't really remember to be honest. Mostly football and music, and girls I guess. We weren't exactly intelligent or like good at talking. It was mostly just being friends and having each other's backs at school.'

This makes me melancholy, as if nostalgic for a childhood I never had anyway. I hunger for these things and it hurts that I missed them, and now it is too late. But he got to experience it, years and years of it, and in a strange, self-tormenting subgenre of living vicariously I say, 'I want to see it.'

'The hockey booth?'

I nod.

'You mean like, now?'

'Yes, it's only three stops. We can go, talk about girls.'

THE TUNNELBANA RAIL in this area is actually not in a tunnel but high over ground so I can see far in both directions. I take in the suburb where Abbe grew up from infant to fifteen, before moving to the middle-class villa. It really is lush, green as a forest, with large grey buildings dropped like lego.

I have never visited this area and from the tunnelbana window the buildings look unreasonably large to me, a set of five identical concrete shapes to my left could well house half of Åhus. 'No way,' Abbe says, so I search Åhus population which is 9,422. We spend a good three minutes estimating how many families fit into one of those buildings but soon realise we really have no idea so we give up. What strikes me is that the simple concrete blocks everywhere do not jar with the green scenery. If anything they look stable and safe, like they could live a thousand years.

We exit the station and go into a non-chain supermarket where I wander around while Abbe shops for 'provisions'. On our way to the hockey rink we take a detour down to the water. The asphalt morphs into a footpath through the trees, strewn with brown bark that crunches under our feet. When we see the water glitter through the tree trunks Abbe takes my hand. He is keen to show me, I can tell. His hand is a little moist. There are cliffs, quite steep, mottled with moss and sprinkled with pine needles. I expect to see litter but there is none, or maybe just one or two things.

He points things out, the long since amputated trampoline, the tree that used to have a swing, the best route down the cliff if you didn't want to jump. 'It was fucking nuts, like we would swing from here and just splash right down into the water. And on the trampoline you'd climb up onto the handrails to get a higher jump.' He grins at me. 'I'm surprised we're not all dead to be honest.' I shudder at this because I can too easily picture cracked boy heads on the cliffs below.

THE GRAVEL IN the booth is grey and grainy. There are cigarette butts, some half-hearted graffiti tags in blue spray paint. We are hot from walking, the sun today is not joking. But the booth is in the shade and Abbe sits next to me on the worn wooden bench. He puts the plastic bag on the gravel.

'So I went for the full hockey booth experience.' He lifts things out of the bag. 'It's actually not that nice, I don't think you'll like it.' In a row between us, he places a pack of Camel Lights, a lighter, a tetrapak of tropical fruit juice, and a bag of pistachios. 'This was the standard fare. I kind of expected there'd still be pistachio shells in the gravel to be honest, the ground used to be covered with the stuff.'

He holds out the bag for me. I take a nut and wait for him. He opens his deftly and I copy. The nut is rough and salty and I suck on it for a few seconds before I chew. Abbe is on his third.

'See the height of that?' He points to the fibreglass barrier in front of us, encircling the rink. 'One time Ville tried to jump it and caught his foot and fell really bad. He had a scratch mark the size of a fist on his face, for weeks.' He shakes the juice to mix the contents. There is almost no breeze. It's warm even in the shade, and I am hangover thirsty.

'Do I drink straight from the carton?' I ask as he hands it to me. A cold drop of condensation lands on my thigh.

'Sickan, we were fourteen. Not like we would bring glasses.'

I drink and it is very sweet, mango and mandarin and pineapple. It might be the sweetest juice on sale in stores. When I hand it to Abbe he drinks for a long time and afterwards he wipes his mouth with the back of his hand which seems like such a teenage boy thing. 'This is making me nostalgic, honestly.' He pauses. 'Actually I don't think I've sat in this booth since last time I was here with Ville and them.'

'Ville was your best friend?'

'Yeah I guess. So annoying though, like such a show off and everything had to be a competition.'

I light two Camels and give one to Abbe.

'We played football together and he was one of those kids who'd be just devastated if we lost a match. Like he would cry and everything, I'm being serious.'

The cigarette smells nice. A small breeze fills the booth. I have some freckles and Abbe's arms are brown against his white t-shirt. It is already August and I don't want summer to end. When school starts we won't spend all this time at Abbe's talking and having sex. It is his final year, he will be busy, he has warned me.

'I think it's terrible, telling kids do to sports,' I say.

'What do you mean, kids should move around.'

'Yes but why pit two teams against each other and say only one can be the winner? And that losing means you're a failure. It's like hunger games but the losers have to live on.'

He laughs. 'Okay but in team sports you have your mates and you're like, learning collaboration skills.'

'But, why instigate conflict between teams to teach that? It's a horrible idea.' I look at the empty rink. 'What about puzzle solving, or personal bests, like, working together without defeating anyone.'

'Yeah, where's the fun in that?' He's laughing but I am serious. Which seems to be a dynamic we have a lot.

'No but it's just, how good you are at football or studying, or being popular, will affect your confidence as an adult so much.'

'So you're worried about the kids who failed at studying, and sports, and being popular?'

'Yes. How are they now?'

'Jesus that's a sad thing to be thinking about.' He presses his cigarette into the gravel with a pirouette motion of his foot. 'So,' he says then, 'how about those girls huh?'

'Yes, girls. Always up to no good.' I blow cigarette smoke and the breeze plays around with it. 'Would you ever move back here?'

He turns to me. 'You know, somehow I've never thought about it.'

'You seem to love it here a lot.'

'I do.' He takes a swig of juice. 'But also, it didn't wind up so great so I feel the place got a bit tarnished in the end.'

'Your parents' breakup?'

'Yeah and like, before that.' He opens a pistachio and throws the shell halves at the rink, one then the other.

I light another cigarette and lean my head back so I don't look at him. 'Did he hit you?'

'Huh,' Abbe says. 'Yeah, he did. But only like, four times. And then she found out and left him and as soon as I was done with ninth grade we moved.' He stands up and heaves himself onto the fibreglass barrier quite effortlessly, holding his arms out for balance.

'I don't know maybe I shouldn't have told you that, I don't want you to look at me differently.' He turns his back to me. 'It's like, I didn't grow up in terror or anything, it was only four times when I was fourteen fifteen so it doesn't feel like part of my childhood, you know? And he never had a reason or never gave me one anyway. He wasn't even angry, no shouting or anything.'

I drop the cigarette on the gravel and step on it. 'Where is he now?'

'Malmö I think. Why?'

'Well I thought maybe I could try breaking into his life and destroying it for you,' is what I think but what I say is, 'What about your mum?'

'No he never touched her. In a way that made it worse, which is a fucked up thing to say, but I just mean like,' he exhales hard, takes a few steps along the narrow barrier. 'It made it seem personal almost. Not sure that makes any sense.'

'You felt like there was something specific about you that made him hit you and not someone else?'

'That's it.'

'And?'

'And what?' He turns to me. I want to hold his legs so he doesn't fall but I don't think I should touch him right now.

'Did you ever find out what it was?'

'No? Of course not.' Abbe looks at me and nods his head upwards. 'What about you?'

'What?'

'Did you find out why they picked you, in school?'

It is so unexpected my mind blanks. 'No. I still don't know.'

'Maybe it's just arbitrary then, the way violence works.' Then he shakes his head and grins at me. 'You know it's weird, I was that age, fourteen, when we started coming here to smoke, and that would have been when all that happened.'

'I'm sorry today got so grim.'

'No I mean I'm just thinking like, can you imagine if I had told them then what I've just told you? Like how incredibly big it would've been and how it would probably have changed our friendship.'

'Yes, there were so many things you could never talk about. It was heavy to carry it all around, wasn't it.'

'We're lucky that way.'

'How so?'

He shrugs. 'We grew up.'

'Yes.' I suck on my lip. 'That's lucky.'

He holds his arms out straight and lifts one foot off the barrier, balancing without shaking. 'Look,' he says, 'still got it.'

I stretch my legs out and feel the sun burn my sandalled feet. And I wonder if he is right, if we grew up and the heavy things we kept quiet are now okay to talk about. But mostly I think he is wrong. Some things I can't imagine ever putting into words. Probably some things will stay this heavy and I will carry them around forever and that's just life.

'Let's go,' I say. 'I want to buy a magazine.'

He jumps down from the barrier and puts the provisions back in the plastic bag. When we leave, the gravel is sprinkled with pistachio.

AFTER NINTH GRADE, I deliberately only applied to gymnasium in Kristianstad, forty-five minutes away by bus. I knew none of the other sixteen-year-olds in the social sciences programme, nor anyone in the rest of the school. I thought I wanted to prepare for a career that would allow me to work with people, I really did think that, until I realised that god no I did not want to work with people. But by that time it was too late to change programme.

Thinking back on my three gymnasium years in Kristianstad I mostly remember the tedious bus rides and even more so the cold bus stop, waiting in the dark, the relentless wind. I kept to myself in class and I was left alone which was new and incredible. At first I didn't believe in it, bracing myself for whatever. Shellshocked, was a word I'd heard. My aversion to noise, my nerves bristling when someone walked behind me. So I skulked the halls soundlessly, making myself invisible, trying to identify threats. But nothing. No one.

So it slowly passed. And then I could walk down the halls noisily and take notes during class without minding the other students, and I would never bristle unless someone slammed a locker door, things like that. Not like it disappeared completely, my nervousness, but it became tolerable. I didn't make great friends but wasn't explicitly excluded either. Maybe at times people looked at me funny or I could hear them laughing and there was no way of knowing if they laughed at me or something else. But no worse than that. And also I noticed that the less scared I got, the more relaxed I could be in my behaviour and speech.

I was braver online because it was terrific to hide behind a screen.

I had never tried it before, back in school knowing that being on apps would be a bad idea. Bringing my classmates into my parents' home. The only safe place. I never begged for a smartphone.

So now in gymnasium, I relished the thought of posting things and commenting. I thought maybe my place would be with the political people since I had many opinions and worried about the planet so much.

I joined a number of socialist groups and in the beginning it was thrilling because I could voice my opinions openly. They took me seriously enough to write back, to turn and twist my statements. It was like this whole anthill of thoughts and ideologies had existed all this time and I had never known. And you didn't have to be an adult or educated or even particularly intelligent to post.

It was fascinating and I overindulged. It was a sugar rush when, after crafting and redrafting a paragraph painstakingly, you clicked post and saw it in real time mingle with the others. But the rush really only lasted a few months because soon I started to get the nerve bristle after clicking post. It became clear that the majority of posters were only in it for the debate, a type of word sparring in political disguise. Often the discussions steered away from the subject into intricate, unattractive in-house intrigue and pettiness. And I couldn't stand it, the fighting. It seemed like conflict was everywhere and I had developed an intolerance.

I researched my strong inclination against conflict. This way I found out about pacifism which seemed to have a lot to do with summer of love and hippies experimenting with acid. Still, out of the isms I had so far met, pacifism felt the most sympathetic. I wondered why it had gone out of style. Even so, that's what I was. Non-violent.

IT IS AFTER ten when he calls me. I am in bed with a Selma Lagerlöf novel, my back against the headboard. It's dark outside and my phone lights up as his face fills the screen.

'I have been thinking of you all night,' he says and the barely-there consonants tell me he is not sober.

'Me too. How's Pontus?'

'They're all good. I am in the bedroom.' He is speaking quietly.

'So, how come you called, do you have something on your heart?'

'I can't believe I told you all that earlier.'

I slowly put the book down. 'Do you regret it?'

'I don't know yet. But it made me think, and I am a bit drunk now so don't expect too much, but don't you find it weird that out there in the living room right now are friends I've known for years and for some reason you and Pontus are the only people I've told. So now I'm wondering if your straightforward way of talking is rubbing off on me? Like I don't want to hide things from you. Is that weird?'

'I don't know. Is it, you think?' This is a lot of information to take in and I am wondering whether what he has told me is a negative or a positive. I think positive, but the word weird always puts me on edge.

He covers a sound like a cough with his hand. 'Anyway I know we are not dating seriously because of Mexico but I'm thinking that maybe I want to try.'

'Try what?'

In the background someone is shouting his name. He turns towards the closed door and shouts back, 'Yeah, god, one minute.'

'Abbe try what?'

He looks at me through the screen. 'To date. Seriously.'

My skin goes hot. 'But you're leaving in May.'

'Mexico City is a big place.' We are both quiet for several seconds. 'I mean if we keep hanging out and we both continue to like it this much, maybe you could come with me? You can still go back and do your master's in the autumn. What I'm saying is, I would really like it if you came with me for the summer. If you want to?'

'Yes, I do!' And I do. Even though Stockholm is a wonderful place I feel at home in, Mexico City seems another creature entirely. Can you imagine. I realise I actually can't. Imagine it.

'How long have you thought about this?' I ask.

'Not long to be honest but once the thought came it came very strongly.' After a moment he says, 'Have you thought about it, coming with me?'

'Not even once!' I say honestly because the idea still seems fantastical.

'I feel I should warn you though, I'll probably be a horrible boyfriend.'

'That's okay. I will be a bad girlfriend too, probably.' And the word is new and scandalous in my mouth.

He sniffs and makes a hm sound. 'Sickan, let's just try not to hurt each other okay.'

'Oh, I won't hurt you.'

'I know, but what if I hurt you.'

But he is so friendly and nice I don't see how he could. 'Let's just do our best.'

'Yes. Okay. I have to go, they're being idiots. But yeah, Mexico City huh?'

'What a time to be alive.'

We end the call and I go barefoot to the kitchen and take a bag of cinnamon buns out of the freezer which I thaw in the microwave. Leaned against the counter in the dark I eat all five of them, one by one, not unrolling like you are supposed to but biting straight in towards the gooey core.

HERE WE ARE, Hanna and I and some people on the slopes of Vitabergsparken, looking out over the rooftops of Södermalm to the clangs of Sofia Kyrka's clocktower. Someone is playing music through portable speakers. My beer is lukewarm.

I use the toilet in the church and as I walk back Bogdan comes up to meet me. He studies with Hanna so two mornings per week we have shared classes. I like Bogdan, he is what grandma would call a proper piece, meaning solid and stout. His head is shaved and I always want to touch it. Walking up he smiles and looks devilish, like he is going to proposition me. I panic a little, blanking on soft turndowns. But I am off mark because he says, 'Hey Hanna told me about the addiction essay,' and boxes me clumsily on the arm.

'The, what do you mean?'

He points back towards the church and we take a stroll away from the group. He lights a cigarette. 'She told me she paid you.' Breath in. 'To write it.' Breath out.

'Oh.' This catches me off guard. 'She wasn't supposed to tell anyone.' And I wonder what else she has told.

'She had smoked a lot.'

'Still. I don't want any trouble.'

'But do you want money?' He is whispering now and it seems to me he is enjoying himself. We are pacing around the church and no one is here so he needn't have lowered his voice. I bite my hand, look at him, then say, 'Yes, I want money.'

What I want is to quit the bartender job. I'm not making much on tips because I never did absorb Ingela's skill for flirting. And since we divide the tips equally it feels bad to stay in a position where I am in effect causing her a pay cut.

Bogdan says, 'How much to write my resit-essay on disability interfaces?'

'You failed?'

'Obviously. Einstein. I need it by next Monday to pass.'

'Four thousand.'

He lifts both eyebrows. 'Hanna said two.'

'Yes well. I like her more.' Four is a ridiculous sum but I know he has money from the brands he wears. Also he has a car.

He laughs like this is all a joke. 'Fine, four. But it has to be good.'

'Please. Don't insult me,' I say, because now I am getting into character. We slowly walk back towards the group. 'You need to send me another paper you've written so I can mimic your style.' He nods. I feel clever and professional for coming up with the request.

Now the speakers are playing worn Swedish summer pop. 'I like your head shaved like this,' I say. 'It even has a tan.'

'Thanks. Yeah it's good in the summer. Cold in winter.'

My neck is moist from sweat, my hair so long it covers like a curtain. I imagine the cut of the scissors.

I see Hanna, her head tilted back from laughing. But at what? Bogdan gives me a high-five and walks away towards his friends. I sit down next to Hanna on the slope.

'New customer?' she whispers.

'Yeah, Hanna, why would you tell Bogdan about the essay?' I whisper too.

'Was I not supposed to?'

'Definitely not! It was private between you and me.' I can't tell if she is playing dumb or if she is actually being quite dumb. We could get caught. They would kick us out. The hugeness of it. I am angry, that's what I am, a wave swelling inside me. I bite down and breathe. Maybe I am overreacting but it feels like a large transgression, like she is taking liberties. Though I'm unsure if this is right since I have no analogous relationships to compare ours to.

Hanna says, 'I'm sorry. But it's only Bogdan. Honestly I thought you needed the money.'

Of course, she is right. And four thousand is no spit sum. I look at the rooftops of Södermalm in front of us, scratch the side of my neck. And as quickly as it surged, the anger recedes until gone.

THE SEAGULLS ARE motionless in the air, sailing the wind without effort. I point at them and say look. Noor lifts her head and shades her eyes with her hand. 'They look like ice cream,' she says and it is true they do, the plumage so smooth and white.

We are walking along the water on Skeppsholmen and it is one of the last summer evenings, I can feel it.

'So Abbe told me,' Noor says, 'about Mexico.'

'Oh. Did he?' For some reason this seems amazing, Abbe talking about me with other people. I would like a transcript.

'Honestly I was quite shocked.'

'Me too,' I say and she laughs.

'But you will go? For the summer?'

'Yes of course. I mean, shouldn't I?' I listen intently because her tone is confusing. I can't predict where the conversation is going, which has so far not been the case with Noor. If anything she is one of the few people I feel naturally simpatico with.

She points towards a kiosk further down the footpath and we walk towards it. 'It's just, you know how he is.'

I stop and look at her. 'Please could you just say what you mean because otherwise I will worry.'

'No that's, I'm just careful about you. I don't want you to go over there and he will be, you know, detached, and you will feel stranded.'

'He is not detached.'

'Oh come on Sickan. Come on now.' She looks frustrated.

'Not with me. I don't feel that.' And I wonder if this is true, do I not feel that? I think we are very connected. Most of the time. Sometimes he has to do something else and leaves rather abruptly. Sometimes he is with friends or playing football and we have to reschedule to meet up later at night. I think this is normal. Not everyone has to be attached at the hip. I am busy too.

Although if I wasn't busy with work, if I had as much time as Abbe, would I not want to see him all the time, attach at the hip?

She touches my arm. 'Well, I mean, you are rather head in the sky yourself Sickan, so maybe that works out.'

I shrug. Noor is a close friend to Abbe and a new friend to me and it is nice that she cares but now I don't want her to say anything more about it. I don't want her planting seeds about Abbe being detached because then I will start looking for it when we are together.

We reach the kiosk and get softserves in waffle cones. The best is the first lick, the cold smooth swirl at the top, that you bite without teeth, just lips. I only ever eat softserve in warm weather because I want to keep it special.

We sit on the concrete edge dangling our feet over the water. On the other side are the grand hotels of Gamla

Stan. There are stationary boats which you can board and eat food on. If it was allowed I would swim now. I roll up the sleeves of my t-shirt and scratch the skin on my shoulder. It is starting to flake. While we talk I flex a bicep at Noor and she makes a so-so face.

I wonder how warm it will be in Mexico City. What their version of seagulls is, their softserve. Although I have almost obsessively researched the city, there are still so many details I can't know before I set foot. Studying a map until you have it memorised won't tell you about the sounds, the air quality. I can't believe I am going. I will learn Spanish. My accent will be Mexican.

I have already saved some money, because after Bogdan I helped another student with her summer resit-essay, and I have one more client lined up. Word has got out but now I don't mind.

Of course there is a risk of getting caught and if I do I will be thrown out, but for some reason I am not so worried. No one can tell on me because they would also be implicated.

Maybe this lack of concern is just being young and feeling invincible, that bad habit. But it is how I have been feeling lately. Invincible.

I take a bite of the cone. 'Are you only bringing up Mexico because you'll miss me so much?'

'Hey, what makes you think I'll be here? I'm graduating.'

'You're leaving too?'

'Maybe London?'

So now we compare London to Stockholm. Noor says Stockholm is boring next to the breathtaking speed of London, the many things to do. 'But I shouldn't forget about rent prices,' she says. 'Knife crime.'

I am amazed to hear Stockholm described as grey and bleak and small. To me Stockholm is what London is to Noor. It is shiny and many things happen here. And yes, breathtaking. Abbe also talks about Stockholm in this grey way. Perhaps it is always the same, the city you are born in is mud next to the green across the border. Luckily for me I am never going back to Åhus so whatever city I live in will have the shine.

Noor gossips for a while, just light-hearted things about people. I relax listening to her, licking the vanilla. I don't even know what time it is, the sun has been up for months.

'Should we go?' she asks, and yes now I want to leave too.

It is late, the air is cool but not cold. A few more nights and then September. I am only a short walk from Artillerigatan so I hug Noor goodbye. There is almost no one out and I hear my own footsteps patting the pavement. I feel alive, that's what I feel.

I push my earbuds in, open the audiobook app, and click *Immanuel Kant in Sixty Minutes* which I am halfway through. There is an old man walking a dog and they are both a bit scruffy. I say gokväll and the man nods his head. The dog lifts his leg to a lamppost. Now I don't mind summer ending because the sooner autumn comes the sooner next summer will arrive. And then maybe I will be the one complaining about how grey Stockholm is. But no, I don't think I will. Because looking around at the beautiful old stone houses and the black glint of water between buildings and hearing the seagulls cry on roof-tops, really I find nothing here to complain about.

WHENEVER I HAVE a quiet moment, in the shower or cleaning the kitchen or at night before sleeping, my mind goes back to the hockey booth. It has made me recon-sider Abbe's and my first meeting, me stepping in with the blond guy, and how we talked about it on the phone later. I told him one night when we were almost asleep in his bed, 'I understand now that you felt you needed to call and thank me and it wasn't just a pretence for asking me out.'

'Well yeah,' he said but he was yawning and maybe not listening so much.

'And it makes me picture you there in the hockey booth and I wish I would have been there then, when you were fourteen.'

'You would have been twelve.'

'Yes okay but if we were the same age, maybe you would have told me? Do you ever think of that, how things would have been if I'd gone to your school instead?' I was careful not to touch him since being intimate both physically and conversationally at once was a little much for me. 'Because sometimes it feels like I had the wrong childhood in Skåne.'

'Huh.'

I looked at his contours in the near dark. His eyes were closed. 'If I'd gone to your school, do you think the result would have been the same, that I would've been singled out in your school too?'

'Yes.'

'But. Why?'

He placed his hand heavily on my cheek. 'I feel like this is an important conversation and I'm already asleep.'

I told him go to sleep, but he already had. What I felt then was envy. I could see Abbe would fit in anywhere because he was never too serious and he asked everyone a question, everyone. I wondered if Abbe's friends liked me at all or if they only tolerated me by association. There was no way of finding these things out, since I knew you couldn't expect someone to answer honestly.

Earlier that night we had met Henrik and the others, and Pernilla said something about Kierkegaard's view on marriage as an ethical union rather than a romantic one and Noor said oh please are we seriously considering moralistic individualism now, and I thought are we supposed to have read Kierkegaard? No one else seemed to react so I said, 'Have you actually read Kierkegaard, like the actual texts?' which was a serious question and at first they looked at me like maybe I was an idiot, but then they decided to interpret it as a joke to laugh politely at, leaving my question unanswered.

I couldn't keep up with them, and felt I never had anything remotely passable to say which made me quiet. When I did say something it disrupted their easy flow. Sometimes, horrifyingly, my Skånska accent would break through, which it did when I was stressed. This made me fear I would never interact well with Abbe's friends though he, for some reason, did not seem to mind the awkward-ness. But I often left these gatherings hating myself a little. I thought I had learned the easy chat by now but the larger the group the more obvious it was that I was still quite an ugly conversationalist.

It was something I had noticed about Abbe's metropol-itan upper-middle-class friends, they were willing to spend time on boring things like Kierkegaard for the sake of intellectualism, or at least online-skim him extensively enough to be able to talk about him in beer cafés. As would I, the very next day. I had in no way given up on learning their way of conversing.

It was my first encounter with intellectualism. At my gymnasium in Kristianstad, if you wanted to impress some-one you did so by knowing things about new music or fan culture. But around Abbe people talked about old music and great thinkers.

Then there was Lottie and Hanna who had gone to the boarding school. It was confusing but coming from the upper class, they had adopted a form of anti-intellectual-ism, as if knowing too much was the same as trying too hard which was in their culture the same as being vulgar.

I had no specific culture because my parents had very little money but we were not working class. There was no salt of the earth pride to capitalise on, neither were they part of elegant academia like the literature professors or psychiatrists. They were devoted students of moths and quarks.

It gave me a headache to picture learning the intricacies of each culture so maybe I should simply pick one to

belong to. Which I had already done, I had picked Abbe.
And Abbe had picked these people.

The bourgeoisie.

Such a pretty word.

I would try my best to befriend them.

I HURRY OUT of the tunnelbana station and across Plattan Square because I am late. Stadsteatern is up a flight of stairs and outside the entrance Noor and Hanna are waiting. It is the first thing I notice when I see them, Hanna's hat. A sailor's hat with a rubber logo at the front. It is my hat. But of course it's not because I am wearing mine. Also mine is blue, hers is black. They have not yet seen me so I pull the hat off my head and push it down to the bottom of my bag. And somehow I can't believe this. I have one nice thing, one.

Noor waves at me and I arrange my face and hug them, first Noor then Hanna. 'What do you think?' she says, meaning the hat.

'Yes great, suits you,' I say and turn around and enter the building.

We were supposed to see *Annie the Musical* but Hanna was sick that week and once she got around to re-purchasing tickets the show had finished. Instead we are watching a one-woman show about sex and the workplace. Groundbreaking, supposedly.

By the time we have checked our coats the woman on the speaker urges us to please take our seats and I am glad for not having to make small talk. We are on the tenth row and Hanna sits in the middle.

A woman is on a near-empty stage delivering a monologue. I don't really register the words.

I hold my thighs and keep my hands there. I feel restless,
upset. My trousers are worn thin and my white acrylic
turtleneck lumpy with lint. On the inside of its collar is a
faint lipstick smear that doesn't wash out. Next to people
like Noor I look cheap, I know this.

I draft a message in my head that I will never send. It is
a message to Hanna, and as I draft I realise it doesn't only
cover the issue of the hat. Other offences surface, the
capricious moods, telling people my private things, taking
liberties. It is frightening because I have only felt this
resentment before towards my parents in Åhus. I remember living there, the smallest overstep causing a surge of
anger, me leaving the room to focus on breathing and stifle
whatever thoughts. Mum dressing badly in ICA. Dad for a
full week not asking how was my day. The cruel things I
wanted to say to them, focusing on my breath there in the
hallway.

I am not stupid, I know this is not about the hat.

In the break we push through to the theatre bar and
order white wine. Riesling. I rush it down. We are standing by the window and it is just before eight in October so
the sky is black and the city below a collection of small
lights. People scurry around like wraiths down there. The
wine has made me cold inside. It is incredibly stiff. Noor
appears puzzled and flustered, she tries to discuss the play
but I have not seen a second of it. Hanna seems offended
as if she is the one who's been wronged and this I can
almost not take.

I finish the remaining Riesling in one drink and I don't care that this is strange behaviour. I excuse myself to the bathroom.

It is too bright in here. I can see dry patches on my skin. My lips look bloodless, like two slugs stacked.

In the toilet stall I bite my bottom lip hard.

I have so far always managed to hide my anger so I am confident I can contain my feelings now. Although the idea of going home with Hanna after the play is daunting.

In front of the brightly lit mirror I wash my hands and flush cold water on my wrists. Then I apply red lipstick and go to join the others.

'AND THEN HE fucked me sideways over the table and it was the best I ever had.'

I shift in my seat. The second half of the play is vile. The monologue is what the culture pages call unflinching. I have trouble understanding why we are paying money to experience something so brutalising.

I hold on to the armrests and wonder how I will stand another hour, but somehow I do because suddenly there is loud applause and I have never been more grateful for the sound of hands clapping.

It seems Noor is also relieved because she says sorry she needs to rush off. She kisses me on the cheek and hugs Hanna and then she is gone.

We are silent, walking to the station. Again it seems like she is in a foul mood with me but I can't understand what she has to be upset about. On the train she puts her earbuds in and this makes it very obvious we are angry.

As soon as I close the door to the flat behind us she says, 'Okay, what's wrong with you?'

She is intimidating standing there in the hallway, aggressive energy, blocking the way to my room.

'Why is something wrong with me?'

'You ask your friend to join us and then you behave awfully the whole night. It was awkward.'

I move past her, brushing shoulders, and go sit on the sofa. My skin is crawling. I breathe calmly to release some steam. She walks in but stays standing, arms wrapping her chest.

'Hanna, are you upset Noor came with us to the play?' I shift my focus to her upset, to force myself out of my own.

'I gave you those tickets for your birthday, I meant them for the two of us.'

'But, we are always the two of us. All the time, the two of us.'

'Is that a problem?'

Slowly I say, 'Sometimes it's nice to be with more people.'

She covers her face with her hand and when she removes it she actually sneers. 'If that's the type of people you want to be with, by all means go ahead. You do know what it says about you right?' She stares at me and I don't want to say any more so I reduce my facial expression to blank. She turns around and walks out the room and I hear her bedroom door shut.

I stay still for a moment and look through the windows across the street. Someone is watching television because the room flickers in different colours. Whatever anger I felt is now fully extinguished by the raw unsorted emotions Hanna just heaved onto the parquet. I feel beaten up.

In my room I turn on the bedside lamp and take my clothes off. I sit cross-legged on the duvet and look at my phone, wishing hard there'll be a notification. There's not. I put it back in the bag, and there is the hat. I take it out and touch the dense fabric between my fingers. Then I go over to the desk and drop it in the wastebasket.

IN THE MORNING, Hanna knocks on my door. I say one second and get dressed.

She is in the kitchen and has made Earl Grey and toast with marmalade. I join her at the kitchen table. Abruptly she says, 'I'm sorry things got weird.' She holds up her hands, palms out. 'No really, I was out of line. And I like Noor a lot so I don't know why I said she is a type of people.'

'So, by that, what did you mean?'

'Like, I guess, fashionable? Popular? I think I was feeling insecure.'

'As in, me being a social climber?'

'I don't think that about you.' And then sincerely, 'I don't.'

I fidget with the dry piece of toast on my plate.

She sighs. 'I don't know, I just thought we were doing something different. Like, being above it.'

'Oh no, Hanna, I'm not above it.'

'Well, okay. That's okay. I'm sorry I made the mistake.' She looks tentatively hopeful, like she wants to smile but needs approval.

I touch my face with my fingertips and I feel fine. I can swallow the tea down like normal. Hanna's hesitance grows because I am not saying anything and her wide-open eyes make my heart swell for her. Although she can be curt with people and stormy in her manners she is kind to me and so painfully undisguised in how much she likes me.

'It's fine Hanna, we're fine.' And in this moment I truly believe we are.

Later in my room I pick up the hat from the wastebasket and tap it with my hand before pushing it far back on the top shelf of my wardrobe.

ABBE AND I walk for a long time across the parks in the city. It is Saturday and mostly cloudy, the air absolutely still. The sun breaks through now and then, making us take off and put on our jackets accordingly. In a tight alleyway, cafés have put out tables and we choose one facing the sun, our backs against the building. Abbe is wearing sunglasses and a navy jacket with brown lapels. I hope people walking by assume we are together.

Once our cups arrive he holds out his hand and says okay, ready. From my bag I pick up a paperback novel and my A4 notebook with the dialogues.

Since that time he quasi-accidentally read my notes while drunk he has not asked to again which is a relief but also a disappointment. I have got used to him and feel more sure as time goes on and sometimes I find myself actively wanting him to read my notes. He had seemed impressed that time and I very much want to impress someone.

This morning I had placed the notebook on the kitchen table when I was organising my bag and he took the hint and asked if he could read some more, please. I proposed the café because of its neutrality.

His coffee grows cold while he reads. I look at the pages of my novel.

He closes the notebook, puts it on the table, and says, 'Of all the girlfriends in the world, this one happens to be mine,' which to me is just the most sophisticated reaction imaginable. A rush of confidence fills me then and I open a pack of cigarettes and light one. Abbe reaches out and takes the cigarette from my lips, puts it between his. I light another and lean back in my chair.

'How am I supposed to keep up with you,' he says.

'Oh, you're doing just fine.'

He laughs then. I am so pleased.

LATER THAT NIGHT, we are on the sofa in Abbe's living room watching TV. He goes to the kitchen and opens the fridge. I change the channel. *The Wizard of Oz* is on, still in the black and white part, pre-tornado.

'My mum's favourite,' Abbe says and hands me a glass of Coke with ice. 'We used to watch it at Christmas.' He sits down and seems content listening to the familiar words.

'I don't think I've ever seen the whole thing,' I say. 'Just parts here and there.'

'Should we watch?'

'We could, if you want.'

'I like it. She's a good hero.'

I drink most of my Coke in one go. It is incredibly sweet.

He says, 'Judy Garland is one of those people you can't help but love, isn't she?'

'Yes. Maybe because of her tragic life and all the drugs they gave her.'

'I think likely she was just born abnormally charming.'

We watch in silence for a while and even though I know the story it is still great when Dorothy goes from black and white to colour. I finish the rest of my drink and swirl the glass to make the ice clink. Abbe hands me his glass and I drink some of his too. 'You want more?' he asks.

'No it was enough, thank you.' I rest my head on his shoulder. He puts his hand on my head and fusses my hair. I might fall asleep. 'The dialogue hasn't aged so well though, has it.'

He laughs a little. 'You're the expert.' Then Dorothy starts singing and he says, 'Have you been writing much lately?'

'I don't really have time, with school.' I haven't written anything in months.

'If I was that good at something I would make the time.'

'What do you mean, you are good at something. You're a designer.'

'I make interfaces more practical, they're not exactly original works of art.'

I yawn. 'Why does everything have to be original? I mean does originality really have intrinsic value? Work can be inspired without being unique.'

'You're skating around me now.' He sits up straight so I have to lift my head off his shoulder which I resent. 'I'm sorry if I'm up in your business but I honestly feel you'd be happier writing than coding.'

There are monkeys flying on the screen. I try to determine if he is right but can't be sure. 'It's a job. It doesn't have to be fun, I can have a hobby.'

'The thing is your writing is funny but like, in a new way. People should see it.'

It feels then like he sees me as a singularity, a new species. It hurts, all the multiple ways he keeps saying: you're strange.

'It's only entertainment, it doesn't do anything. With software I can change things.'

'I don't want you to settle though.' He roughly runs his hand through his hair. 'And sometimes I feel like you're hiding.'

'But, is that so bad?' I sound upset now, I can tell. 'Is it mandatory to expose yourself to humanity all the time? Because I sort of can't handle that.'

'Hey,' he says and reaches for my hand but I pull it back. My heart feels too strong. 'I think I'm ruined that way.'

'Hey, I'm sorry I brought it up, okay. I didn't know you felt that way.'

I see he is uncomfortable but still I say, 'It's like I'm skinless.'

He breathes deeply. 'You're not skinless.' He touches my wrist. 'You're just sensitive. It's fine. I can get that way too sometimes.'

But I think, it's different, him sometimes getting overwhelmed by the world and my ceaseless watchfulness, my flinching at sounds, expecting violence. It's not the same.

I AM HIGH above ground in a truck going west. I can see everything. The driver is a single male but old and frail enough to be harmless. Three hours from here on the motorway is Båstad, and the summer house of Noor's friend's friend.

Abbe and Noor and the others took the train early this morning but I said I would come on a later train, which is euphemism for hitchhike. Abbe told me he would stay sober and come pick me up at the station in 'one of the cars'. There is a party in the summer house with people from all over Sweden. I am happy to be on my way because this is one of those see-to-believe events with a pool but also because it is nice to get away from Artillerigatan for the night.

The hitchhike clears my head and there's the familiar sense of freedom from being in between places, invisible. No one in the world knows where I am except for this frail truck driver.

He breaks the quiet. 'So do you have a boyfriend then?'

'Yes,' I say, for the first time answering this question in the positive. I can't help it, it fills my chest, having someone waiting for me at a train station. Staying sober for me.

'And he lets you hitchhike all by yourself?'

Generously, I do not roll my eyes. 'It's not really up to him to let me.'

'But it's not safe, a girl alone.'

I hold my hands up as fists. 'What, you think you can take me old man?'

He laughs for a long time. 'Well you have some spunk.'

I hope that's the end of it but then he says, 'I think it has gone too far now. When I met my Lisbeth I would make sure she was always safe and taken care of.'

'You're not a danger to me,' I say and remind myself he is one hundred years old and a little sexism is to be expected.

'No indeed. But I don't mean just danger, it's only polite to look after each other. You couples nowadays, looks to me you're just two individuals sharing a bed, thinking too much about yourselves. That's what I say.' He taps his hand on my knee and I actually let him. 'You tell your guy from me to take better care of you.' I resent the conversation but choose not to argue. I look out the window and spend the rest of the hike silently watching red cottages dot November-mudded fields.

What I don't tell the driver is that I'm not nearly as frustrated with Abbe's independence as with Hanna's overfamiliarity. Maybe it is inevitable when living together but I feel we have entered a stage of codependency I never gave the nod. Last week she came into my room without knocking. I wasn't doing anything, just at my desk, but still. It is risky to hint at boundaries because she is so easily hurt. I tiptoe around her frail ego and try not to get sucked in. But I already am. I owe her, I know that. And sometimes it seems like Hanna and I are the ones behaving like a couple. I don't like that at all. If what the driver has with his Lisbeth is anything like me and Hanna, I gladly choose individualistic bed sharing. In contrast to Hanna, Abbe seems a breeze. And with time we will grow closer, his skittishness settling, my trust building, as long as I don't chase him away or push too hard.

'How long have you been married?' I say.

'Forty-seven years we had.'

I pause a moment, then gently I ask, 'So, your Lisbeth is not still with us?'

'Four years gone this summer. But yes, she's still with me.'

I ask the driver to drop me at a bus stop behind the train station and then I enter the station, walk through the building, and exit onto the pavement in front. There on my left sitting on a park bench is Abbe. His arm is stretched along the backrest and I can see the outline of his torso through his shirt. 'Don't get up,' I say as I approach and he laughs. I take a photo with my phone. It is not warm but there is a weak sun out and even one seagull calling somewhere. I can smell the sea.

Abbe gets up and says, 'Sickan are you ready for this? It's fucking intense,' and although I am certainly not ready I nod my head and get hit with the anticipation.

ALTHOUGH SCHOOL WAS always bad, art class was worst. Something about the free form bred anarchy, no benches in orderly lines, no teacher by the blackboard. Instead two long tables in a large room and one small room for paints and things, and the teacher, Åsa, walking around looking over our shoulders. Her hair was short and somehow we all knew she only had one breast.

You couldn't tell she only had one breast, according to rumour she had a rubber copy in her bra. But we knew and she knew that we knew. This one weakness was enough to nullify her authority.

Throughout the ninety-minute class every Friday afternoon there was a threat in the room, a promise that if Åsa tried to reinstate order the rubber breast would be brought up. Now I can't remember the breast ever being mentioned which likely meant the threat of it was enough. Like a dog kicked once left forever wary.

Two boys took over the class. One boy's dad had killed himself and the other dad was frightening. Those two boys always pushed things too far. Every Friday afternoon they would pick a target to harass for the entire ninety minutes. If a girl, there was often touching involved and sexual words. If I was the target there was no touching or sex because I was repulsive.

This particular Friday they targeted Erik. Erik lived on a farm and his clothes were not modern, even I could tell. They sometimes teased him for smelling of manure but I never smelled it, although he would usually have mud on his shoes and the cuff of his jeans. Another thing about Erik was that at the slightest attention he turned bright red, which made the harassment a sort of measurable sport. I stayed away from him.

We used water colours to paint a still life Åsa had prepared in the centre of the long table. Different fruits and a stuffed bird. She told us about shadows, that if an orange is orange, its shadow will have the opposite colour, blueish purple. I am not sure if this is true but the concept has stayed with me because I find it neat.

Erik was concentrating on his paper so he didn't notice one of them, Jocke, picking up a pencil and slowly moving the tip with the eraser towards Erik's ear. I saw and others saw but no one said anything. When the eraser entered Erik's ear canal he jumped as if struck and screeched his chair back from the table.

'Fucking gross,' Jocke said and held the eraser up to the class. Of course we could see nothing but we understood the sentiment. 'He must be fucking deaf.' Jocke clapped his hands near Erik's ear and the pang made many of us jump. Erik froze stiff. Åsa pretended to help someone at the other end of the classroom. Erik stared at his brush and paper and said nothing but his face was so red it looked painful. Sitting across from Erik, merely spectating, I can't say I felt compassion. Instead I was fixating on this one thought: better him than me.

HUMANS IN DIFFERENT stages of intoxication move around the rooms and up and down the stairs like erratic schools of fish. Everyone seems to be looking for someone, in a perpetual state of low-level impatience. The house is large enough to lose yourself in. Abbe was right, it is intense. It is now six in the morning and I have been drunk since yesterday. I am told some guests have been here three days and no one seems to leave. Earlier I saw two people have sex in the pool in front of everyone. That made me feel nauseous or maybe it was the gin. I made a note not to go into the pool which was a shame because I had brought my swimsuit and everything.

Although most of the houseguests look the same, fresh, tanned, boaty, the accents are from all over. As if a network of veins and arteries connect the members of the small upper class. There must be summer camps they go to. Or they are third cousins.

For hours now my head has rested against the large cream sofa in one of the lounge-type rooms. Noor is here and Pernilla and her childhood friends, who all seem to enjoy her sarcasm. When a person comes in looking for someone she makes us laugh by sending them off in random directions. And this is what I notice, when you are angry with someone and also drunk, Pernilla carrying on is fun to listen to and not upsetting. And it is nice to be included, not to sit by myself or wander around.

It surprises me that this is all, the party. Just being continually high while ignoring personal safety, this is it. I had expected more substance, a new level of aliveness. But it is the opposite. A disregard for life. Contempt for the body.

Abbe is not always around but he checks in with me often and we make out or drink water together. Earlier people were dancing and when the song changed Noor said, 'Oh yes please,' and took my hand to pull me up from the sofa.

'Don't bother,' Abbe said. 'Sickan doesn't dance.'

Right on beat I said, 'Saving myself for the wedding,' and the whole group laughed, Abbe too. They were drunk and high so they laughed easily but even so I had meant it as a joke and they took it as a joke. It pleased me and I wondered if this was what it felt like to belong to a group? From then on I relaxed and talked a lot, my conversations running smoothly, even with Pernilla.

Although, if I can tell they are all upper or upper middle class, I assume they can tell I am not. I must stand out, accepted as a conversation piece or to prove they're not snobs. Abbe seems unfazed. If anything he encourages my eccentric side and always wants me to behave like myself. I hope it is because he likes me and not because it makes him more interesting to have a weird girlfriend. Maybe it is both. In bad moments I think he is going through a phase, the creative couple type thing, wanting to date the gifted she-writer, not the quiet anxious code mouse. In bad moments I think even my financial status is exotic to him. I know these thoughts are unfair and only emerge because deep down I question what someone like him is doing with someone like me.

Maybe an hour ago Abbe went to the ocean to sunrise with Pontus and he is not back yet. I am outside smoking with a blanket and those radiator lamps when the sun comes over the horizon and the heated pool steams beautifully in the cold. I am sweaty and my pulse feels strange but also I'm so happy I'm soaring. It seems perfect now, all of it. I look towards the sun to see if maybe Abbe is coming back.

'Where's your friend by the way?' Pernilla asks me, reclined on a sunchair.

'Which friend?' I think maybe she means Abbe but no because Pernilla says, 'You know, the strange-looking one,' and immediately I know she means Hanna.

'Pernilla!' a girl says, and some of the people show mock shock.

'Sorry, no offence.' Pernilla blows smoke out her nose.

'No no it's fine,' I say. 'She looks strange on purpose, like a defence mechanism. You know like broccoli tasting so bad to avoid being eaten by rodents?'

Someone says oh my god and the laughter that erupts is equal parts amused and aghast. It is enormous, the thrill of creating laughter and directing it at someone who isn't me.

But the laughing ends abruptly and the others are not looking at me anymore but behind me. I feel a shiver. I slowly turn around although I don't want to. And there is Abbe. His face right then, it breaks me.

ON DECEMBER THIRTEENTH my universitet throws a St Lucia Ball for third-year students. I have asked Hanna to be my date since Abbe is busy.

'Sure but don't expect me to wear a dress,' she said. Instead she wears black trousers and a white tuxedo shirt. She looks nice. Polished shoes, hair slicked back, heavy black eye makeup.

I have toyed with the idea of buying a dress, keeping it clean, and returning it the day after. But on principle this seems immoral. Last week Hanna said just borrow one from me, and we went to stand in front of her colossal built-in wardrobe. Without hesitation she pulled out a black full-length gown. 'This is oversized, like a tent. Valentino. It will fit you.' I loved it instantly.

Now I slip it over my head and it does fall like a deflated tent, soft as tissue paper. It has a strap tight around the neck and deepcut underarms, revealing the sides of my breasts when I move. I wear it with a high tight braid and discreet makeup and it is the best I have ever looked.

She has ordered us a taxi as a surprise, one of the expensive ones with quiet drivers and miniature bottles of water. I ignore that this is indebting me even more to Hanna. My conscience is wretched enough for saying she is repellent

like broccoli. Even though I have spent my whole childhood at the mercy of mean people, that night I behaved
like one of them. It had happened, and so easily. Today, in
a normal state of mind, this seems impossible.

In the days after the party I had written it off as hubris, as
taking too much pleasure in finally fitting in with Abbe's
circle, even with Pernilla. But I'm not stupid. I deep down
knew, even as I was saying it, that the broccoli comment was
not simply me sacrificing Hanna on the altar of popularity.

These months living with Hanna have not been easy. In
my parents' home, swallowing my feelings and never voic-
ing my anger had been possible because they left me alone
and never probed about my mood. But Hanna never leaves
me alone. She always probes about mood. And Hanna
does not have many boundaries. I knew the broccoli insult
was me being quietly angry for long enough to make it
boil over. And apparently I am the type of coward who
boils over only when the other person isn't in the room. If
Hanna had been sitting around that pool with us, I would
not have called her broccoli. Yes, a coward.

I need to come clean and apologise, though I know it is
crueller to come clean. And also I am afraid. What I'm
thinking is, this might end our friendship. Hanna is a fragile person, already she thinks she's not very loved. A
disloyalty this unkind might hurt her in a way I can't repair.
She could break up with me, ask me to move out and then
not pick up when I call her on the phone to talk about
things. Without Hanna, my life would go very quiet again.

It is one thing to want a friend but not have one, and
another thing entirely to find a best friend to keep all that

company with, only to lose her. Going back to the loneliness, having no one to call on the phone.

But. I can't go on with the dishonesty. I can't do it, it's unbearable. I think about it all the time. So I am waiting for the moment to have the conversation. I will do my best to repair it. Until then I have solemnly resolved to be a good friend and flatmate and to smother my irritation over the small things. Tonight I will show her a good time.

IN OVER TWO weeks I have only seen Abbe twice. We met at a café a few days after the big house party. He seemed distracted and we couldn't get our talk to match. The longer we sat the more difficult we got. I had planned to bring up the thing I said about Hanna but the mood was very much not there. My anxiety grew throughout our conversation, I felt things were slipping and tried hard to not show this on my face.

He told me he wouldn't be able to see me much before Christmas because he had his big thesis and also there were two exams so he needed to buckle down and mug up, that's how he put it. And I myself always considering schoolwork a priority tried to reassure him how much I understood. And I did. It was just unfortunate timing he had to mug up right after the house party and that one uncoordinated coffee. We seemed rocky and I wanted us to be in the same room or on the phone a lot to become stable again.

Some days later I was sleeping when he called. It was Friday but still he was not the type to call and wake me up at 2am.

'Hallå?'

'Sickan. Heeej. What are you doing?'

He sounded sloppy, sentimental, which were things he never sounded, so I was concerned.

'Hello, min vän, where are you?'

'I'm out! We had some drinks.'

'Oh yes, I can hear. You outside?'

'I wanted to talk to you and to see you so I called.'

'Okay yes. Are you close by? Do you want to come?'

'No, you come here! We should go out!'

I was already putting on jeans. 'Yes okay, I'm coming. Where are you?'

He was sitting on an empty side street behind Stureplan, a fifteen-minute walk I made in ten. He had settled on a low marble doorstep and when he saw me he didn't stand up but raised his arm wide in welcome. 'Kom, kom,' he said and waved his hand to hurry me up. I sidled in under his arm. He pulled me close and I leaned my head on his shoulder. 'There you are. Sickan sickan sickan.'

'You okay?'

He lifted my chin and stared into my eyes in a way he thought sensual. His drunk eyes couldn't focus. 'You are so beautiful,' he said. And then he kissed me, with tongue.

I drew my head back. 'Oh wow, jesus.' I wiped my mouth. 'Did you vomit earlier?'

'Oh yes I did.' He chuckled softly.

I looked him over but he seemed clean. 'When?'

'It was two times.'

'That's okay. It made you feel better? Should I go get some water?' I searched the street for a kiosk.

'No! No. Stay here. Stay here.'

I had chewing gum in my pocket so I handed him one and took one myself. The vomit taste lingered.

He pulled me close again. My head on his shoulder, we looked across the street. No one was here. Even in my winter coat I was freezing but Abbe was drunk beyond cold.

'Did you have a good night?' I asked.

'It was so much fun, you should have seen.'

'You sure?'

He let go of me and turned to see my face. 'Why do you ask if I'm okay so many times?'

'Maybe you don't seem that okay?' I swooped my hand to indicate the situation.

He paused, as if taking it in, and then his shoulders dropped. He looked defeated. I felt bad.

'Should we go home?' I took his hand and moved to stand up.

'No, let's sit here a while. Just talk.'

I pulled my coat closer and drew my hands into my sleeves. 'So what did you do today?'

'I saw mum.'

'Oh, how is she?'

'Yes she's fine but, I feel like, it made me strange to see her.'

'Really? Why.'

'I don't know, just a lot on my mind lately. And I wanted to talk to her but I chickened out.' With the sloppy sweetness now gone he just sounded sort of sad. I waited him out.

'Do you remember when we were at the hockey rink and I told you that stuff about my dad?'

I nodded.

'I think that was the first time I'd talked about it in years. Mum and I don't talk about it. Not since I was, I don't even know, fifteen? But since you and me talked about it I have been thinking on that. And I had something I wanted to ask her about, but it's like I just can't.'

I tried to keep my voice normal. 'Like what?'

'I wanted to ask her if, after all that, if it had changed, you know, the way she looks at me?' And he fell apart.

His face a grimace, exposed. Large, unrestrained crying. It was frightening. The vulnerability so naked.

'Abbe, please,' I said but I didn't dare touch him. 'Please.'

The thing is, I could understand. The care I had taken for my parents to never know or see me like that. The victim. Pathetic. Misused. But his mother had seen it.

If my parents had, of course it would have changed their opinion of me. But I had hidden it. I wanted to be the capable strong Siv with the intelligence and the grades. Not the pathetic one.

Had it changed the way I saw Abbe, when he told me? Yes. It had.

He wiped his face and looked at me. 'Hey Sickan?' He sounded calmer, some tears in his eyes but breathing normally. 'Do you think we're too fucked up?'

I winced. 'No? What do you mean. We're not fucked up.' I backed away a little. 'We're doing really well! I mean, we outlasted it, it's over.' I was hurt, it seemed unfair. 'Everyone goes through things, they get past it.'

'I don't think, not everyone goes through things like ours.'

'They do. Not exactly but everyone has some thing.'

He blinked his eyes free of tears and frowned. 'Don't you ever like, think maybe you should talk about it?'

'No. No I don't want to talk about it. That's the last thing.' I held my elbows. 'I never wanted that.'

He stood up slowly. 'I get it.' He raised his hands. 'No I do.'

I stood too.

'I won't bother you with that anymore, sorry I'm really drunk.'

'You're not bothering me. I just, I see you're sad and I wanted to comfort you but I'm not sure how to other than to just let you know that I think you are a wonderful person and you make me feel so so good and like, this is important to me! You, are important to me.'

He sniffed. He looked down at his shoes. 'Thanks, yeah that's good to hear.'

'Come, let's go home, I am cold, let's go okay?'

'No that's alright, I think I'm going to head.'

'Head home?'

'I need a shower.'

'Shower with me.'

'Thanks for coming out to see me anyway.' He wiped his face with the back of his hands. 'And sorry, being so fucking dramatic. Call you tomorrow, okay.'

He started walking and I panicked. 'Is this about Hanna?'

He stopped. 'Hanna?'

'Are you mad at me?'

'No? I'm not mad.'

'What then?'

'I don't know, it's a lot of pressure.' He uhmed. 'Right now I think I need to focus on passing my classes, so I can graduate and move.' He turned to look at me as if making an effort. 'So, would it be okay if I'm a bit out of it?'

And of course it was okay. He needed to study and pass his classes, and I didn't want to distract him just because I was feeling insecure. 'Of course it is,' I said. 'Just, like, don't disappear okay?'

IN THE TAXI with Hanna I say, 'I figure this is the only ball we'll ever go to. People don't normally go to balls.'

'Let's make the most of it then. Spike the punch.'

'Okay. But I don't want one of those ugly flower bracelets.'

After a long dinner there is dancing. First the slow songs, waltzes and everything. I dance with Hanna once but we don't like the waltz. Anyway we are too drunk by now to keep the rhythm, out of sync and dizzy. Then there is normal music. In the bathroom I wash my hands and can't believe I have taken a friend as my date to my only ball. I have not seen Abbe since that night on the doorstep. We have texted and I have called but he hasn't called.

I smoke weed with Bogdan outside and then we dance together. We get into it and it is fun and then flirty. His shaved head shines under the moving lights. We dance close together as a joke and his hands feel nice on my arms and lower back. At one point I wonder if he will slide his hands even lower and in my inebriated state I can't calculate how I would gracefully exit such a situation. But he never does so it's fine. I want someone to tell me I am beautiful. There are some shots with people in the bar and I even talk to Konrad who is here but not as drunk as us students and whatever I say to him blissfully doesn't make it past my short-term memory and is thus lost to me although maybe not to him.

Then I am outside in the delivery truck alley and I need to vomit. I keep the dress safe scrunched up in one hand and lean against the brick wall with the other. But nothing comes up. I put two fingers down my throat and wonder why we put two fingers, not one or three, if it is instinct or learned through TV. But still nothing comes up, only ugly dry hurls. I don't even feel the cold although I know it is there. The shape of the alley makes for superb acoustics and my hurling echoes back with resounding clarity.

Hanna texts me. *Where are you? The car is here I have your coat.* And then, *See you out front.*

I give up on vomiting and round the corner to the carpark and there, just by the doors, is a cluster of girls. I don't know them, not from any of my classes. They are smoking and must have heard my retching in great detail. I am not drunk enough to not care. The flush rises up my scalp, and I can tell they are talking about me and I am expecting unkindness so I try not to listen but I am wrong, because as I walk past I can make out the words 'but weird as in modelesque'.

Modelesque.

I soar across the carpark and grin at Hanna where she stands beside the taxi looking at her phone. I kiss her on the cheek and she says what happened to you, mm you smell nice. In the taxi I lean my head back and we talk over one another about everybody and the outfits. I feel so safe, so perfectly at peace with her that I say, 'I love you Hanna,' knowing full well it is the first time I say this to a person and now forever Hanna will be my first. She says you're drunk, but she takes my hand and holds it hard enough to stop my bloodflow.

Back at Artillerigatan I fall onto the sofa and Hanna fetches a bag of crisps from the kitchen. Dill, which isn't my favourite but quite good. We hand the bag back and forth and although I thought I was happy I say, 'I can't believe it was my only ball and I didn't go with Abbe.'

She stops midchew. Then she says, 'You didn't ask him though.'

'No I know, I thought I would but we have been weird and now we haven't talked for days, only texts. Who does that, not talk for four days straight.' My voice is mushy.

'I think it's fine, it's not like you're fighting? He's just, you know how he is. Just leave it for a while.'

'But Hanna I think about him all the time. All the time! And he must do as well so I don't understand.'

She sighs. 'I mean, maybe you're wired differently. It's like, if you and me didn't talk for four days, how much would you worry about it?'

'Ouch.' I sit up and wipe my face.

'What?'

'Obviously I hope Abbe thinks more about me than you and I think about each other.'

She stands up then, places the crisp bag on the table and says, 'You just said that to me, didn't you,' and turns her back. I say Hanna wait, come back, but she goes to her room. It confuses me but that makes sense since I am so drunk. Even before I met Hanna I knew female friendships were supposed to be intense. Still I had wanted the experience, ached for it. It seems like quite a lot of these womanhood exploits, once you're up in them, they aren't so lovely as all that. These two years in Stockholm, as thrilling as they have been, I would lie if I pretended to not have been bruised.

I go to the bathroom to rinse my mouth.

THE NEXT MORNING, I apologise to Hanna in the kitchen and ask if what I said hurt her feelings, but she is a ray of sun and laughs loudly and says, 'Oh I was just being drunk and dramatic, seriously don't mention it,' and I say okay and hug her and we take the tunnelbana to school together talking about the things we had seen at the ball.

I think we're drinking too much. But also I think we are supposed to at this age?

After class Konrad asks me to wait for him. I help carry his things and we walk together through the ice-cold brick building, making chitchat about the ball. There is no snow yet so the ground is brown outside where the grass used to be. I am careful to stay on the asphalt because I don't want to muddy my white shoes. Maybe Konrad has the same idea because we walk so close our upper arms brush. 'So I wanted to ask you,' he says, 'about your work this semester.'

'It has become a bit shit, hasn't it.'

He scoffs softly. 'I would rather put it as a slow but steady decline. It's still good, just not as good.'

'I think now you're being polite.' We keep walking so we don't look each other in the face.

'I'm just wondering about the cause of it, you know, if you're distracted for a specific reason, because you're sad? Or because you're happy?'

I think about this. At first the decline was because I only wanted to be with Abbe and stay up and have sex and also there had been many social things. It was hard to care as much about studies when I cared more about Abbe. Now it is hard to care so much about studies because I still care more about Abbe, but not in the fun way. And I am also busy writing some other people's essays and making money for Mexico but I can't tell Konrad all that. Diplomatically I say, 'I've been enjoying myself a lot this autumn.'

He sighs, nicely. 'Oh I'm glad, Sickan. I was worried something was up. And I've wanted to tell you this since last time we spoke, that you shouldn't care too much about school, there are other things you know. At your age especially. So, maybe your goal shouldn't be to ace your classes, maybe your goal should be not to?'

Because of the cocktails last night, suddenly I feel a bit sick. I want to sit down right there on the asphalt. 'So this means I'm no longer your best student?'

'It means, you shouldn't care.'

But I do.

I can't stomach the tunnelbana, so I walk even though the air is wet and dismal. 2pm and already dusk. No one else in the entire city seems to be outdoors, the streets echoing my steps and the birds long since fled south. Who can blame them, the wind so hard and mean in my eyes I have to wipe my face many times. Despite the streets being lonely and my stomach so sick, I have enough sense not to call Skåne.

THE WATER IS cold but I don't change the temperature. In my hand the potato feels odd because my numb fingers are not gripping properly. I am peeling one kilo. Mum is next to me, slicing onions and rubbing her eyes, hunching her back more than usual.

'You look tired mum,' I say. 'You shouldn't work so late.'

'I'm just fine.' She wipes a wisp of hair off her face with the back of her hand. The radio plays Christmas choral music and the old speakers rasp at the high notes. I am tired from working late too but maybe on me it's not so visible. I need to write Petra's ethics essay on artificial intelligence IP. Also I have PMS cramps. 'Why don't you take a pause,' I say. 'Lie down a while.'

'That's nice, but there's a lot to do still.'

We are making a Janssons frestelse gratin. Tomorrow is julafton and I arrived late last night. We have agreed to make this year's Christmas a simple affair. It is our first winter without grandma and she was a Christmas person but my parents are not. I am not sure what I am yet.

'It's okay I will finish the Janssons, and the rest is not so much.'

'Maybe just for an hour then, thank you Siv.' She moves towards the kitchen door and as she passes behind me I can tell she stops. I don't pause my peeling. After a few seconds she leaves the room.

I am glad to be alone in the kitchen. The pale noon sun sends shafts across the floor, low and slanted as if dusk. Soon the sun will recede behind the neighbour's house and by three the sky will be dark again. There is no snow but the naked tree branches have a delicate film of frost.

It is a respite to concentrate on preparing food because it has been taxing to keep my face looking happy. Whenever mum and dad sense I am in not a nice mood I worry they will think it's because of them. In the past it sometimes was because of them, but today it is not. Today it is because I haven't heard from Abbe in two weeks.

Numbly I rummage the peels for any straggling potatoes but it seems I have peeled them all. I rinse my cold hands and pat them dry. Up on a high shelf in the pantry is the food processor. I climb a chair and then plug in the machine on the counter.

Without wanting to I check my phone for notifications before replacing it in my trouser pocket. The morning after the Lucia ball I sent him a photo of me and Hanna all dressed up. I was so certain he would say we look nice together that I didn't start to fret until that evening. Since then there has only been fretting. He never did reply. It is not pride, the reason I haven't texted again or called. It is fear. I know this is the moment where if I push he runs.

I check again. No notifications.

I grate the potatoes in the food processor then finish slicing the onions mum left on the counter. They are very potent and soon I am crying too. I hum along to the radio.

The oven whirrs when I twist the knob and I hold my hands close to the grill where it is warm. The Janssons frestelse doesn't need many ingredients. I place them in a row on the counter. Margarine, oat cream, capers, salt and pepper, breadcrumbs. When I open the packet the crumbs have morphed into a loaf and the expiration date says two years ago. I need tampons anyway.

After turning the oven back off, I pour myself a small snaps from the bottle in the freezer. I sit at the table and sip, my shoulders folded forward. The alcohol hurts my stomach but otherwise it is good. In the hallway I put on my cap. Then I wrap a scarf tightly so it covers my chin and mouth.

It is miserable outside. Here in the south it rarely snows on Christmas, but always there is the wind. Wet, punishing. Sometimes there is hail that pricks your skin, turned horizontal by the gale. Now the ground is bare but slick and my feet crackle on the anti-slip gravel. It is two o'clock but looks like six.

In the ICA I take a basket although I am not buying much. There are Christmas decorations here and there, scruffy from many years of being packed and unpacked. I get compostable tampons in regular size because they are out of large size and then I go searching for breadcrumbs.

It takes some time to find them because I am distracted. I am wondering whether Abbe will wish me god jul tomorrow because if he doesn't I will know it is not about his studies. If you are in love with someone or if you care about them you will always wish them god jul on julafton, I strongly believe this. The shop seems warm after the cold outside so I unwrap my scarf and push it into the basket and cool my cheek with my hand.

Finally I find the breadcrumbs on the bottom shelf in an aisle I have walked up and down twice already. I crouch and search for the own-brand packet and while I sit there on the floor someone says, 'Siv, hej!'

Instantly my nerves bristle.

I look up and lose my balance, placing a hand on the floor. Above me is an adult version of Jocke, my classmate whose father killed himself. It is pure reflex, the three seconds reminding myself what I am wearing and what my hair and face might look like. I place the breadcrumbs in the basket and absurdly I am thankful the shop had been out of large tampons. I stand up and say, 'Hej?' like a question. And I wonder if I could get away with it, simply pretending I don't know him.

He points at himself. 'Jocke Lindqvist. You don't remember me?'

'Jocke, yes. Hi.'

'So how the hell are you, I heard you moved up to Stockholm?' He angles his feet outwards and folds his arms as if making himself comfortable.

'Yes, a few years now.'

'Åhus's not good enough for you?'

I say nothing. I fear he might see the scar on my left hand gripping the basket. A long white line along my ring finger and up the back of my hand which whenever I look at, makes me think of Jocke.

'I'm only joking,' he says now. 'I'm sure you're doing great things up there.'

And I can't reply, I just stand there.

Here he is, the rightful recipient of my controlled anger. I can tell him this. If I want to I can get the weight off me and on him. Out of everyone, it's him. Not my parents, not Hanna. Him.

I say nothing.

Now he is not so comfortable anymore. He drops his arms. 'Anyway, I should get going. God jul yeah?' He walks past and casually pats me three times on my bicep, each tap an earthquake. He turns a corner and the aisle is empty. I walk straight to the self-service checkout without turning my head. I pay for the crumbs and tampons and I don't wait for the receipt and I don't look behind me as I exit through the automatic doors.

Was Jocke pretending or does he actually not remember? Is it at all possible that his memories are so fundamentally different to mine? No, impossible. Stunning that he was able to talk to me just now, like normal. As if nothing.

But of course, I have left no white line along his ring finger. He has no reminder.

I put the tampons in one pocket and crumbs in the other and lean into the wind. I walk back home to the maracas of crumbs on cardboard.

UNDER THE TREE I place two wrapped gifts. I usually place three but this year grandma is dead. I try not to notice her almost audible absence, the lack of saffron smell and routine touching. I also try not to think about the twelve thousand-kronor bills.

I look over at the hand-me-down antique sideboard and no one has put out the bowl of nuts and wooden nutcracker. Since she died this is the most I have missed her, the house feels like a body without a beat.

Today is julafton and as per tradition we have watched Donald Duck on TV, at no one's insistence. I am setting the table for three and dad boils potatoes and Brussels sprouts. The Janssons frestelse is in the oven for reheating and it is the only thing not storebought this year. Even the rödbetssallad, although none of us can stand it prepackaged, the beets overcooked, too sweet.

We are all wearing aprons. Mum and dad have thick socks on and my feet are cold in stockings because I have dressed up. Grandma always wore heels indoors even when it was not jul because her tendons were too short.

By the time I untie my apron, hand it to dad, and sit down at the table it is 5pm. I still haven't heard from Abbe.

While mum gets the snaps and glasses from the freezer and dad hangs our aprons I send a text before I can think.
God jul Abbe!

And then, *Wish I was up there with you not down here in stupid Skåne.*

My stomach is cramping but no period yet. The checkmarks tell me the messages have been delivered but not read. When we eat I try being Christmas-spirited because we see each other so rarely and they should see me happy and not worry.

After the first course mum says, 'Are you alright Siv?' and this throws me.

'My stomach hurts,' I say, grateful for the cramps.

'Why?' dad asks.

'Just PMS.'

Mum says that's tough, and dad gets up from the table. I chew a piece of beetroot. Dad comes back with a white oblong pill and I swallow it with my spiced julmust. He nods, once. Although the pill takes twenty minutes to work the cramp is easing already.

After clearing the table we exchange gifts. There are two under the tree that weren't there this morning which means they haven't forgotten. I give mum a porcelain teapot with a tealight stand because she is a great tea drinker when she works and complains about it cooling.

For dad, a heavy-duty flashlight because he walks at night. He gets uncharacteristically excited and reads the miniature instruction booklet for several minutes. I have wished for textbooks because they are goddamn expensive. I also get a memoir by some important man I don't know but dad thinks I should read. Mum and dad don't give gifts to each other. He says she is the biggest gift in and of herself and we all roll our eyes.

I collect and fold the wrapping paper to recycle. Dad says, 'Should we take it for a spin?' and clicks the flashlight.

On the beach the wind is worse. It is lucky we have dressed in layers and hats. Dad walks ahead of us and the flashlight is remarkable, we see everything. He flashes light here and there and we follow the beam with our eyes. There are whitecaps on the sea and the sand is wet so we leave footprints in arbitrary curlicues. It is hard to talk in the wind. We use loud voices but no one else is here because why would they be in the punishing weather at eight thirty on julafton. Tomorrow I will go home to Stockholm.

Mum steps badly and grabs my arm for support. I hold out my elbow for her to hook her arm through but she doesn't, she lets go and points at the shaft of light. I drop my elbow back down. Dad is now directing the light straight up into the sky. Above him are tiny specks, momentarily flashing white before rushing on in the wind. 'Look it's snowing,' mum says. And although it isn't snow, it's hail, I say, 'Oh yes will you look at that.'

In the house, after locking the toilet door, pulling down my trousers, and sitting down to pee, I take out my phone once more. No notification. I replace the phone in my pocket and refuse any emotion. When I wipe, the tissue turns red.

MY FEET ARE deaf with cold. It is nyårsafton, 23:00, minus eighteen degrees. I am wearing loafers and worry I might lose toes.

'Okay so he's a bastard not picking up his phone,' Noor says. I shrug my shoulders and stamp my feet. Hanna says nothing, preoccupied with the map on her phone.

We have been searching these houses for twenty minutes. Up and down ploughed streets lined with crystalline snow piles. The houses all look the same, same pastel colours, same rosehip bushes and obsolete white satellite dishes. But we have not heard or seen a party.

We should have stayed at Lottie's. Elaborate cocktails, toasting the new year at twelve, maybe some games, then falling asleep to whatever black and white film. Waking up not terribly hungover and eating fresh breakfast with berries instead of the slimy pizza. But Noor got a text from Pontus and we knew there was no stopping her when she said, 'I'm going,' and so the night took a turn.

Hanna and I went with Noor. Lottie and her new tall girlfriend didn't seem to mind staying behind. Now I think of them in the flat, Champagne, ice cream and cloudberry sauce, public service television, feet nice and warm. My left loafer has a tear in the back seam.

There are two reasons I followed Noor on this bus trek from the southern suburbs to the north-west newbuilds. Firstly, I wouldn't want her crossing the whole city by herself. Secondly, I know who else will be at the party.

I didn't text him to ask, but if Pontus is there, Abbe will be. I have not seen him in five weeks, not heard from him in three. I am not even sure I want to see him but of course I really really do.

'Should we just go home?' Hanna asks, her voice shivering. She is wearing a thin coat. I go over to rub her arms. My legs are in nothing but nylon but at least my coat is long and padded.

'You are joking I hope?' Noor says to Hanna. 'It took us an hour to get here, if we leave now, do you want to count down to midnight on a bus?' She sounds irritated and I feel her frustration is misplaced.

'No need for testiness,' Hanna says and I remember I never really have to defend her. Since our night at the theatre Hanna has decided she likes Noor and now they get along famously. Sometimes I think they are even better suited as friends and this is a little unnerving.

There is a slight sting in my small toe and then it dies. Minus eighteen is not to mess around with. I start to worry in earnest. I picture taking off the stiff loafer, rolling down my stockings, seeing the frostbitten black knob that used to be my toe. I dread getting inside, growing warm again, feeling the surviving toes get the tingle then the heat then the unbearable pain of nerve reanimation. Like local shocks of electricity.

'Okay you know what it's fine I'll call Abbe,' I say. They look at me, take in the largeness of what I have just said. Noor nods. Hanna smiles gently.

The dial tones are like a warning. Hang up, they tell me. It's not too late, hang up before he answers. But what about the missed call notification, I think. He will know anyway. Besides. It is either this or the toe.

'Hello, is that you,' he says.

'Yes. I'm here. I think.'

'Here? You're here?'

'I think so. But we can't find you.' And then to make sense, 'Pontus invited Noor. I came too.'

'Oh. I'm sorry, Pontus is completely packed. Running all over the place.'

I wonder why this conversation is so hard, somehow lagging. The many small pauses make me nervous and I am not sure anymore if I want to see him. But of course, I really do.

'Where are you, exactly?' he asks.

'Sirapsvägen thirteen.'

'Wait there, I'll come get you.'

He will come get me.

I put my phone in my coat pocket and blow on my hands and Hanna squeezes my shoulder like I just lost a match but at least with good effort.

Then we see them, slowly approaching down the street, Abbe one head shorter than Pontus. Pontus swaying a little, thumping into Abbe who routinely holds out an arm to steady him. When Pontus notices us he jogs in our direction, picks up speed. Abbe keeps to a walk. Pontus reaches Noor and lifts her up. 'Well aren't you pretty,' he says. Noor can't choose between laughter or indignation so she attempts both. But I no longer care about them because Abbe is here now, in front of me. He kisses me on the cheek, shyly. 'I'm happy you're here,' he says. If I lose a toe it is worth it.

'So, where's this party?' Hanna asks.

'The party's dead,' Pontus says.

'Yeah, it's quite bad, Pontus shouldn't have told you to come. And they're running out of drink anyway.'

'Then, we could make our own party,' I say. Abbe smiles and his eyes reflect the snow crystals. I wish I knew what he wants because I would give it to him.

He orders a taxi and while we wait I stand as close as I dare without us touching. I can feel his heat through our coats but I am probably imagining. Our mouths breathe smoke. The sky is pitch black and the ground is white and sometimes yellow because of dogs. I almost can't take the many emotions.

I wonder what Abbe did on julafton, who he got gifts from. I reach for his hand and when our fingers meet he brings my hand to his lips and blows lukewarm air. I want to touch his lips, put a finger in his mouth, feel his warm tongue.

He sits in the front of the taxi. Noor is on Pontus's lap and Hanna and I sit tight and still like schoolgirls. My nerves must be triggering hers because she is never like a schoolgirl but tonight she seems afraid to speak lest she says something to ruin things for me. Which means I am not imagining his skittishness. Any small nudge and he might open the car door and simply walk away.

PONTUS LIVES IN a one bedroom in a large building in a new suburb. The house is white and flat like cardboard. In the elevator Abbe doesn't touch me. We stand there perfectly platonic while Noor teases Pontus about his unattractive building. I feel like cardboard too, flattened, and nothing is natural. I want us back to talking a lot saying yes yes exactly to each other. I want his eyebrows to shoot up, him wetting his lips before kissing, his hips pressing me into the mattress. It takes some self-control not to reach for him again. The elevator doors open. Floor seven.

We are shuffling to get our shoes and coats off in the narrow hallway. Pontus takes up most of the space. Abbe hangs his heavy coat on the coat rack, and underneath he is wearing a suit, a real suit. White shirt, black jacket and trousers, skinny tie, the formality only pronounced by his wild curly hair. He sees me staring and shrugs his shoulders, then he smiles. The scar on his cheek appears as it only does when he is smiling, like a dimple. I don't know how he got it.

Without shoes, my numb feet struggle to keep me balanced, the sensation now completely lost. My stockings are black with reinforced toes so I can't tell what colour the small toe is. White, safe. Red, harmed. Black, dead. So I've heard but if that's even true I have no idea.

There is a slight tingle in my footpads. So here we are. Soon the heat, then the pain.

'Hallå,' Hanna says. 'It's eleven fifty.'

This gets Pontus excited and he ushers us to the large living-room windows which he opens fully before going to the kitchen for Champagne and flutes. Up here on the seventh floor there is nothing between us and the fire-works. Close and far away, the flashing lights and the sharp bangs bring the world back to 3D. My chest expands outwards, I see depth again. I think I can see forever. I lean out, rest my hips on the windowsill and spread my arms, sensing Abbe tense next to me, ready to catch hold. The ice-soaked air is fresh but painful to breathe, the moisture in my nostrils freezing solid. I better not cry.

The heat has now almost reached my toes. A red unnat-ural fever beating like a heart. Soon there'll be the pain.

Fireworks are everywhere and the sound is deafening. So many bangs they melt together into one massive roar. The explosions far away are minuscule but minutely detailed, in green, blue, purple, red. Like tiny branches and twigs in the sky. I don't know why we shoot fire-works, why blowing up things is a celebration. But now yes I do feel it. I breathe and smell the gunpowder. It sticks on my tongue and I wonder if I will taste like firework.

We count down from ten and toast gott nytt år and hug in a circle, the five of us. Pontus puts on scatty big band jazz and Noor and Hanna dance a mock Charleston. I lean the small of my back on the sill, cross my arms, watch them dance and I love them. No matter what happens this nyårsafton, Hanna and Noor and I will go home together and eat pizza for breakfast and it will be fine.

'Aren't they great,' I say.

'They're great.' Abbe stands still, his thigh against mine. 'Should we go to the bedroom?'

'Yes.'

He walks ahead and switches on a bedside lamp with an orange shade. I close the door behind me. The jazz spills in but he clicks his phone and soon 'Northern Sky' fills the room. For a moment we just stand there. 'Do you want some more wine?' he asks.

'Yes, why not.'

He leaves for the kitchen and I go to the ensuite. I wash my hands and smell Pontus's selection of cologne. I love the Polo Sport, god help me.

When I return Abbe is sitting on the bed pouring two glasses of Champagne. His tie is loosened. His left foot on his right knee. I get shy. I resolve not to ask where he has been. He will tell me, probably.

I sit next to him. We touch glasses and drink. The fireworks are still exploding but the midnight frenzy is subsiding. There is silence between the bangs now. I finish half my glass in one swallow and the moment it leaves my mouth he wets his lips and he kisses me. His lips are cold from the wine, his tongue is warm and wet and moves inside my mouth. I reach to touch his hair and he pulls me closer until one of my legs is around him. And I wonder what are we doing? He bites me softly. I choose not to ask.

'Do I taste like gunpowder?' I say.

He laughs a bit. 'Sure.'

'You look very nice.' I nod at his clothes.

'Don't tease.'

'I'm not.' I look at my own cheap black dress.

He touches the hem of the skirt, slides his hand up my thigh, lifts the fabric over my head. He stands up and hangs the dress on the back of a chair. I am not wearing a bra. In only my stockings. I resist the urge to fold my arms. He looks at me. And now we laugh a little, both of us. Which is a relief.

He starts taking his jacket off. 'No leave it on,' I say and nod. 'Straighten your tie.' I lean back on my hands and watch him tighten his tie. 'You look good. I like you like this.' He is sexy but also somehow vulnerable in his nice clothes, though I don't tell him that. He comes closer until standing between my knees, my legs angled wide. We drink straight from the bottle. I hope he finds me sexy too. He trails a finger up a run in my stockings.

'Ruined,' I say.

'I like you.'

I feel pain like electricity in my left foot now, outer pad, just slight. We kiss on the bed and his face lights up now and then from the fireworks. I feel the heavier bangs in my chest. I sit up and take his tie off and drop it on the floor. My hands are still cold and his shoulders will be warm. I am unbuttoning his shirt when he takes my hands in his. 'Before you do that,' he says, 'there's something I should tell you.'

I pull my hands back.

'So, something happened.' He stands and backs up. 'Why I haven't been around.'

I sit very still.

'Don't get worried now okay, I'm fine.' He unbuttons his shirt one button at a time. His Adam's apple moves up then down. He pulls the shirt off his shoulders and holds it in one hand. He is covered in bruises.

I close my eyes. I want to speak but I don't. I look at him again and take in the damage.

Horribly, he laughs. 'It looks bad, doesn't it.'

'Yes.'

'I got beat up.'

'I can see.'

'You should have seen me at first. I could barely move.'

I wince.

'Sorry.'

'That's okay,' I say and my voice shakes.

'Do you want to know what happened?'

'Do you want to tell me?'

'Maybe not tonight. Let's keep it light, it's the new year.'

'Sure,' I say slowly. And now the sadness is so heavy I can't take it. I don't know where to look.

'So the last few weeks I've been staying here with Pontus, on the sofa. He's been gone a lot anyway for Christmas. I couldn't see anyone because I was in kind of a bad place, but Pontus has been great.'

I want to ask him where he spent julafton. The urge to comfort him is incredible, but I don't know how. And he doesn't want me to anyway. He wants to keep it light.

'I thought you should know. That I didn't disappear because of, because of you, or us, or something. I just couldn't talk to anyone. Anyway it was a low point. But I am sorry.'

'That's okay. I am sorry too.'

'No don't be, I'm fine now promise. I'm strong.' He smiles and he doesn't look strong, he looks fragile. Soft parts that bruise and hard parts that break.

'Are you going to kiss me or am I too hideous?' he asks.

'Does it hurt?'

'Not to kiss.'

I stand up and go over to him, on feet now full of electricity.

I THINK ABOUT him in Henrik's grandmother's bedroom, his bruised rib. I think about the hockey booth, watching him balance on the barrier talking about being fourteen fifteen. I think about him saying he might have wanted children, but now doesn't. About the look on his face hearing me say those things about Hanna.

MY STOCKINGS ARE still on my legs, I never did take them off. He is in only underwear, his skin warm under the duvet. In the end he decides to tell me anyway, about the bruises. I have entwined his legs with mine, like a braid. I stay mostly silent and he talks. I don't know how to help any part of him. So I stay mostly silent.

'But you walked up to them? Could you not tell what they were?' Now I sit up slowly and he does too. Opposite each other, the duvet over our legs.

'I could yeah. They had flags and leaflets, and the clothes.'

I am wrapping my brain around the fact that a slim brown boy would walk up to six protesting neo-Nazis.

'It didn't dissuade me really, someone had to say something. I mean it's just a beating.' He touches my knee. 'I'm not afraid of that kind of thing, is what I mean.'

I pause, consider my words. 'Because you've had practice.'

'Yeah well. Turns out it's one of those things you get used to.' A thin smile and then a shrug.

'What about your rib that time, drunken football.'

'Yeah sorry it was drunken, but not football.'

I process this information. 'You get into fights?'

'No, I mean, I get into like verbal arguments.' He rubs his neck. 'But yes it has happened that I get beaten up for it. Not like I fight back though,' he says as if highly important. 'I just, kind of, take it.'

But I can't picture it, this lovely person with the brown eyes, I can't see him arguing, with anyone. This is wrong. My chest hurts. I think of his dimple scar. I am rewriting Abbe now and it is devastating.

'Anyway with the Nazis, it had been a rough day and I wanted to speak my mind, and honestly I didn't care that I'd get punched for it.'

I pause. 'So, you are saying, that, what?'

'Yes, I knew it would likely get violent. And I decided I didn't mind.'

'Do you mean, it was on purpose?'

He looks at me then. His eyebrows tense, he moves his head back and searches my face for something. He seems confused, or disturbed.

'Was it on purpose?' I say, my pulse beating my ribs.

He shakes his head a little. 'That's a strange thing to say.' And I know it is done then, the talking. I say sorry I didn't mean, and he waves his hand and retracts to normalcy and the almost eerie openness between us closes again.

He taps his phone for a Peggy Lee song. 'Do you think you can forgive me disappearing like that?'

'Yes,' I say and I mean it, I really think so. Although I can tell my trust is a little scarred. But also, awfully, in the middle of all this I think a clear thought: there was a reason for his disappearance, another than him not liking me anymore.

'Are we still together?' I ask him.

He bites his bottom lip. 'I'm bad at being a boyfriend Sickan.'

'But Abbe, I don't mind!'

He sighs and nods. 'Okay then.' He wipes a rogue tear off my face and changes the subject to new year's resolutions but neither of us have any. I make some up to amuse him and contribute to the normality. Salt consumption. Single-use plastic.

We lie down, close our eyes, talk some more. The fireworks subside and the jazz in the living room stops, the world grows quiet and so does he. I am on my back next to him, our fingers laced. His breath gains weight and slows. And then it is just me. By now the pain in my feet is loud like a scream. It keeps me awake but I am glad for it. Better than the quiet anaesthesia, the fear I've lost them. They were near death earlier but are now coming back to me. Excruciating, but at least not gone.

IT IS EARLY now and I am still awake. His breath is calm and deep so maybe he is sleeping. The sky is black. Soon the light of dawn will show the celebration leftovers. The bottles and cans, plastic firework wrappings, grey craters from children blowing miniature bombs in snow piles.

It is hard to know when night turns into day this time of year. The morning lasts until nightfall, if there is sunlight it is crooked. For months you never fully wake up and it is hard to tell things for certain. It is a brutal thing to force on a human. When the sky is more grey than black, there is a tap on the door. 'Time to go,' Hanna whispers.

Abbe must be awake but his eyes are closed. The atmosphere is different in this reluctant daytime and I wish he would give me my cue. I unbraid myself from him. He opens his eyes.

'Did you sleep?' I ask.

'A little. You?'

'I think they want to leave. You go back to sleep.'

'I'll walk you to the station.' He stretches his arms then stands up and reaches for his trousers and even in the winter half-light his bruises are stark. Last night they were black but now they are many colours. Green, blue, purple, red. Exploding on his body like tiny branches and twigs.

He sees me staring. He doesn't say anything. Neither do I. Instead I go to the bathroom and scrub a little at the black makeup under my eyes. I wash with water under my arms, rinse my mouth, then drink many times from my cupped hand.

We put on our coats and I force my feet into the hateful loafers. The pain is gone and the sensation mostly back, I keep balance just fine. The overground station is a short walk away. My phone says minus sixteen, no wind.

Outside is sort of postapocalyptic, nothing but empty bottles and firework packaging to show we were here. A powder snowfall sometime during the night has covered it all like dust, as if last night's waste is centuries old. Noor is laughing about how hungry she is and lists the different foods she will eat today. I am shattered and a little nauseous.

Abbe and Pontus are walking behind us, I can't hear what they say. I want to walk with Abbe while holding his hand. Even though it is too cold for packsnow I scoop some up and try to pack a snowball. I don't succeed and the snow cascades like powder onto Abbe's face. I laugh and so does he, a little, politely, and he dusts the snow off his face and he looks sad. The others are staring at us, this strange scene. I don't know what I thought his reaction would be but it is not this. I feel the flush up my neck and cheeks.

Normally Abbe would be the one throwing snow, so energetic and over-caffeinated he can't sit still. I would be the one waving him away. 'You looked like you needed a cooling off,' I say but I can't smile. And I know to give it up. He takes my hand and tries to make it good, walking together to the station, talking about normal things.

They wait with us for the train. When it arrives, we hug goodbye. I stay in the hug as long as I can.

On the train I sit opposite Hanna and Noor. Before they ask a thing I hold on to my shoulders, try to breathe, and say, 'It feels like I'm being crushed.'

IN THE FLAT on Artillerigatan Hanna makes sparkling water in the machine and puts glasses on the coffee table while

Noor takes a shower. I just sit there on the sofa, unhelpful, filled with a tenderness so acute it is painful. I wonder if him showing me his bruises from getting into fights is an invite to grow closer or a warning to stay away.

Noor walks in wearing Hanna's sweatshirt. I go to the bathroom. With the door closed I hear Hanna ordering pizza and setting plates and Noor turning on the TV and talking loudly about something. The mirror is covered in steam and it is still warm in here from Noor's shower. I sit on the toilet lid and flex my feet. No pain now. I roll my stockings down my thighs, over my knees, down my shins. I look first at my right foot. It is bright pink, as if scalded, not frozen. When I touch the skin it feels hot. They are fine. Then I take a breath, brace myself, and roll the stocking off my left foot. Which is just as pink and hot. No black. Two toes are still numb. I pinch them hard and feel a tingle in one. But the smallest toe is completely silent. Maybe I never will get the sensation back, the nerves dead and lost. They say the small toe is important for balance and I wonder if I will stumble more now than before.

ONIONS ARE SIZZLING in a pan and then the smell of garlic. The knife cutting through tomatoes makes a steady knock on the wooden board. I asked to help but have been planted on a stool with a glass of red wine, while Hanna moves around putting things in her mouth and generally getting in the way of her sister, Viveka. It is coal black outside which is a shame because I want to see the stairs leading down the cliff to their private deck into the sea below. What I want is summer, the sun still up and swimming before dinner.

It is my first time meeting Viveka and seeing her home, although Hanna has described it to me with much humour. Bohemia-posing she called it and I see her point. The oddly shaped furniture, the whimsical art, the colour clashes seem chosen with careful deliberation passed off as inspired spontaneity.

It was a nightmare getting here. Viveka's house is in a steep part of the archipelago, over bridges and up ice-slick roads. Hanna said let's do bus instead of taxi because the bus will be safer. Still, the large vehicle had moved forward with great hesitation and every time it opened its doors the air flooding in was bone-shivering.

We are ten days into January and like every January in this country there is wintersickness in the air. People not normally contemplating suicide picture it, a collective consideration, before brushing it aside once remembering that by end of March the clock will turn forward and from there on it's really just one joyous freefall towards summer and the midnight sun.

Viveka is telling me a childhood story about Hanna, how she would give away her toys to classmates to make her look like a good girl but how Viveka saw through it as a clandestine ploy to get new toys. Hanna says, 'I'm not embarrassed by this story try again.' To me it seems Viveka hadn't tried to embarrass Hanna but to make me feel welcome by way of having Hanna in common.

Viveka doesn't have children but she has a husband who is expected by the time the pasta is al dente. Hanna has told me Viveka and Calle want children but can't have any and this is a thing no one mentions in the family. It makes me view Viveka differently. Like her sociability and good humour come with a tinge of blue. I like her a lot. She is warm and makes me feel at home in the large steel house on the cliff. My limbs are loose. I am happy here. Hanna smiles at me like a question and I shake my head a little to say no, nothing.

After stirring the sauce Viveka tastes it straight from the ladle and offers some to Hanna. Then she spoons up more and reaches the ladle across the kitchen island for me to taste, a hand underneath for drips. I blow on the tomato sauce and it is hot and garlicky. The three of us in turn licking the ladle has a touch of the communion.

Leaning over the island, Viveka looks so much like Hanna it is stunning, I can't stop staring. The same muscular build, the same clean broad face with the perfect eyebrows. But in a loose white shirt and hair a slick neck-bun, she is a scaled back, elegant version of Hanna. Hanna the caricature of Viveka. I imagine it must be painful, being a messier version of someone who is right there for constant comparison. I remember what Hanna said, that having a sister is not so great.

I love Hanna. I love her naked armourless warmth, the offbeatness of her, even when she is annoying and sometimes because she is annoying. But I can see that for most people, Viveka would be the easier pill.

Calle comes home and I am sure he is fine although he does make me instantly more timid. I would prefer to be with just Hanna and her sister. I want to see more of them interacting because I am curious whether I'm still aching to have a sister of my own or if that part is over.

The food smells nice and there is bread with walnuts inside it. The pasta itself is simple, tagliatelle with tomato sauce, large pieces of mushrooms and courgette. I don't know why the simplicity makes it more luxurious but it does, which is something I have noticed often around rich people.

We drink wine moderately and Viveka's husband Calle is dry-humoured and oscillates between giving us neo-liberal and conservative everyday observations. There is a social democrat journalist living down the street who Calle has thoughts on. Hanna openly makes fun of him which both Viveka and Calle appear to enjoy.

When I go to the bathroom there is an infrared sauna and a freestanding bathtub and somewhere in the room there are speakers because the Fela Kuti song reaches me here too, while I wash my hands.

And who also reaches me is Abbe. I get texts.

SINCE NYÅRSAFTON WE have been in touch a lot. We talk on the phone and have seen each other three times, communicating only in sweet anecdotes and what we had for lunch, no difficult things. We have kissed but not naked. There is a new mood, a softspoken carefulness. As if we have survived some catastrophe together, a shipwreck or a plane crash, and are now back in normality processing the absurd fact that life is still going on.

After a lecture on online harassment, I read about Freud saying that meaningless trauma sometimes makes people deliberately put themselves in similar situations again and again, as if looking for clues, trying to grasp any at all meaning in the senseless. Adrenaline junkieness, toxic relationships, physical altercations, a perpetual loop of pain. I think of myself and of Abbe, our individual brands of bad situations. I can't even imagine putting myself back there on purpose, in school. Then again, this is only what Freud says and he was wrong about many things so maybe we are fine. Also, I know about victim-blaming and I don't want to do that to Abbe or to anyone.

I am worried about him. I want to shake him and say please stop this because he was supposed to be the well-adjusted one. I keep picturing it, the crack of his ribs, the hateful slurs. Do I wish he hadn't told me? And what I have been thinking is, can I handle it happening again? But we don't talk about this. We talk about cats with human voices and the actual weather and he hasn't teased me once. I have yet to solve how to get back to us before the big house party, when we confided things and whatever I said he said yes yes exactly. I think I have to give it time probably. Or maybe I have ruined it, making him like me less by being cruel to Hanna. It feels surreal I said that about her and I don't like thinking about it and still I keep thinking about it.

But now Abbe has texted me. I dry my hands and unlock my phone. He says, *Do you want to come over?* And then, *Bring a condom.*

I feel a pulse between my legs. My thighs contract. I wonder how long I have to stay at dinner to not be rude. I look up bus routes on my phone. It will take me almost an hour to get to Abbe's and also I don't have a condom.

I reapply makeup to cover my flushed face. By the table I say I'm sorry I have to go very soon, something important has come up. Viveka says we better serve dessert then, and I eat the tiramisu although I don't want it, the coffee cream thick on my tongue. With the phone in my lap I text Hanna, *Do you have a condom?*

In an exceptional act of bastardliness she smiles sweetly and says, 'No I don't,' out loud.

Viveka says, 'You don't what?'

'Maybe ask Viveka,' Hanna says. 'I'm sure she'd be happy to help with your important thing that just came up.'

I carefully put down my spoon in the dessert bowl and remove the napkin from my lap. 'That's okay. Thank you so much for dinner and sorry again to rush off, I feel rude.'

Viveka doesn't look at me, she looks at Calle. 'To be twenty-two,' she says and he grins and even my ears are red, I can feel them.

I wait for the bus in the ice-cold air and my body is dizzy with the possibilities, all of them.

ALTHOUGH WE HAVEN'T talked about the future lately my Mexico City preparations are progressing. I have been accepted to an intensive Spanish summer course and there are two software master's in English I could take in autumn, if I want to prolong my stay. I spend hours looking at flats in different areas and then research which areas best combine vibrant and safe. High on the safe–vibrant axis are Roma and Polanco and San Rafael, according to the forums. I am nervous but many young people move there and then stay because they love it so much. Most of all I am curious to find out if I will be one who loves it so much. Twenty-two million people. Twice of Sweden in one city. I don't know how this is possible or what it means in practicality. But I will be one of them.

The Spanish summer course costs some money but I am saving ruthlessly. Students come to me to cheat and I have no scruples taking their money. I find every available short-cut and it feels like I am writing one essay over and over. Same format, just different keywords. Confident sentences a camouflage for topical ignorance.

It is not sustainable, I know this. When I turn off the desk lamp at night my head feels boiled, my eyes too large for their sockets.

Also my own studies are suffering but I don't care that much anymore and I wonder why I ever did care so much? Perhaps it's what Abbe and I talked about in the hockey booth, your adult identity being informed by your childhood talents. Sports, studies, social competence. So far I have never been able to picture academic failure or mediocrity but ever since Mexico City my Swedish university career seems a thing of negligible importance. Maybe my identity is changing from studious to something else, I don't know. School has started looking more like memory than present moment. I walk the corridors but I am not really there.

HE IS WAITING for me in a heavy winter jacket and mittens. The bus doors open and the snow swirls everywhere, sticking to my eyes and lashes. I feel self-conscious even though I checked my makeup and teeth in the compact mirror on the bus. I get off and he places his mittens as a frame around my face and we kiss and I bite his lip a little. The bus ride has been long. Although I have brought no condom there are morning-after pills in the bathroom cabinet on Artillerigatan. It will be nice this way anyway, nothing between us.

His flat smells the same as usual, his kitchen table is empty and there are dishes drying on the rack. My socks are wet at the toes. It is so intimate, this scene, that I can't tell if comforting or heartbreaking. No music is on but I hear the TV.

He asks if I want something to drink and I say later. He says, 'We should talk,' and I say, 'Abbe, later.'

I walk up to him leaned against the counter and I kiss him. I take my time. His hands are low on my back and I push my hips forward. We know each other already, we know how to do all this, and right now I don't care about anything else.

He is on top of me and although we move slowly it is intense, almost brutal. I breathe so hard I feel drunk. I push my hips off the bed to get closer, he sits up and lifts my waist. We have not had sex in weeks. This is not how I remember it. This feels large, naked, we are being very serious. I grip the pillow under my head and he holds my arms then my shoulders and then around my neck and he pushes into me. His grip isn't hard, I can breathe fine, so maybe it is the newness of it or the intensity but I think I might come. Then he looks at me and suddenly pulls his hands back and says fuck sorry I didn't mean to do that. He looks taken out of it. Again he says sorry, and I say no it's fine don't stop I want to finish. He lifts my hips and I put my hand on his stomach and then I use my fingers and almost instantly I come. Then I come again when he does. When he pulls out I calculate how many hours I can safely stay before taking the pill at Artillerigatan.

He pours hot water from the kettle, places two cups of Ceylon on the kitchen table, and sits opposite me. My naked feet are cold and I hug my knees to my chest. Some loose hair tickles my face. 'I'm happy you're here,' he says and I say, 'I love you.'

He is quiet for an endless second then he says, 'I love you too,' and my heart now races and I can feel it, the nerve bristle.

I tell him, 'We don't have to talk. It's nice to just sit here.'

'I think we should talk.'

'But, Abbe I'm tired now. Maybe just sit.'

He looks at me squarely as if deliberating. Then he says, 'I have some news.' I close my eyes for him to stop but he doesn't. 'I talked to my supervisor and they're okay with me writing my thesis from Mexico. I can go early, in late February.'

'Late February.' I wonder if I have to be happy for him but I think not because he looks miserable. 'Is there a reason you want to leave early?'

He holds his shoulders. 'Honestly, I'm dying here. Like, I can't stand it.'

My eyes burn. 'But why. Why is it so bad?'

'I don't know.' He twists his teacup left then right. 'Sorry I really don't.' He wipes his face and looks at me. 'But you'll visit in the summer, it's not so long till then.'

I want to ask, what do you mean by visit.

'And I'll already have so many places to show you and I'll already have a flat sorted, and you'll get a nice Mexican tan to show off at school next term.'

'Oh no,' I say and he looks at me with such alarm, such pleading, I say, 'I don't tan.'

He smiles faintly and nods in recognition of my charity, my not causing a scene.

And it seems I have finally learned it, the correct use of niceties and vagaries, the kindness of treating difficult conversations as if easy.

'I can't stay,' I say. 'I have to take the pill.'

'Right.' He stands up. 'Listen, we still have weeks. And then the whole summer.'

In the hallway we don't kiss we hug and then I take a taxi home that Abbe pays for with his app which only makes everything worse.

Hanna is staying over at Viveka's so the apartment is blessedly dark and still. In the bathroom cabinet are two packs of emergency contraception.

I look at the purple letters on white cardboard and god help me for a moment I consider.

Then I slap my face, hard.

I push the single pill through the foil and swallow it with water from the tap before opening another pack and pushing another pill and swallowing this as well.

I sit on the lid and pull my knees tight and bite my hand and breathe. I stop thinking about anything. It doesn't matter, my face turns wet just the same. I stay where I am until the stomach cramps start.

I AM IN the backseat of a Saab SUV, two men to my left, two men in the front seats. I have broken my primary rule of hitchhiking. They are drunk, as am I, although it is not late, only eight thirty. We make jokes together and the speakers play one of the DJs.

It is the day after the morning-after pill and it has not been a good time. I needed to get out of the rooms on Artillerigatan so I walked straight through Gärdet to Frihamnen harbour with the cruise ships. It was good to walk with all the adrenaline in my thighs and I wanted to do something drastic so I took the first car that stopped at my thumb. They've told me their names but I can't remember. Doesn't matter. There has been a sports match, a momentous one to win or join a league, and the four men are now driving home to Uppsala. Their excitement about their team destroying the other team is unflattering but infectious.

The man next to me, Tim I think, hands me a can of beer which tastes good. I am thirsty so I drink most of it without coming up for breath. Outside the swishing of scenery evokes the familiar sense of freedom from no one in the entire world knowing where I am. I have come to the conclusion that I have not much to lose. I breathe in and feel lightheaded.

I think Tim is making advances and there is much too much energy in the car but my nerves are so wrecked I don't get alarmed. I feel good, I do.

Then Tim pinches my waist. 'Stop,' I say and twist away from him.

'Why?' He pinches me again and comes closer, his lips wet. The other men are watching our display with that specific tension, the need for something to happen. I know this scene. It is threatening, the tension, the size of his body, but I am not frightened.

What I am is angry.

'Did you not hear me?' I say and push his shoulder hard and he says, 'Why are you being weird?' and it floods me then, the rage.

'Stop the car,' I say, loudly.

The driver says what we're on the motorway I can't just at the full strength of my voice I scream

stop

the fucking

car

and I open the back door and the car is moving fast and freezing air hits my face.

EARLIER THIS MORNING I woke to a quiet apartment. I stayed in bed till after noon, then filled a glass of orange juice and lay flat on my stomach on the sofa, the emergency contraception cramps dull echoes of last night. I clicked on the TV but muted it. Replacing its sound was a distinct tick tack, meaning that somewhere was an actual clock. I had never heard the clock before but it must have always been here hidden among the books and glass bowls and stuffed birds. The clock somehow intensified the silence, highlighting the absence of sound after each tick, each tack. It drained my energy.

Paradoxically this sound of time passing made me feel stuck in a perpetual moment, and if I stayed here not moving the world would not either. I couldn't lift my limbs anyway. It was Tuesday but the TV showed Sunday morning mass, the church near empty. It was one of the loneliest I've been. I texted Hanna.

I'm stuck.

She replied.

On my way home be there in fifteen.

Soon her keys in the lock and after searching my face worriedly she sat on the floor with her back against the sofa. Her hair was newly washed and incredibly fine, like a baby's. And she was here. In the room with me. I breathed a little deeper.

'Yes church on mute is always a good time.'

'Do you hear it?'

'What?'

'Ticking.'

'No. Maybe?'

'Do we own a clock?'

'I mean, we might.'

'Why aren't you in class?'

'Cancelled. You?'

'Skipping. I'm acting out.'

'Huh.'

We stayed like that, just sitting.

Finally she said, 'Did something happen last night?'

'Oh no, I'm not talking about it.'

She finished what remained of my orange juice while I breathed slowly in and out two times. The glass clinked on the table. 'You spooked him?' she asked, gently.

I closed my eyes and hated all of this. 'I didn't know I was so frightening. Why, I mean why am I?'

She sighed deeply. 'It's nothing to do with you. He was always going to get spooked, is what I think.' She kept looking at the TV. 'This isn't like a barometer on how easy or hard you are to love Sickan.' She took my hand and massaged my knuckles and I was comforted by her sheer presence.

'Maybe he'll come around,' I said.

'Yeah.'

I was still on the sofa when she left for the library. For the remainder of the muted mass and long after I considered her words, that it had nothing to do with me. But I couldn't believe this. I wondered where it came from, her need to reassure me I wasn't hard to love. I hadn't said I was. It felt like she'd assured me I looked fine before I even asked do I look ugly in this. So, likely I looked ugly.

Mimicry had been my defence mechanism since coming to Stockholm. A copy, that's what I was trying for. I had made friends. I was in a relationship with a beautiful person. But the worry I felt, of him dating me for the novelty, today it seemed true. Because it looked like he was pulling away. I was too big a bite to comfortably swallow and the thing about novelty, it wears off.

I dreaded it but I needed to know, finally, why I was too big to swallow. What, exactly, was wrong with me.

The only time I had been told straight to my face was back in school.

In the desk drawer was my notebook. I hadn't touched it in months and picking it up I ran a hand over its cardboard cover. All dialogues I had written were overheard conversations, strangers talking about things that didn't matter to me. Not once had I written down my own conversations. I never thought back to school in Åhus because I had buried it, forgotten the details, the exact words. But now I was going to look at it, that's what I was going to do. The details, in exactness.

I filled pages. It came back so easily, as if not buried at all but simply left under the top layer of skin. I moved on from kaffe to red wine. The cramps or the writing made me nauseous so I didn't risk eating. My head swarmed with words and self-loathing and humiliation. Picking the scab of a wound that refused to heal. I wanted to glue it sealed or burn it clean once and for all, let it scar.

When I put down my pen, the wine bottle was empty. I knew I should give it a rest, take a shower, close the notebook unread. Eat something. Instead I filled a tumbler with vodka and read the whole thing through.

I didn't trust my memory, no saying how many of these words had ever been uttered. I thought about running into Jocke at ICA, him acting as if nothing had happened. I had a scar on my hand he may or may not remember giving me. And it hit me then, that no one had acknowledged it happening. Ever. No one had once said I saw that, that was bad.

Now reading my notes back, yes a pattern did emerge.

Disgust, that's what it was.

Flaky skin. Bad breath. Unclean home. Idiot speech. Charity clothes, ugly parents, many speculations on genitalia deformations. It was amazing to me, how clear it was. How I had wondered all this time what it was about me, specifically, that made me not fit and it was right there. I was disgusting. To other people. My skin was clear, my speech intelligible, my genitalia completely fine. But there was something wrong with me, as a person. And other people could tell. I had brushed my teeth, dressed better, but they just found something else. Because the core of me was repulsive. I couldn't do anything to change this, not hide it with clothes or slang.

The only one who loved the real me, not the copy, was Hanna. And it was because she was wrong too.

I was hot, my armpits wet, my top lip salty. Without the rasping of pen on paper the silence came back, intensified by the ticking of the clock. It made me fall apart, that sound. I was stuck. I was still in Åhus. I never really left.

I CRAWL FURTHER into the field, my hands and knees cut on the frozen mud. I hear stop the fucking car echo in my ears. He had stopped, the driver, letting me stumble out onto the motorway, before driving home to Uppsala. Now I am in the field and I am dizzy. My muscles contract and I vomit red liquid until my stomach is emptied and the retching turns dry. My head is tilting and my face is wet from tears and snot but I have no tissue. I don't have a bag. I feel my pocket and yes I have a phone. The screen lights up, a text from Abbe. *Hey just watching the game with Pontus but maybe talk later?*

It is Tuesday, it's not 10pm and I am not in the corridor, but still I scream the anxiety out of me until my lungs turn raw.

MY PHONE RINGS. Mum. I don't pick up. I am on my back and can smell the vomit next to me but I am not cold yet because of the vodka. I wipe my face with my coat sleeve. My throat hurts from acid and screaming.

The phone rings again.

I don't want to answer but her ringing twice could mean something is wrong.

'Mum, what's wrong?'

'What's wrong?'

'Yes, what's wrong.'

'Why is something wrong?'

'You called me twice.'

'Ah, yes, I thought maybe your phone was in another room and you didn't have time to pick up before it rang out.'

I take a long indulgent breath. 'Mum, no one is that far away from their phone anymore.'

'Your voice sounds bad.'

'It's just hoarse from screaming.'

'The football?'

'What do you know about the football?' I say.

'The neighbours were shouting so I assumed football.'

I tsss and the utter absurdity of the situation is not lost on me. Here I am in a frozen field somewhere between Stockholm and Uppsala, slurring with alcohol and snot caked on my coat sleeve while my mother is filling the kettle for tea, I can hear her.

'Mum?'

'Yes.'

'How come you stayed in Åhus?'

'Why not. It's a nice enough place.'

'Yes but you grew up there, you see people you went to school with at ICA.'

I hear scratching of chair legs and her telling Malin to get off the table. 'So?'

'I always thought you didn't have a nice time. Back in school.'

'I had a decent time. Like everyone else I suppose.'

If I don't say it now I will never say it. 'The other parents used to talk about you. Katrin's mum.'

'Marie-Louise?'

'Yes, Marie-Louise.'

'She was always like that. She's not a nice person.' She blows on her tea. 'But there are rude people everywhere, moving to another town I would just have met other Marie-Louise types.'

'But Marie-Louise, those people, they still see you that way. Like who you were back in school.'

'So do I, I think. I haven't changed that much?'

I close my eyes hard. 'I can't understand why you choose to be neighbours with your bullies. It's humiliating.'

'It's not humiliating, I'm not humiliated.' Quiet for some seconds and then she hmms. 'Maybe if I wanted to be like Marie-Louise. But I never did, she's not a nice person. She likes to gossip. I could gossip about her too but I don't want to.'

'Mum, I'm drunk.'

'The obvious society has taken note.' This is a favourite expression of hers and hearing it makes me miss her. Deep to my core miss her.

'You have gossip on Katrin's mum?'

'We live in the same town.'

'Please?'

'I just told you I'm not a gossip.'

'But oh it would be good for me.'

She sucks her lip a few times. 'Well, apparently Katrin has an online-casino problem.'

'Oh yes that makes sense actually.'

'And she is borrowing money left and right and Marie-Louise had to sell the cottage to pay Katrin's creditors and then Marie-Louise got in touch with that TV show, the Money Trap?'

'The Luxury Trap!'

'Yes that one, and they even considered doing an episode on Katrin but apparently she was so unpleasant on the phone with the producer they didn't want to do it after all.'

The image of Katrin on a debt-clearing show certainly makes me giddy. 'How do you even hear about these things?'

'You know? I have no idea.'

There's a pause and then I say, 'But you are happy then? With how you turned out, as an adult?'

'Mild heaven, I swear you say the silliest things.' I hear her emptying her cup into the sink. 'Eat some bread now, before sleep. Soak up the alcohol.'

'I will. Okay. Thanks mum.'

After we hang up I let myself stay on the frozen mud for twenty solid minutes. I hug myself when I start to shiver. Then I app a taxi and pray I look decent enough to be allowed in.

His foot pumps the pedal and I go up, up, up, up. He looks into the mirror in front of us and ruffles my hair. Then he flaps a black cape over my body and fastens it around my neck.

'You've never bleached or dyed, have you?' he asks.

I shake my head no.

'It's in great shape. We don't have to take much off, maybe just four centimetres?'

I look at my own hair, hanging limp over my chest and stomach. It is light brown or dark blonde. Rat coloured, they say. Midpart, no bangs, straight. Very conventional.

I say, 'Actually I was thinking maybe doing something.' I know it's not recommended, a drastic cut when your heart is aching. But I think it will be a good time to try, see for myself.

'Doing something what?' He speaks youth Stockholmska, many Arabic and Spanish and Turkish slangs, which sounds just lovely. His name is Yuusuf, tall and slim, head shaved. Maybe Somali? Brown shirt tucked into brown trousers, very self-assured. I trust his aesthetic completely.

'I don't know what exactly,' I say. 'Maybe, you tell me, what you think?'

He tilts his head in the mirror and looks at the different parts of my face. This makes me self-conscious but I endure it. There are many other mirrors and chairs in the room, some occupied some not, but my chair is back in a corner so it doesn't feel so exposed.

'Is there one haircut you always want to do but not many have the guts to try?' I say.

He stops and looks into my eyes. 'I have two.'

WHEN HE SHOWS me the first style I begin to change my mind. The photos on his phone are of a seventies round bob, everything smooth and folded in towards the face. Which is not me at all. But I remind myself this is why I am here, because what is me? So preoccupied with not being weird I always err on the side of caution. My clothes and my hair, although perfectly modern, say nothing about my personality. Truth is, I am not sure what my personality is, or if I even have one, after all this time copying others. Today is an experiment, to see if I can find it, my style.

But the seventies bob, I am sure it's not it. I shake my head and hope I don't hurt Yuusuf's feelings.

'Zero worries,' he says and goes back to tapping his phone. 'The next one is better.'

I feel jittery so I sit on my hands.

Yuusuf turns the screen so we can both look. First is a photo of Faye Wong in *Chungking Express*. Then Mia Farrow in *Rosemary's Baby*. Then Jean Seberg in *À Bout De Souffle*. Three women with extremely short hair, sheared so close you can see the head's exact shape. I tap my finger at a photo of Jean Seberg, a cigarette dangling from her lips. 'This one,' I say. 'I think this one.'

'You will crush this cut.'

'Are you sure? I can pull it off?'

'Oh yeah.'

'Very sure?'

'You can pull it, look at me I'm confident.'

'I won't regret it?'

'No you will. At first you will freak a little I think but that's natural. I mean it's identity-shifting this type of trans-formation. But calm, after like two days the shock will pass. You'll feel liberated.' He touches his own shaved scalp.

Liberating, identity-shifting. Maybe this is what I want. And maybe now I don't have time anymore, to worry so much about what others will think. There are mean people everywhere.

I nod my head in assent and Yuusuf cuts my hair off.

THINGS HAVE NOT been normal between me and Abbe, I can see that. Even though the idea is still I will visit him for the summer, we don't talk about it anymore. We sleep together a few times per week and the sex is always nice, if a bit gentle. I don't really like gentle sex, but it is how it is.

I know Abbe is skittish so I have always worried I will startle him and push him away. But this is my opinion: what use is a relationship if I can't ask him straight when I am worried or confused? I don't think that is what a couple should be. Couples should be the most honest. And the least worried. And the least confused.

There is still a chance I can turn it around. The summer is half a year away, a lot can happen. We can grow closer again and forget about this horrible winter. I am certain we can have a wonderful month together in Stockholm, then a spring apart with the video calls, missing each other and being lonely. I will show myself from my best side, and then it will feel natural to be in Mexico. He will be emotional seeing me at the airport. You're here, he'll say. We'll be excited again.

BEFORE I LEAVE the hair salon I want to give Yuusuf a hug because now I feel sentimental. As if to test my identity shift I ask, 'Can I hug you?' and he says, 'Of course you can,' and slaps my back a few times.

'Thank you,' I say, strangely touched by it all.

'This was fun. I will think up ideas we can try next time.'

'Oh! Yes okay, next time.'

And with this hellraising attitude I hit the street and start walking north towards Sergels torg.

The sun is strong but it is only late January so the cold is biting. I pull the lapels of grandpa's coat tight around my neck and walk fast.

Yuusuf had said I would freak out the first two days so I decide to avoid mirrors. Instead I try to notice how I feel. The breeze is everywhere around my neck and the top of my scalp is freezing. My ears have air in them. I understand Bogdan saying it's not so great in winter. I shake my head and nothing happens. I pull a hand through my hair but it just stops. I rub the shortest neck hair and my fingers tingle from friction. Crazy. I can't believe I just did this. I want to show Hanna.

Hanna. I have been an ugly friend, first swallowing my anger, then letting it out behind her back. Someone so vulnerable as her, who might sometimes be clumsy towards me but never on purpose. I think about me moving in, her clearing half the shoe rack for my shoes. Today I will talk to her and come clean. If I lose her I feel it is deserved.

But, I don't want to lose her.

I used to think I wouldn't want her as a sister but now I sort of do. Because one thing about sisters, they don't break up with each other.

I hurry into Hötorgshallen. I buy a hot tea to warm my hands. The market is not busy, I can peruse each food stall and take my time. Everywhere is a new smell. Bread, coffee, garlic, citrus. Fish. Weird cheese. The smoked red muscles of farm animals. I use my tea as smelling salts. At the mushroom stall I buy many kinds on the recommendation of the mushroom woman. Then I find the fresh pasta stall, the vegetable stall that puts your items in small brown paper bags. Still cold, I consider the bus, but decide no I will walk home to Artillerigatan. It gets cold in January, this is something we have to accept, all us Stockholmare.

I HEAR THE door in the hallway. Hanna is home.

It is dark outside and I have set the table, put tulips in a vase, lit the candles. Pasta water on the boil waiting for me to cook the fresh linguini, mushroom sauce ready to reheat. Cooking steam is fogging the windows. Every time I catch my reflection I jump a little, my hair so short I think I see a boy.

Hanna walks in and drops her bag on the floor and then she sees the table setting and stops, surprised, and then she sees me and she also does it, the jump.

'Wow Sickan. You've done it now haven't you?'

Instinctively I touch my neck. 'Do you like it?'

'Obviously! Come here!'

She touches my head everywhere. I touch too, we are shocked.

'Are you happy?'

'I don't know yet. We will see, in a couple of days.'

Before I cook the linguini, we sit at the table and I pour us each a glass of Malbec that has been left to breathe. Hanna hugs a knee to her chest and tastes the wine. I put a leaf from the salad bowl in my mouth. My head is loud with nerves.

'I've never had hair that short,' she says.

I chew the leaf and swallow, then say, 'But Hanna, can I just say, this is my haircut. It is not up for grabs.' I look at her face, awaiting her reaction.

'Oh. I didn't mean. Are you talking about the hat?' She is speaking gently, showing we are far from animosity today.

'Yes about the hat, but other things too.' And so we are having it now, the talk. 'Because, sometimes you are not so good with boundaries.'

'Okay.'

'And I think I go along with too much since I owe you. You have more money and sometimes you pay for drinks and I live in your home, we're not on equal terms. I don't think it's a healthy situation for a friendship.'

'No I hear you. We can create boundaries.'

'And the more I go along without speaking my mind, the more resentment builds up and then it happened that I did something bad that I haven't told you about.'

She takes a deep breath and narrows her eyes. The flickering candlelight throws shadows here and there. 'What did you do?'

'Do you want to know?'

'Yes.'

'You sure?'

She nods.

'At that house party on the west coast, remember I went with Abbe in autumn?'

'You had a bad time.'

'Yes, because I did something. I made a joke about you in front of Pernilla and those people.' I pause to give her a chance to interrupt but she doesn't. 'I said you make yourself look weird on purpose to put people off coming close. Like how broccoli tastes bad to keep rodents away.'

She shakes her head a little. 'You said that?'

'Yes.'

'Wow. Wow, you know, I can't really picture it.'

'It was by the pool. Anyway, I am really sorry.'

'Okay.'

'I should know better, me who's been bullied my whole life.' And I think this is the first time I say it out loud.

She pours herself more wine. 'You know, it wasn't nice what you said.'

'I feel so bad.'

'But you have a point. I do make myself look off-putting on purpose.'

'But, why?'

'Piss off my mother?'

'Actually I think that's why I cut my hair. I've been trying so hard to look a way everyone will like that I don't even know what I myself will like. I am curious what our real style is, if we have one.'

'Yeah. I don't think I know either.'

'Maybe it's hard to know when your wardrobe is filled with your mother's old clothes?'

'I should probably get rid of those.'

I smile and shrug like, maybe.

'God, sometimes I feel my whole life is just a rear-kick reaction. Whatever she expects of me, I do the opposite.'

'Only some things are a rear-kick, not your whole life. And Hanna I think you will always stay very punk, I think this is you. Just maybe less sad punk.'

She laughs a little. 'Thanks.'

I go to the stove and drop the thick strands of linguini into the boiling water. I stir with a spaghetti ladle and am amazed how well we are communicating. 'But I really am so sorry for saying you taste like broccoli.' I set the timer on three minutes and go back to the table. 'And you know, I thought this conversation would be quite different.'

'You're surprised I'm not more upset?'

'Yes. I thought I would really hurt your feelings and maybe you wouldn't want to be friends.'

She sighs. 'Sickan, you're allowed to make mistakes. Like, you're not perfect, I'm not perfect. It doesn't make you a bad person.'

'It was just anger over other things that came out in an ugly way. And that's my fault for not telling you straight away when I felt annoyed.'

'Okay so lay it out for me. What things?'

'Oh.' I purse my lips. 'It's nothing bad. I have just been feeling a little cramped. Like if you walk into my room without knocking. Or you tell my secrets to other people as if they're your secrets. You're not being mean, I think you're just overfamiliar.' I pause a moment. 'How does that sound?'

She rubs her eyes. 'I mean, it's not nice to hear.'

'I don't want to hurt your feelings.'

'I'm not in love with you.' She locks eyes with me and I don't look away. 'Let me be clear, I don't love you that way.'

'Okay.'

'But I do love you. It feels like we're special.'

'I love you too.'

'But it's different.'

'Yes I think because I also love Abbe and Noor and I want to be with different people but maybe you would be happy just being the two of us.'

'I love living with you.' She is not crying because she is Hanna. 'But from all this I gather you're telling me you're moving out.'

In the silence I can hear the pasta water. 'I don't think we would stay friends if I go on living with you. It will be better for us, me living someplace else.'

'I guess you're right even though it doesn't feel right.'

'It will. But, even if we don't live together anymore I wanted to say, if it's true what you told me that time, that you can pick your own family as an adult, I would pick you.'

She looks at me simply. 'I know that.'

In the kitchen I pour the linguini into a colander then onto pasta plates. I stir and scoop the mushroom sauce.

'You look like a movie,' she says, leaned back on her chair taking me in. 'It's a success, that hair.'

I am happy to be serving her food after such a talk. Likely we are both a little shattered but it went okay I think. Now we seem silly with relief. We twirl the linguini around our forks, drink a little but not much. And I can't wait to spend time with her, to be together all this spring, now that we are on equal terms and our identities are shifting.

I DON'T HAVE many things, so unpacking takes little time. Just hanging clothes and piling things in the kitchen, skincare on a too small bathroom shelf. I place the hat from Abbe in the hallway and my candlestick on the desk in my new bedroom where it looks ridiculous but okay then.

It is lucky someone dropped out of universitetet and moved home, because now there is a free room in Noor's friend's flat. I have never met her before so we are not friends. It is nice, I will keep it this way, cordial but impersonal.

The flat is not bad but it's not Artillerigatan. Two bedrooms, a living room, one galley kitchen with a small breakfast table by the window. No balcony. It is in Enskede, so no more morning walks to campus but perhaps in spring I will buy a bike if I get up the courage to cycle in Stockholm. It doesn't glitter this flat, no ceiling height or grand entryways or hand-me-down china. But it will do. It is a reasonable place to live when you are twenty-two.

Hanna made me kaffe and breakfast and lunch when I was packing but she didn't help me pack or touch any of my things. She is being respectful because of our talk last week but she is overshooting. This is fine, we will find a good balance as we go along. And now I am out of there. No more creaking herringbone under these feet.

IT IS MY first weekend in the new apartment and my flatmate is visiting parents, so I invite Abbe. I have been busy finding a place and then moving, so he hasn't yet seen my new haircut. I haven't told him because I want to see his face.

At first I had planned to cook something but then I decided we should order in because it has been a big month for me, with the bad hitchhike and the haircut and then talking to Hanna, so I am a little tired.

Yuusuf had been right, it took some days of freaking out before I got used to the mirror. But now I like it. Maybe this Jean Seberg short hair is not my thing, maybe no particular hairstyle is. Maybe my thing is trying all of them.

These few days, walking around with short hair, I have noticed that people looking is not so bad. I'm realising I've been bored miserably, making myself invisible. But I am a hungry person. I want to try a lot. And fortune favours the bold, so the story goes.

The buzzer rings and I say hallå and Abbe says hallå and I press the button. I hear the cables in the elevator. He is on his way up. I run my tongue over my teeth because today I am wearing lipstick. I fuss my hair in the hallway mirror even though it is too short for fussing.

When the elevator arrives I am standing in the doorway. Abbe comes out, sees my hair, and his eyes go round.

I laugh a little at his face. 'What do you think?'

'You're outrageous.' He shakes his head. 'Just outrageous.'

I back into the flat and he closes the door behind us and puts his bag down.

'Do you love it?'

He lifts his eyebrows. 'I love that you did it.' He kisses me on the cheek as a hello. 'Do you love it?'

'I think so!' I touch my neck reflexively. He touches it too. And that's enough, his warm hand on the back of my neck, to make me furiously want him. I pull him closer and I am so tired of the gentleness lately and I just want to let myself go.

In the bedroom I take off my top and drop it on the floor. I kiss him and pull the shirt over his head and maybe I am being too fevered but I don't care, so he submits to me and I am mostly on top, moving us around the bed and I feel audacious. I have multiple jolts to my stomach when he looks at me or does something unexpected. I pin his arms to the mattress. He tilts his head back. Everything is heightened and I don't want to stop.

In the moment I forget about the lipstick. Afterwards he has red marks on his neck, arms, chest. But that's it. Red. Not blue, not purple.

'WHAT DO YOU feel like?' I ask, scrolling the food app.

'I don't mind, you go ahead.'

It's late, I have showed him the new flat, we have talked about Hanna, my hair, his thesis. We are on the sofa, in our clothes again, drinking beer from the bottle. I am deliriously relaxed.

'Wok?' I ask, because the wok place has those tall white takeaway boxes you see in movies, which I find romantic.

'Sounds good.'

But Abbe doesn't seem relaxed. He looks out the window then at his phone then he wipes his hands on his trousers.

'Are you okay or?'

'Um. Maybe not completely okay.'

'Oh.' I turn to him slowly, so slowly like time is stopped.

'I feel shit bringing it up now, but I kind of feel I have to.' He sounds agitated.

No. No no.

'I think you shouldn't come. To Mexico. I don't think it would be a good idea.'

I say nothing. I notice I am not surprised. And also that this does not lessen the pain.

'I don't think we are ready for this. I'm not anyway.'

'Is this about Hanna?'

'Hanna?'

'The thing I said about her at the party.'

'What, no. Or, maybe in part?'

I desperately don't want to cry so I just sit very still and say, 'Explain.'

'I think, one thing that happened this summer when we went to the hockey rink is that you're always so up front with me and I love that so I have been trying to be up front too.' He looks down. 'But talking about that stuff, it brought up a lot of shit. And I can see that some of my behaviours are linked to that and I hadn't thought about it before.'

I consider this. 'Like me always sitting with my back against the wall.'

'For me it's like, not caring if I get hurt? As if I want to prove I can take it, like it's no big deal.'

I look at him. My eyes fill now, I can't help it. 'Please don't say things like that.'

'But, you must know how that feels, not wanting to be the victim. And the only way I could think of was to show that people can be violent but it doesn't touch me. Which is ridiculous. And so backhanded I'm embarrassed to tell you.' He smiles faintly.

I sigh. 'I know. It's like, if I think about school and take the blame for it, I feel I can change so I don't end up that way again. But if it was not my fault, then what?'

'That's it.' He pauses, looks at me. 'Anyway I think we both have some dealing to do before we're good in relationships.'

'But, I thought maybe we could deal together!' I feel an unbearable pity for us both. I don't know whose sadness to attend to.

He sounds close to tears. 'I don't want to push my issues on you, it's unfair.'

'You can push them on me I don't care!'

'Sickan, I don't think we fit.'

This is new information but also not. I think about his friends, all the rooms he has brought me into, where I just, stand out. 'Am I not good enough?'

'What?' He looks at me, upset. 'No I'm not good enough! I was always not good enough.' He moves to face me square-on. 'I feel like I'm trying to keep up with you. But I don't think I can. I'm not like, special.'

'But, you are wrong, I have never felt even once that you are not enough. I feel I am too much!'

He draws his eyebrows together. 'But isn't that the same thing then? I've been trying to show you that it's okay to just, be yourself, with me. It's like you relax sometimes but then you catch yourself and sort of, hide again? And yeah the thing you said about Hanna, I feel like, am I making you think you need to be like that to fit in with us? And that made me question who I hang out with. Because yes, some of them say things like that and some of them just aren't very nice people.'

'But Abbe, this is all fine.' I place my hands around his face. 'Look at me, this is all fine. We know this now. We can go to Mexico, find new friends, and just be us.'

Gently he takes my hands off his face. 'So why do I feel like we can't?'

'So why?'

The look of him then.

'You are always honest with me, so now I feel I should be very honest with you.' He pauses and I can't take it so I say, 'This is not about Mexico. You would break up with me anyway.'

'I think so yes.'

'You don't love me?'

'I do.' His eyes fill. 'But maybe not as much as you love me.'

I wipe my face with my hands because now there are tears. 'I hear what you're saying and I understand but the thing is I'm in love with you so much and Abbe you are breaking my heart now.'

'Mine too.'

I look at him, his face blurry through tears. My heart aches for him. 'What can I do,' he says.

I take a long, shaking breath. 'Oh. Not much I don't think.' I sniff. Then I wipe my eyes. 'Can you stay a while? I don't want you to leave.'

'Sure. I can stay.'

We talk about neutral things, his mother, my flatmate. Later I go to the bathroom and wash my face. Back in the living room he is standing up and has connected his phone to the speakers. 'Just My Imagination' comes on. He lifts my arms around his neck and holds me. We kiss like that for a long time but it makes me cry again so I have to stop. Then we dance for a while. I am grateful to him for not commenting it's the first time he sees me dance. I don't care about dancing badly. After all these months finally I am in a room with Abbe without worrying about making a good impression. I wish I had tried it more.

I AM HOME alone. There is a song on repeat on the living-room speakers, loud so I can hear it walking around. I refill my wineglass, closing the fridge door with my hip, and drink while I go to my room and there, on a hanger, is my new dress. Because when you save for a long time to move to Mexico and then get uninvited you end up with a lot of money, many thousands, sitting in your account without a destination which means that, yes, yes, you can totally if you want buy that dress for two thousand kronor and that's exactly what I did this afternoon and now I am already feeling the two glasses of wine in my head in a way that makes me desperate to put it on and take it out around town. I remove it from the hanger and it is light as paper and so tight I have to shimmy to get my body into it, and it is daring, the material matte white, so see-through you can see the shape and colour of my nipples and white underwear underneath which is on trend, although not a trend made for shy people and I am thinking that maybe my days as a shy person are not only over but forgotten, as I look in the mirror on the inside of the wardrobe door where I see a tall person with ungainly limbs and a head without almost any hair, earlobes heavy from big gold earrings, which I throw left and right a few times, and with that, I am ready, with a final look in the hallway mirror, and I wonder what he would think of the way I look right now, in this see-through dress for two thousand kronor, he would say something in the vein of herregud Sickan come here, but also I know what the influencers say, it only matters what you think yourself, don't dress for anyone else, least of all some boy! and this is true of course and I myself think that I look deadly, which is the last thing I think before I put my debit card, keys, and phone in my bag and walk out the door to the flat and into the club under the bridge where I am meeting Noor because she is already here somewhere in the sweating mass of human body and exhaled breath texting me that she is bored with her people and come get wrecked which is exactly what I want and oh Noor how beautiful does she look leaning on her elbows there in the bar, nonchalant and glamorous and let me be vulnerable here and say I have maybe not ever been happier to see another person than I am to see her now when she hands me her cocktail and I drink deeply while she orders four shots of cranberry vodka that we down at once before she takes my hand and leads me to the dancefloor telling me that I look scandalous which I do, I know I do, and we dance together in a funny way, sort of headbutting the air, and the next thought I have there on the dancefloor is that Noor is a wonderful person and also so pretty and I want her to be rightly appreciated so I ask her who do you want? and she laughs and looks around and points at a man in a loose black t-shirt so now I take her hand and pull her over and I think that immediately it is a success so I leave them to it and make my way back to

the bar to order something anything whatever you recom-
mend herr bartender sour not sweet and please a strong
one I can take it I am a woman who has just been broken
up for the first time and now, what I want more than
anything, is to have all the cliché, all the romance, of devastating ruinous heartbreak, cry on public transport, I want
to cancel everything, and I want friends, and lovers who
are not friends, what I want is to walk through different
bedrooms, so many they lose contour, without anyone
caring or saying a word, which is maybe why when a boy
in the bar looks at my body and my arms and asks me are
you a dancer, I honestly say, I don't know, and he says do
you want to find out, and yes! I do! so I take his hand in
mine and he is so good at this and he screams his name in
my ear but I extremely don't care because I am only interested in his torso really, which is dramatically taut like a
cage but enough about the guy because now they are playing that song, you know that one, the one I love but can
never remember the name of that we played over and over
that time on the . . . and so okay I am going to dance, I
throw my head and arms, my legs willing to do whatever I
ask and I want to tell you this: you think I don't dance but
I do.

Just not in front of you.

I have been wondering, were we good for each other?
Bad?

I don't know how to tell, but there is no one in this
club who I care what they think about me, so now, here,
it is a release, a freedom, deliverance, to simply stop thinking about it, and somehow I have gone over all this in my

head even before the boy with the torso kisses me which is incredible, in that complete abandon, death or glory type of way that I hold on to with white knuckles while I go to pee and in the mirror see that I could very much be a dancer with these long limbs and I wash my hands and my neck with cold water and walk out the bathroom into some boy's bedroom who turns out to be another boy but does it matter, can I go home with anyone, absolutely anyone, will anyone ever say no to me? because it doesn't seem like it here on his bed wide enough for both of us and I am on top, my new dress on his messy floor seeming deliciously lewd to me, expensive white fabric on filthy carpet, inspired like this I go faster and he leans his head back and then he moves to change position but I push him back down because I am not being under him, no way, I am over him, out for blood because my appetite tonight, it is insatiable, I am an open wound, I know this, so I embrace the skinlessness, what other option, and hold his wrists hard and he bites my breast and I lean back on my hands and I come, selfishly I come, and he says oh god and maybe he comes too but who cares, the rules are so off and I can do what I want which I tell him and he says, yes seems like you maniac, and I walk home to Artillerigatan for some reason, which is not home anymore, but I still have keys, grateful to not have been raped but in my current state honestly who would have tried, let them try I think as I take off my shoes and walk barefoot on the asphalt because there is only so much my body can take, and soon I am on the right street and the elevator brings me up home and I look utterly weird in the elevator mirror like an alien not even human, which makes me laugh, full-heartedly, because how ridiculous are we, which is the inspiration for the song I play on the kitchen speakers, on low volume though, because Hanna is likely sleeping considering it is a . . . four in the morning, äsch, that's not so bad and I am only playing music in the kitchen, a long way away from her bedroom, which stays quiet and closed as I pour myself a glass with shaking fingers and okay I drop the bottle but neither the bottle nor the floor tile break so it's fine, honestly it's fine, and I lean back on the counter by the window moving my tired head a little to the music, quite pleased, and drink my drink but this is when all of a sudden Hanna is there, at the other end of the kitchen looking at me like the alien I am, but SO WHAT, and she says

hey.

and I grin insanely in a good mood and I say hej you and she says, you okay?

and I say, Hanna I'm in the best mood. Please please

She says come here

and I resent her serious voice and no way am I letting her destroy this formidable feat of strength I have performed tonight so I say have a drink with me but she says Sickan come over here and I say no way man and display with all my might that I do not want her to come any closer but she walks up to me and backed into a corner I have no escape and she cups my neck with her hand, pulling my head forward until our foreheads touch and standing like that, head to head, no one between us, the song so grotesquely upbeat in our ears, I break utterly, wretchedly, irreparably apart,

not in a philosophical way,

in a devastating human physical way with liquid leaking from eyes, nose, mouth, Hanna's hand unmoving on my neck, her forehead hot on mine, and all I can think is fan också

fan också

fan fan fan fan fan fan fan fan fan fan fan fan fan fan fan fan
fan fan fan fan fan fan fan fan fan fan fan fan fan fan fan fan
fan fan fan fan fan fan fan fan fan fan fan fan fan fan fan fan
fan fan fan fan fan fan fan fan fan fan fan fan fan fan fan fan
fan fan fan fan fan fan fan fan fan fan fan fan fan fan fan fan
fan fan fan fan fan fan fan fan fan fan fan fan fan fan fan fan
fan fan fan fan fan fan fan fan fan fan fan fan fan fan fan fan
fan fan fan fan fan fan fan fan fan fan fan fan fan fan fan fan
fan fan fan fan fan fan fan fan fan fan fan fan fan fan fan fan
fan fan fan fan fan fan fan fan fan fan fan fan fan fan fan fan

I SEE THE email in my inbox while looking at my phone waiting for the kettle. I pour my cup of oolong and sit down on the bed with crossed legs. Then I open my laptop.

It is a formal email telling me my application has been received. A ten-week scriptwriting course this summer, at a private school so it costs a lot of money. Forty thousand kronor. But I have Mexico City savings.

I have no idea if it is hard to get into the course. You have to send writing samples to show you are good, but considering the cost they might well not get many applicants and so accept everyone, or everyone who is a little bit good. This is what I am hoping.

For the last month I have been looking over my notebooks, choosing my favourite dialogues and reworking them on the laptop late at night. I don't mind not staying true to the overheard conversations, I am going very off-piste, making up new lines and taking the conversation in unexpected and sometimes wild directions. I didn't know I had an affinity for making stuff up. It is a distraction, of course.

This last month has been the saddest so far. Sometimes he calls or texts to see how I am but those days I become very upset and I can't concentrate on much else. Hanna says we need to cut ties for me to heal so I have told him not to be in touch right now. I miss Artillerigatan, the cocoon created by all that velvet, muffled and intimate. But they say sadness is good for your writing so I am trying to make the most out of my ripped-apart heart.

I think the dialogues are good and would be a bit offended by a rejection but who knows. I read the email again. Starting June. Some of the lecturers are quite famous writers.

I picture myself there in the lecture hall. I am not sure I will like creative writing, maybe coding is more me. But I won't know unless I compare. Maybe neither is me. I am open to that. So this course would be a start, an appetiser. To see if I have an appetite.

I want to celebrate sending my application in some way. I go to the kitchen and look around and take a bag of cinnamon buns out of the freezer which I defrost in the microwave. Then I put all six buns on a plate. I open the kitchen window and straddle the narrow sill which is a reckless thing to do with a fifth-floor window but I am being bold. There is no wind today and the sun is gently warming even though it's still February. I pull my cardigan up around my neck. Then I tear a piece of the sweet dough and chew slowly. It melts inside my mouth. Dough sticks to my teeth, making my mouth smack as I chew. It is warm and so familiar, the pearl-sugar crunching between my teeth. After I have unrolled and eaten two, I light a cigarette. When I inhale, the smoke picks up the cinnamon and I think of Hanna that time, smoking while eating. As if inhaling cinnamon. I am not sure I like it.

I wonder who to call with the news. I text Hanna and ask if I can come over for dinner.

Then, I call Skåne.

'Hej mum, are you busy?'

'Always busy, you know me. But I have time to talk, go ahead.'

I exhale cinnamonsmoke and say, 'I applied for summer school today.'

'Oh? Like an extra course?'

'Not precisely. A scriptwriting course.'

She is quiet for a moment. 'Scriptwriting?'

'Yes.'

'What in all the world. What do you mean, creative writing?'

'Yes.'

'As in, making up stories?'

'You know what creative writing is mum.'

'I didn't know you like to write.'

'I'm not sure I do like it yet. But I have been, doing it sometimes.'

'Should I get dad on the phone too?'

'Mum no one has died, this is not a crisis in the family.'

'What about school? You are doing your master's this autumn?'

'Yes, that's the plan. Don't worry I have not lost my mind.' I touch the buzzed hair of my neck and am glad this is not a video call.

'Okay then. That's fine.'

I look down the five floors to the pavement below. I dangle my foot. 'Mum I didn't call to get your approval.' I breathe out fully and then I just say it. 'What I want is for you to get impressed.'

'I see.'

'Could you do that? Please.'

I hear her pull out a kitchen chair and sit. 'Well. I haven't read anything you've written. Can I see something?'

'Oh no. No I can't show you.'

'It's hard for me to praise you then.'

'How about you get impressed I got the application together? I had to send writing samples.'

'Is it hard to get accepted?'

'As in, numbers?'

'Yes. I think if you give me numbers it will be easier to get impressed. It would be fun to see.'

'I'm not even sure I got in yet. But sure. I can find out. I'll send you numbers.'

'Siv?'

'Yes?'

'For now, even though you haven't been accepted yet, I can still feel impressed. I never knew you were creative. Gods know me and dad aren't.'

'Are you telling me I'm adopted?'

She tssks. 'You look exactly like me.'

Which has never once crossed my mind but now that she says it maybe yes actually I do. 'And what do you, I mean, do you like the person, I have become?'

'Oh Siv,' she says. 'You're a lovely girl. Just lovely.'

I soak it up, soak up all of it. 'Mum?'

'Yes?'

'I'm not a loner anymore. Maybe you don't know this about me, but I have a best friend and other friends as well and I had a boyfriend, his name is Abbe. But we broke up.'

'Well! Sounds like big things are happening in Stockholm!'

'Indeed.' And I tell her some more stuff on the phone because now I'm thinking that okay, we don't know each other so well but that's not just their fault it's my fault too.

I HAVE BOUGHT a new notebook. A4, lined, black boards. I bring it to the kitchen table and refill my teacup. I have two cinnamon buns left. It is cold in the room now so I close the window. Then I pick up my pencil.

Even though the characters are not named I know who they are. I know her bristling nerves. His curly hair and easy manners.

What do you feel like?
I don't mind, you go ahead.
Wok?
Sounds good.
Are you okay or?
Maybe not completely okay.

I try my best to remember our breakup verbatim though it's hard because I am emotional. But it is good, filling pages, the rasping sound of lead on paper. In two places the letters smear because drops fall on the page. It goes on for lines before the final few words.

What can I do.
Can you stay a while? I don't want you to leave.
Sure. I can stay.

Over these weeks I have come to think that things were said that time I should look closer at. I know what he meant, me hiding myself to fit in. But it is hard to show who you are when you don't know yet.

I turn to a blank page and start on a new dialogue, with the same people. I have never written a piece not based on an actual conversation before. But it turns out I can do it. The pencil stays on the paper, filling each line. It is easy. This specific conversation between the two people has never taken place, it is fiction. But perhaps one day it will. We don't know.

I TELL THE taxi driver to stop outside the train station. 'I'm waiting for someone but don't know exactly when they'll arrive. Do you mind, just sitting here for a while?'

The driver turns off the engine and sighs. Then he clicks off the meter. 'How about I go get some coffee. Like fifteen minutes?'

'Okay yes. You do that.' I rub my hands on my trousers.

'I'll lock the doors from outside but if you want to get out you can open from inside like normal.'

'Thank you.'

It is here now, late February. The 27th. Mid-morning, the sunlight very slanted. The car ride into central has been magical, the city golden, the water glittering like mad. It is still winter but here in the warm car, the sun through the window heating my thigh, it is easy to forget.

Yesterday he posted a photo of a plane ticket. Arlanda airport to Mexico City, departure 14:12.

I have done a calculation on Arlanda Express train departures. There are three likely trains he could take, at fifteen-minute intervals. Of course, he could also take a bus or a car to the airport, or he could oversleep or anything else. It is a fool's errand but okay then yes I am a fool.

I have no plan. If he does walk out of the tunnelbana station and cross the short stretch of pavement into the train station I do not know what next. It is a compulsion, this sitting here waiting in an empty taxi. I want to see him.

The minutes in the car stretch out, my eyes fixed on the tunnelbana entrance. It takes so long even my brittle nerves start to settle. My hands stop sweating. I can swallow just fine.

I am getting bored.

I wish the car radio was on but it is completely quiet. I can't do anything or look at my phone, worried the moment I look away is the moment he will appear. So I wait.

And then he does.

He walks out of the underground entrance towards the train station. He looks awkward with his luggage and in his mouth he is biting the edge of a small brown paper bag. The ground is icy and he slips a little. He stops by a roadsalt box, drops his bags and sits down. From the paper bag he picks up a bread roll. He takes a bite and squints at the sun.

Slowly I place my hand on the door handle. The doors are locked but I can open them from inside like normal, if I want to get out.

I think about that time, my birthday. I was drunk that night but I had been looking at the two of them dancing, Hanna saying that they love me even if I'm messed up. I remember thinking, we are perfect.

And we were. We were perfect.

I let go of the door handle and just enjoy looking at him.

He takes two more bites and throws the rest to the pigeons. Then he picks up his bags, walks into the station, and leaves.

I stay here.

Later the driver comes back and waves at me through the window then sits on the hood and lights a cigarette.

What has it been? Fifteen minutes, not much more.

Ten months since I first saw him.

Not a very long time whichever way you turn it. But I am thinking that some things need to be measured in other units than time.

My phone rings.

'Hej.'

'Are you on the way?' she asks.

'Yes. In the car now.' I shiver a little and rub my nose.

'And you're up for it?'

'I'm wearing my bikini under my clothes.'

'I thought you might have chickened out.'

'Oh no. I'm not a chicken.'

'It will be cold.'

I laugh a little. 'It's a hole in the ice, of course it will be cold.'

'It will be worth it after.'

'I brought beer.'

'Good. I'm in a great mood to get drunk.'

'Me too.'

We hang up and I knock on the car window with my knuckle. The driver turns his head and I mime let's go.

Swimming in an ice hole. What are we thinking. But I am twenty-two, this is Stockholm, who knows what could happen.

Acknowledgements

Thank you to my fantastic agent Peter Straus, as well as Emer Walsh, Stephen Edwards, Tristan Kendrick, Sam Coates, and the wonderful team at RCW.

Thank you to Ansa Khan Khattak, for her perfect balance of kindness and scalpel-precision. And to Nico Parfitt, Olivia French, and everyone at Sceptre, as well as the tireless Lizzie Dorney. Thank you to Claiborne Hancock, Jessica Case, and everyone at Pegasus for believing in my work.

Thank you to my phenomenal film agent Emily Hayward-Whitlock, as well as my foreign publishers, editors, and translators, above all Jutta Wallrafen and the terrific team at Eichborn. Thank you to Shannon Cartier Lucy for lending her stunning artwork for the cover.

Thank you to Molly Aitken, Rowan Hisayo Buchanan, Chloë Ashby, Cecile Pin, Yan Ge, Lucy Caldwell, Ayşegül Savaş, Niamh Mulvey, and Caoilinn Hughes for reading early and generously.

Thank you to everyone who has produced, distributed, recommended, or sold this novel. And to my readers, followers, and subscribers for the means to pursue a creative life.

Thank you to my family, friends, and to my parents, for not being anything like the parents in these pages.

Most of all I thank you David. Like always, for everything.